DEAD
BY
POPULAR DEMAND

DEAD
BY
POPULAR DEMAND

A HARLEM *NOIR* FEATURING
DEVIL BARNETT

TEDDY HAYES

KATE'S MYSTERY BOOKS
JUSTIN, CHARLES & CO., PUBLISHERS
BOSTON

FIRST U.S. EDITION 2005

Originally published in 2000 by The X Press, London

This is a work of fiction. All characters and events portrayed
in this work are either fictitious or are used fictitiously.

ISBN: 1-932112-23-5

Library of Congress Cataloging-in-Publication Data is available.

Published in the United States by Kate's Mystery Books,
an imprint of Justin, Charles & Co., Publishers,
Boston, Massachusetts
www.justincharlesbooks.com

Distributed by National Book Network
Lanham, Maryland
www.nbnbooks.com

10 9 8 7 6 5 4 3 2 1

PRINTED IN THE UNITED STATES OF AMERICA

To the memory of Marc Ralph Fitzsimmons
and to my mentor, Melvin Van Peebles,
who blew on the spark, fanned the flame,
and started the fire.
Thanks, Baby Boy.

Acknowledgments

Special thanks to my cousins Minnie Marshall and Elaine Ebose for their nonstop love from across the pond; and to Jennie Rosenthal, Monserratt Fas, Luz De Armas, Brian and Jill Nihad, Dave and Yvonne Roberts, Terry Fraser, Valerie Pressley, Rhea Madison, Bill Madison, Mike Abbott, Alan Cutler, Sergio Carioca, Luiza Terto, Lamont Burrell, and Nanesh and Tim Fry for their support and friendship.

A very special shout-out to my press agent, Jaqueline Asafu-Adjaye, who keeps on pushing on.

DEAD
BY
POPULAR DEMAND

PROLOGUE

London.

This was the stuff that dreams are made of . . .

The seven young men riding in the back of the long black limousine were on top of the world. In only a few months they had made the leap from living in one of the poorest housing estates in the East End of London to becoming pop stars and renting luxury in upmarket Holland Park, where their neighbors included bankers and Internet millionaires.

Nobody had expected this kind of success, least of all Rebel, Waxie Maxie, Shogun, Man O War, Goldfinger, Wicked, and Filthy Rich, collectively known as the Dancehall Dogz. They couldn't believe it wasn't all still a dream. Their debut album had gone triple platinum within its first two months of release, generating millions of dollars.

The flavor of their music was Jamaican with a touch of hip hop. Radio stations played their album nonstop all over the world. From America to England to Germany to Japan, people knew their faces and their music. They were living the dream life that magazines wrote about—all provided courtesy of their New York record company.

As the limo crawled along London's crowded, neon-lit West End heading toward Marble Arch, the boys relaxed and dared to dream of the things that awaited them: big money, beautiful women, fast cars, the best gear, gold credit cards, the works.

"What you reckon this is all about?" asked Filthy.

"Don't know," answered Duncan, the big bodyguard who was their constant companion these days. "Max rang up about an hour ago and said to get everyone over to the meeting, yeah."

"I bet it's about the tour, I hope it is, I'm ready to break out of the UK, yo," chimed Rebel, who had traded in his natural Cockney style of speech for that of the American hip-hop culture.

Twenty minutes later the limousine pulled to a stop in front of the Cumberland Hotel in Marble Arch. The pop stars rushed from the car under Duncan's guard into the hotel lobby, where they quickly entered a waiting elevator that took them up to one of the hotel's best suites where they were met by Shogun and Wicked. Wicked puffed on a big spliff and blew smoke across the room lazily as the other members helped themselves from the drinks tray loaded with whiskey and wine. On the cocktail table in front of the ivory-colored sofa were two more trays. One was laid out with lines of cocaine, the other piled high with Jamaican-size spliffs.

"Wha'ppen," Shogun hailed the others.

"Safe," "cool," "just chillin'," came the various replies.

"What kinda fuckin' meeting we havin' at twelve midnight?" Man O War wanted to know.

"That's because there's a six-hour difference, remember it's six o'clock in the evening New York time," reminded Duncan.

Rebel checked his Rolex, which was also a gift from the record company. "Then let's do it," he told the bodyguard, grinning through a set of teeth adorned by gold markings.

Duncan dialed the number and put the phone on speaker. On the third ring a husky female voice answered.

"Grooveline Music, may I help you?"

"Hiya Monica, girl, this is Duncan."

"Hey Duncan," she cooed in a sexy voice hot enough to melt the receiver.

"We got a conference call with Max." He grinned into the phone.

"Just a sec," she answered as she switched the call.

"What's up, my brothas across the pond," the voice came on the line from New York. It belonged to J. T. Brown, the American manager of the Dancehall Dogz. If there was any one person who could claim credit for their success, it was J. T.

The group in London shouted their return greetings.

He had discovered them in a small dance talent competition. He liked them so much that he arranged for their demo recordings the following week and, soon after, had left London with the demo tapes and was back in New York talking to record companies. Within a month of shopping the demo tapes, J. T. had landed a deal with Grooveline.

"I hope everybody is sitting down or lying down or something, because if you ain't, what I'm about to say is going to knock you off your feet," J. T. announced.

The Dancehall Dogz exchanged glances in greedy anticipation, like a wild pack of canines on the scent of a pork chop drop.

"Y'all ready?" asked J. T.

"Go on, then," shouted Waxie Maxie. All this tension was making him nervous.

"Well, the new single just went to number 3 with a bullet over here."

"RAASCLAAT, a bullet! Yeah, mon." Shogun grinned and clicked his index and middle fingers together with a flick of the wrist.

"Kiss me neck," echoed Waxie Maxie with similar gleeful enthusiasm.

"Wait, wait, hold up, that ain't all," J. T. continued. "So far we've already got forty dates locked down for the U.S. tour."

"Forty dates, fuck me silly." The words rolled out of Filthy Rich's mouth as naturally as his own breath.

"How we travelin'?" Man O War wanted to know.

"First class all the way, baby," J. T. answered. "We also got spots on *Soul Train, The Tonight Show, David Letterman* . . . We bustin' out."

"When do we start?" Rebel inquired.

"Hold on . . .," J. T. said.

Then a white man's voice answered him. It belonged to Max Hammill, the president and owner of Grooveline Music.

"We have you guys scheduled in to begin rehearsals next Monday. The first date is two weeks from then. You guys are the hottest thing since pussy was invented, I'll tell you."

"This is Thursday—are we talking 'bout Monday coming?" Goldfinger asked. He was the quiet one of the group. He seldom spoke—well, not verbally, anyway. He did his talking on the wheels of steel. He was the group's funky deejay.

"That's right, I'll see you fellas four days from today," Max answered.

"How long we in America for?" Shogun inquired.

"The way things are looking, fellas, I think we're talking a permanent move, at least for a couple years. I've got some apartments in the city for you to look at. Nice places, too—swimming pools, satellite dishes, maid service, the works," Hammill said.

"Damn, moving to America. Damn," Shogun said, hardly able to believe his own words.

"Maxin' and relaxin' in the Big Apple." Rebel laughed.

"Listen, you guys get going and I'll see you in a few days. Gotta go, gotta go," Max said.

J. T.'s voice came back on the phone. "So, what it look like, brothas?" he said. You could hear the smile in his voice. Like a magician who had just pulled off a magnificent feat, asking the audience if they liked what they just thought they saw.

Wicked broke the silence.

"I think I gon' be living in America, that's what I think." He beamed.

Filthy Rich stepped to the center of the room, holding one of the hotel's complimentary bottles of champagne. Duncan handed everyone a glass, and Filthy poured some bubbly in each. Offering up a toast, Filthy simply looked around at the other Dancehall Dogz and said, "Here's to America."

The members all drank in silence as the excitement of their triumphant moment twinkled in their eyes like stars in the skies of a soft summer's night.

CHAPTER 1

New York City.

Shogun relaxed in the warm flowing water and thought about miracles. He had previously never believed in miracles, but if someone asked him now, he would have to say that he had gotten it all wrong. After all, wasn't he living proof that miracles happened? Here he was under twenty-five and livin' extra large already. He was in demand. Like now as he sat in the Jacuzzi with these two beautiful women freaking him off.

"You like this, Gun?" Chandra asked as she stroked his penis back and forth while licking his left nipple.

Shogun simply nodded and smiled. Peaches kissed his face intermittently and thrust her long pink tongue into his ear.

"Stand up," Chandra said.

He did as she asked without question.

She reached out with a manicured hand and took a dollop of honey from a jar on a table near the edge of the Jacuzzi. She wiped the honey on his organ and then began to suck it off.

Peaches held a glass of champagne up to his lips and, as he drank deeply, bit his nipples, first one and then the other.

Chandra eased him down into the water, straddled him, and placed him inside her and began to gyrate vigorously. Of the two women she was the more aggressive. She didn't really like Peaches, but what could she do. Shogun liked threesomes, and she knew if she didn't play it his way, he would get someone else who would. So she took what she could get. Peaches on the other hand was more laid-back. She never pushed. Just did all the right things at the right times. To Shogun, they complemented each other perfectly.

Peaches positioned herself directly behind Shogun and reached around each of his shoulders and started to squeeze his nipples. To be honest, he was tired. They had been going at it most of the day. As a result of the two women's expert manipulation of his body parts, Shogun had been ejaculating like it was going out of style. He felt sleep coming on just when the phone rang. Peaches handed him the mobile.

"Yeah," he spoke lazily into the phone.

It was Man O War.

"Don't forget about later," War reminded him.

"What time?" Shogun asked.

"Four thirty," War said.

"What time is it now?" Shogun asked.

"Almost four," War told him.

"Shit. I'll be there, don't worry."

"Don't be late, Gun. This is a big move, yeah, we're going to make a serious move that's going to kick us right to the top of the music production food chain, yeah."

"I feel you," Shogun stated, using his latest bit of rapspeak.

"OK," Man O War said, and hung up.

Shogun relaxed back into the Jacuzzi.

"Gotta go, got an appointment," he said.

"You coming back, right?" Chandra wanted to know.

"Yeah, but it's going to be late. I'll check you later."

He was satisfied sexually. Now he wanted to get into a creative frame of mind.

He and War had business to do. He thought about this as Peaches washed him down. As he stepped out of the Jacuzzi, Chandra dried him off with a thick green double fluffy bath towel. He thought about what kind of lyrics he would use for their new project. He was a first-class rap lyricist. Everyone said his skills were a gift. He wasn't sure how he did it himself. He just did it. A gift from God. Even as a young kid back in London, with his uncle who was a calypsonian playing melodies on the guitar, Shogun would step up and make up lyrics. At ten he was as good as some popular calypsonians. Once he even got to meet the greatest calypsonian of them all, The Mighty Sparrow, at the Notting Hill Carnival. They even did a tune together. Yeah, words were his gift. He had started writing rap and dancehall lyrics using the name Shakespeare, but decided that Shogun fitted him better. After all, back in the olden days of Japan, no one was mightier than the Shogun.

He walked into the other room and started to pick out an outfit for the day from his seemingly endless wardrobe of designer clothes. He always tried to match his gear according to the place he was going. Today *he was going to Harlem. The home of the funkiest brothas in the world. They loved him in Harlem, even though he was from London. His acceptance in America's number one famous black ghetto was something he was extremely proud of. A few months ago he was invited to a cipher in Harlem at the world-famous Apollo Theatre. In the rap world an invitation to the uptown cipher was like being invited to a command performance in front of the Queen of England. At the cipher, all of the Harlem rappers would get together and freestyle. On the day he was asked, he was on the stage with the elite of the rap world. There was a boxing ring in the middle of the stage and rappers would jump in two at a time and try to knock each other out with lyrics, the crowd being the judges. The rappers started to freestyle, throwing lyrics this way and that, twisting, bending, breaking, and turning words and phrases inside out. Shogun found himself in the middle of the ring doing his thing and holding his own. When he finished, even the other rappers gave him a standing ovation. Yeah, Harlem, New York, was the place to be.*

For his gear that day, he choose a black and gold FUBU top with black corduroy pants, black and tan Nikes, and a black Kangol cap. He checked himself in the mirror and knew he looked good. Damn good. As he heard an old man in a Harlem bar say once, he was "ready for Freddy." He felt good, too, as he began to spout lyrics as naturally as rain falling from the sky on a cloudy day.

"You remember what we talked about?" Chandra said, sticking her head inside his bedroom and interrupting his flow.

Damn, he was tired of her now. He wished she would just hurry up, get her shit together, and go, but the silly cow kept on talking.

"I need something so I can come to you whenever you want me. Something dependable. Just a Chevy or Ford, nothing fancy." Chandra looked around over her shoulder to make sure Peaches wasn't lurking around the door, listening.

"Like I told you, I'll take care of it, yeah," Shogun said.

She ran her hand against his crotch and kissed him on the neck. But his mind was on other things. She sensed it and backed off. Shogun's mind reverted back to lyrics. As he finished dressing he continued humming one of his latest creations.

"Got to get the goodies while the goodies are hot

Depend on me to hit your G-spot
I'm a poet, a prophet a guru a sage
Expandin' your consciousness, takin' you to the next stage."

He decided not to take his new Jeep up into Harlem because if he decided to get high, he didn't want the police to stop and hassle him. As sure as not they would see him, a young black man driving a new Jeep, and automatically think he was a drug dealer. So he had Peaches call to get him a limo.

Uptown it was still early, only 4:45 p.m., but the sun was already showing signs of starting to set in the clear January sky. Even though it was the middle of winter and cold as hell, every now and again rays of sunshine would bite through the frosty urban wilderness to share a little of its warmth with the residents of Harlem, like the pope giving absolution to a group of jailhouse sinners.

Part-time minister Sister Sally Henley stood on a Harlem street corner with her sixty-seven-year-old eyes cast up toward the sky. What worried Sister Sally was that it might rain before all of the food she had prepared had been served out. The weatherman had forecast a clear day, but the rheumatism in Sister Sally's hands had told her differently and they never lied. Her hands were aching between her finger joints. Rain was definitely on the way. She just hoped it would wait until the food had been served.

Sister Sally was what you might call a professional do-gooder, if there is such a thing. For the past five years, on the second Sunday of each month after service, she would drive the church van filled with five or six different dishes she had prepared to some street corner location God had guided her to, where she would set up the church van to feed the hungry. It wasn't an elaborate setup by any means. Just a few tables, some steaming pots of food, paper plates, plastic cups, forks and spoons. But over the many years she had been doing this, the people of Harlem had come to know her. Most people called her Sister Soul Food, which was the phrase coined by the Amsterdam News, *the African American newspaper that had featured her several times. These articles helped Sister Sally raise donations from big corporations, which had enabled her to have several hundred turkeys slaughtered for Thanksgiving and put on a feast for the needy of Harlem.*

With Sister Sally it was always the same routine. Her slogan was "Take a plate and thank the Lord." Her mission was a pure one. She just wanted to give a few hungry souls a little nourishment as an enticement to see the guiding light that would take them straight to Jesus.

She squinted up into the clear sky again and then back to the food she had prepared. Sister Sally was an excellent cook. In fact, she had worked as a cook in a private school for over twenty years to support and raise her three children. She took the job after her husband, Henry, was killed in a knife fight over a green-eyed Creole woman named Esther Jackson from Baton Rouge, Louisiana, back in the late sixties.

Sister Sally surveyed her handiwork on the tables before her. There were five pots altogether. One pot was filled with stew beef and vegetables, one with smoked neck bones, one with cabbage, one with rice and another huge pot was full of black eyed peas.

There was a patter of excitement among the hungry as a long black limousine drove up in front of the building where Sister Sally had set up her tables. When a young man jumped out of the car somebody yelled:

"Yo, it's Shogun y'all."

Sister Sally was too busy dishing out food to pay much notice. Besides, in her sixty-seven years on this earth she had seen enough limousines to last her a lifetime. She also knew that some of the fanciest cars were owned by some of the worst people God ever gave breath to, so she wasn't the least bit impressed or interested in who the handsome young man was or wasn't. Besides, she knew that limousine or no limousine, it wouldn't matter much on the Day of Judgment. On that great day, when whoever the young man was stood before the good Lord in heaven, he would be as naked as the day he was born. All the limousines, big houses, important jobs, and everything else most people accumulated in this world and held near and dear wouldn't amount to a hill of pinto beans.

She only looked up and took any notice at all because of the noise. She saw the young man wave and then quickly run into the building, before turning her mind back to food, rheumatism, and rain.

Shogun took the elevator to the fifth floor. He glanced at his gold Rolex. He was twenty minutes late. He readied his mind for a dirty look from Man O War.

He loved War like a brother. They had been mates since they were barely old enough to walk and were as close as blood and bone.

The door buzzer was answered by a smiley-faced man whom he knew.

"Hey, wha'ppen," Shogun greeted as he crossed the threshold into the nicely decorated and furnished apartment. "Where's War?"

"Not here yet," the man said.

"That's good," Shogun said, and relaxed.

"Want to see it?" The man gleamed at the briefcase in his hand.

"You got it?"

"Right here."

"Ain't we going to wait for War?"

"Of course. I bet you've never seen that much cash before, huh?"

"Yeah, OK," Shogun said expectantly.

The smiley-faced man led Shogun into the next room, where he opened the briefcase in the light of an open window. Inside was filled to the brim with green bills in neat bundles.

The smiley-faced man grinned. "It's exciting just to see it and it's nice just to touch it, go ahead," he coaxed.

Shogun smiled. He picked up one of the bundles.

The smiley-faced man was right. It did feel nice to touch all that cash. Nicer than Shogun had expected. It sent a tingly feeling through his body. Shogun leaned forward to pick up another bundle when suddenly everything went black.

The blow from the ax severed Shogun's head cleanly from his body. The severed head fell off his shoulders and rolled out of the open window.

Sister Sally was still looking up into the sky for rain when she saw something fall out of the window above. She wasn't sure what it was, but she knew Harlem well enough to know people were liable to throw anything out of a window — shoes, garbage, TVs . . . But when it dropped right into the middle of her pot of black eyed peas, Sister Sally couldn't believe her own eyes.

A human head with eyes bucked out and looking straight at her, as big as life itself.

Sister Sally couldn't even find voice enough to scream, she just fainted on the spot.

CHAPTER 2

Cowboy stood at the end of the bar and looked out on the street. He was dressed in his usual outfit: a grease-spotted green plastic rain poncho, combat boots, battle fatigue pants, and a Stetson cowboy hat wrapped in a covering of brown plastic tape. The expression on his deeply lined face was one of permanent irritation. He clenched a thick, dung-colored cigar between his uneven and broken yellow teeth, fidgeted with a black leather pouch strapped around his waist, and mumbled something unintelligible to himself. As he polished the glasses, Duke Rodgers, the bartender, had his small portable TV tuned to a news story about a crooked politician who had been caught taking bribes in the form of prostitutes from organized crime figures. Cowboy glanced at the TV, frowned, then quickly downed half of his drink with the usual one-gulp decorum.

"Damn shame," he said out loud.

Duke looked up and waited for the follow-up. With Cowboy, one could never be sure. His normal commentary ranged somewhere between outright lunacy to highly intelligent. Depending on how the spirit hit him.

"They act like them politicians ain't got no dick. Hmph, they got dicks same as you and me, don't they? Sho do. Damn sho do," Cowboy stated unequivocally.

'Nuff said. It was hard to disagree with that one. Duke glanced in his direction and smiled, but opted to say nothing.

"Ain't I right?" Cowboy asked again, this time in my direction.

I was cleaning the beer taps.

"Yep," I said, looking up into his dirt-stained features.

As quickly as he had sprung to life, Cowboy receded back into the solitude of his personal hell as I served two customers who had just entered.

In most other parts of the world, Cowboy probably would

have been considered a certified nutcase worthy of free room and board in a mental institution. But this was New York City, where nutcases not only walked the streets freely but were elected to high office, hosted programs on TV, and ran the biggest and best institutions. Besides, this was Harlem, where too long and too often people had been cheated and shortchanged. So to even things up, maybe somebody somewhere along the line decided to give Harlem more than its fair share of nutcases and make it a model community for nutcase equal opportunity. Cowboy was just a very small potato in a very large pot. He looked down at the baby stroller he always pushed around and smiled indulgently. Strapped into the baby seat was a dirty teddy bear with one eye missing. This was his son Gerald. If you didn't respect that, you could be sure to expect trouble from Cowboy. Gerald was his pride and joy, the heir to his personal madness. According to Cowboy, Gerald liked peanuts. So on some days Cowboy bought his kid a bag. Neither Duke, myself, nor Christine ever questioned him, we simply sold him the bag of peanuts.

For as long as I had owned the Be-Bop Tavern, Cowboy would come in twice a day like clockwork and order his usual: a double double Jack Daniel's and ginger ale in a tumbler, no ice. He never ran a tab, always paid in cash, and was always accompanied by Gerald. One day some smart-ass had had a few too many and got up the nerve to ask Cowboy what he was doing about Gerald's education. Cowboy told him that he had Gerald in a special school that trained him how to cut the balls off people who fucked with his father. After that story went around the bar, nobody seemed too interested in Cowboy's relationship with Gerald. Cowboy generally minded his own business except for his occasional lunatic comment on life every now and then. Somehow Cowboy just melted into the fabric that had become the Be-Bop Tavern. Nobody seemed to mind. Least of all me; he was a good customer.

It was mid-January and things had gotten back to normal after the Christmas holidays. Christine had become the manager of the bar and was doing a great job. Duke was holding down the daytime shift from 8:00 a.m. until 5:00 p.m., Benny Sweetmeat worked part-time making sandwiches during lunchtime, and Christine had hired two new people, Lonnie and Sarah, to work in the evening on her shift. Business was good.

Po Boy and Goose Jones, two old-timers, sat at their usual booth sipping coffee and reading the *Amsterdam News*. They were having a conversation with Benny Sweetmeat, who was cutting bread behind the counter.

"Muhammad Ali in his day was a revolutionary man—he stood up to the whole doggone U.S. government and won," explained Goose, pointing to a story in the *Amsterdam News* about the ex-heavyweight champ.

"Yeah, that's right. They tried to take everything he had. They even took away his title and his right to make a living, but the more they tried to take, the more the people loved him and the bigger he got," Po Boy chimed in.

"That just goes to show, ain't nothin in this old world set in stone. Things change all the time in ways people can't never predict," Sweetmeat said.

"He was a real man. They don't come along like that no more," said Goose.

"Like my daddy used to say," inserted Benny Sweetmeat. "If you gon' be a man, be a man in full. Let your balls hang down like a Jersey bull."

"Quit tellin the truth, brotha," said Po Boy, holding up his glass and toasting Benny Sweetmeat's words of wisdom.

"Hey, Devil," Goose called over to me. "I bet you don't remember the Rumble in the Jungle, do you?"

"Yeah I remember, Ali verses Foreman in Zaire. That's when he did the rope a dope. That was also Don King's first big international promotion."

Goose smiled. "I'm impressed. You know your stuff, huh?"

"Damn skippy." I smiled back.

Cowboy paid up, adjusted his hat, made sure Gerald was comfortable inside his baby buggy, and left.

Betty Logan, one of the regulars, made her way to the bar and stood where Cowboy had vacated.

"That man need to be in the crazy house," Betty said. "Give me another beer, please."

I started filling another glass for her from the Budweiser tap.

"I'm gonna shock you, Betty," Benny Sweetmeat said.

"What?"

"That man got a college degree and he used to own and manage lots of property right here in Harlem."

"What kind of college, the college for crazy folks?" Betty wanted to know.

"Nope, he's an accountant. If you don't believe me, ask Duke."

Betty glanced over at Duke and scowled at the thought that he was part of the joke obviously being played on her.

"He's telling the truth," Duke confirmed her questioning glance.

"What happened to him?" asked Betty, taking a swig from the freshly drawn glass of beer.

"Woman trouble," Po Boy said matter-of-factly.

"Woman trouble?" echoed Betty innocently, as if it were the first time she had heard the phrase.

"Caught his woman cheating on him and it drove him off his nut."

"He was pretty well-to-do, too, from what I can understand," Benny Sweetmeat added.

"That's what happens when men start to thinking with that little head instead of that big head," Goose commented, and adjusted his trademark, which was an old-style porkpie hat.

"Hmph, well I'll be damned," was all that Betty could seem to say at the thought of such a thing. Without further comment she went back to her table and continued reading *Ebony* magazine while drinking her third beer of the day.

Winston, a crackhead and beggar who was selling stolen dresses, walked into the bar looking around. Duke spotted him before he had gotten halfway into the room.

"Not in here, you know better," was all Duke said.

The crackhead saw Duke meant business and turned around.

Just then Shelby Green walked in. Winston stopped Shelby.

"A little something for a brotha," the crackhead said, holding out a dirty palm in Shelby's direction.

Shelby shook his head. "Fight poverty, get a fucking job."

The crackhead left, and Shelby came over to where I was wiping down the bar.

"Hey Tuffy, what's up?" he greeted me.

I had known Shelby Green all my life, and all my life he had called me Tuffy. Shelby Green had been a longtime friend of my family's since before I was born. He and my father had been the best of friends for over forty years. Shelby was in his sixties but appeared younger because of his high energy level and youngish features under a close-cropped bush of salt and pepper hair.

"Can we talk?" he asked me.

"Want to go into the back or sit at one of the booths?" I asked.

"Let's go in the back."

I took two coffees and we went into the back room that I had made into my office, complete with computer, filing cabinets, desk, telephone, my coveted CD jazz collection, CD player system, and a sofa.

Shelby sat on the sofa while I took a seat behind my desk. He unfolded the morning paper.

TWO DANCEHALL DOGZ FOUND DEAD IN HARLEM.

The newspaper article told of the decapitation of one rapper named Shogun, a.k.a Alan Leeds, and the drug overdose of another, one Man O War, a.k.a Lee Mainwaring.

"One of those boys is nephew to a friend of mine."

"Sorry to hear it," I said.

"The cops notified him of the death, but when he started asking specific questions, they just turned off. You know, just another couple niggers dead in Harlem," Shelby said. "I don't know if you can do any fucking thing but, if you don't mind, as a favor to me I'd like for you to meet with him. You're smart, so I figured you might be able to at give him your professional take on the thing," Shelby stated. "You know yourself it's a bad thing to be bullshitted when your people get killed."

How well I knew.

"I ain't trying to pin no fucking roses on you, Tuffy, but you're better than any of these cocksucking Harlem detectives, hands down," Shelby said.

"These rappers must have been pretty big to make the front pages," I said, showing my ignorance.

"Big! Big ain't the word. The biggest on the scene right now, and making more money than God. Put it like this, these boys make more fucking money in one weekend than the average person makes all year long. All they got is one album out, but that one album has been selling like muthafucking hotcakes," Shelby explained.

We finished our coffee and set a time to meet up with his friend later in the day. Then Shelby left.

I felt chilly. For the past days it seemed that I had had to wear an extra layer of clothes just to stay warm. I didn't like to think about it, but I knew that the unpredictable weather could affect my sickle-cell anemia. Could send me into a crisis, too, if I wasn't careful. But what could I do? Sickle cell isn't the kind of disease you can do much about. My fate was in the hands of the gods.

I wasn't as yet experiencing any of the signs usually associated with an attack. None of the normal background pain and no fatigue. I figured that maybe what I needed was some TLC. I smiled to myself as I thought about a place where I knew I could arrange some, no problem.

I got into my car and drove east to Spanish Harlem. At the corner of 135th and 3rd Avenue sat the Cruz empire. A super-market, funeral parlor, beauty salon, restaurant, and twenty-four-hour bodega all located in one block. The Cruz family had emigrated from the Dominican Republic fifteen years earlier, and through hard work had built a number of successful businesses in the neighborhood. Rudolpho was the patriarch of the family. At seventy-five, he was still strong and capable of running the day-to-day operations. His second in command was his eldest son Paco, who had become a friend of mine as a result of my dating his sister Sonia. Paco was about three years older than me. He was short and built as solidly as a bull, always dressed sharply in immaculately made-to-measure Italian suits and shoes. Paco was the financial brains behind the operation. He had received his MBA from City College and had used the knowledge to grow one business into the other. We took to each other right away because we both shared a love for jazz as well as an interest in martial arts. Paco had just received his black belt and he was good for an amateur.

As for me, martial arts had been more than just an interest; it had been part of my training as well as part of my survival kit during those years in the Agency.

"My man Devil, what's up," Paco said, smiling up from a plate filled with yellow rice and sausages. I sat down across from him at the table as he ate. Paco motioned for the waitress to come over, and I ordered a cup of coffee.

"Sure you don't want nothin' else, you know, it's on the house, you almost family, you know." He winked.

I smiled back. It was no secret that Sonia was pushing to change our steady dating into something more permanent.

Paco and I talked about the latest CDs. He mentioned a new musician on the scene named Siraj Al Hasan.

"I swear, this boy is awesome. He plays all of the saxophones as well as the flute, plus he plays the hell out of some Latin percussion, and he writes and produces his own music. I saw him live the other week at the Knitting Factory. He's the best I've seen and heard in a long long time. Real talent, not like some of these bullshit guys who have to do it all in the studio. Guess what else? He lives right here in Harlem."

"He has his own band?" I asked.

"Yeah, this guy named Paul Chaplin is on keyboards and he's awesome, too. Nice gospel and jazz feel. Good fucking band. I went right out and bought the CD. If I had known the night was going to be slammin' like that I would have called you up, but I just went on the spur of the moment, you know."

I nodded.

"Speaking of music, ever heard of the Dancehall Dogz?"

"Who hasn't—that's all the kids around here are talking about. One of them got his head chopped off and another one died from an O.D. It's like they were royalty or something."

"Why, you know them?" inquired Maria, Paco's seventeen-year-old daughter, who worked the cash register within earshot of our conversation.

"No, just a friend who knows one of the dead boys," I told her.

Paco finished his meal and washed it down with coffee. "I haven't heard the kids around here so upset since Tupac and the other one, the fat one, Big Daddy croaked," Paco said.

"Excuse me, Poppy," Maria chimed in authoritatively, "get the name right, please: Biggie Smalls, OK?"

"Big Ass, Fat Ass, Small Ass, it's all the same to me." Paco smirked, enjoying his own joke.

Maria just twisted her mouth in disgust and gave her father a look that exiled him from the human race. A look that sent him to that place that all teenagers at one time or other will invariably banish their parents. To that great vast wasteland of un-hipness and know-nothingness, where only squares exist and nobody knows their ass from their elbow.

Paco gave her a patronizing look, and we started talking about going to the amateur karate competitions that were being held upstate in a couple months.

"You know it's a conspiracy, right?" Maria said.

"What?" Paco said.

"They just killing them off because the lyrics they dropping is telling the truth, and certain people don't want the truth to come out so they killing them all. First it was Tupac and Biggie, now they killed Shogun and War 'cause they lyrics was just too strong," Maria insisted with adolescent indignation.

"Both those rappers you talking about was murdered by members of their own gangsta rap community. So tell me who is this so big that they running some kind of conspiracy against them? You must think these raggedy-assed rappers are as big as Communist China," Paco quipped.

"Poppy, you don't know the real deal out here on the street. Of course they gonna make it look like rappers are doing it to themselves—that's part of the game."

"Whatever." Paco sighed and shrugged his shoulders like most parents do who have consigned themselves to the reality of the communication gap existing between themselves and their teenage children. Then Sonia came into the room. She was thirty-one, five foot six and slender, with a beautiful, even smile that danced against her smooth bronze skin. Her shoulder-length black hair was neatly tied back in a bun.

Paco took his sister's arrival as his cue to leave.

"I don't know what you doing, brotha," he said, dropping the volume of his voice, "but Sonia is in love. She wasn't this much in love with her husband, know what I'm saying? See ya later," Paco winked at me as Sonia approached the table.

She was dressed for business in a dark two-piece pantsuit with a cream blouse. By profession, Sonia was a bookkeeper. She kept the books for all of her family's businesses (as well as many other Latino businesses in Spanish Harlem) on a freelance basis.

She motioned me to a table farther toward the back of the restaurant, away from Maria's ears.

"Nobody's interested in what you're talking about, anyway, you know that." Maria grinned.

"I know, sweetie." Sonia smiled back at her niece, then turned to me. "This is a nice surprise. How did you know I'd be in?"

"Didn't," I said. "Just took a chance. Plus, I figured Paco would be around and we needed to catch up."

"Oh." Sonia sat down at the table, crossed her legs, and looked dreamily into my eyes.

We usually saw each other on the weekends, and maybe once during the weekdays I'd have dinner with her and her twin daughters Angela and Erica. They liked me and I liked them.

"Do you have a bathing suit?" I asked.

"A very nice one—why?" she answered flirtatiously.

"I was just thinking," I began slowly, "that it would be nice to get away for a couple of days, maybe to the Bahamas."

"The Bahamas?" She beamed an award-winning smile and caressed my hand. "Why not."

CHAPTER 3

At 4:30 p.m. I pulled on my thermal-lined hooded winter coat and went to see a man about two dead dogz. As I turned the key in the ignition, a homeless winehead named Boy Billy came up and knocked on the window. I rolled down the glass to hear what he had to say.

"Hey baby, I'm hungry, you need anything done around at your place? Taking out the garbage, polishing the floors, a little dis and dat, you know," he said through lips parched from the cold.

"Nothing today."

He shrugged, grimaced, and looked out toward the avenue. I fished down in my pocket and pulled out a five-dollar bill.

"God bless you. When you need somethin', you know who to call," he said, looking straight into my face.

I nodded, and Billy Boy walked away. As I turned the powder blue Jaguar toward downtown while listening to Bill Withers singing "Can We Pretend," something about the words made me think of the changes in myself since I had come back to live in Harlem after leaving the Agency.

Earlier in my life when I saw the Billy Boys of the world, especially in America, I thought their conditions were of their own making, but I quickly learned that the slings and arrows of outrageous fortune could touch anyone at any time, especially if you happen to be black. One misguided step and life could have you sliding back down a hill it had taken years to climb. With just one slip of the foot, your soul could be lost. In any case, I had come to a different place within myself. Now I found myself thinking a lot more about the book behind the cover more than I had before. Maybe it was maturity. Maybe it was the daily exposure to Harlem's environment and understanding the hopes, dreams, and disappointments of the people better than I had before. Maybe it was a combination of all of those things together, or maybe it was what I really suspected but didn't want to admit to myself.

Maybe I had grown a conscience and realized that all of the years I'd spent doing someone else's dirty work and protecting other people's money-motivated interests and accepting all of the racial slurs that came with being one of the few black agents in the CIA wet works department had pretty much been a wasted life.

I pulled up to the address Shelby had given me. It was in a block dotted with large brick buildings ten or twelve stories high. A bronze sign on the outside of one of the buildings read L. H. REALTY BROKERS. I pushed the doorbell, and a muffled female voice answered. I announced myself, and a buzzer sounded allowing me to enter. A secretary met me at the door. The office was done up in the traditional dignity of mahogany desks, tables, and chairs against cream walls. The room's style spoke "money" in a cool and quiet way. Adorning the wall behind the secretary's desk was a single photograph of a large black man smiling and shaking hands with the president of the United States.

The secretary showed me into the inner office where Shelby Green was waiting with Livingston Holmes, the man in the photograph, a chocolate-complexioned giant who stood about six feet seven and weighed at least three hundred pounds.

"Thank you for coming, Mr. Barnett," Holmes said in a deep, sonorous, cultured voice that carried slight traces of a West Indian accent. He was dressed in a conservative, expensively cut gray suit, a red and orange silk tie, and a starched-collar white shirt.

"I'm sorry about your nephew," I said.

Holmes nodded his appreciation, and motioned for me to take a seat on the sofa. He then took a seat in one of two chairs opposite the sofa. Shelby handed me my third cup of coffee of the day and seated himself in the other chair.

Shelby began. "Livvy, tell Devil what you told me."

The big man sighed and relaxed back into the chair.

"Man O War, the young man who the newspaper says died of a drug overdose, was my nephew Lee Mainwaring, my sister's eldest son. The last time I saw Lee was three days before he died. He came by to talk with me about some property investments that I had encouraged him to become involved in. At that time he made mention of some money that was coming his way. Said he was spreading his wings, diversifying his interests."

Livingston paused. I took the opportunity to speak. "Diversifying into what?"

"He didn't say."

"Were you and your nephew close?" I asked.

"Yes. Very close. We've always been. Lee called me on the morning that he died and said that he wanted to see a property in Jersey that he wanted to buy for his mother. That's not the action of someone planning to take his own life. He sounded really upbeat. The newspaper said Lee died of an overdose, I couldn't believe it. So I asked to see the coroner's report. It indicated that the cause of death was the result of mixing amphetamines with alcohol, which couldn't have been right."

"Why not?"

Livingston Holmes leaned forward in his chair and extended his huge neck toward me like a great black lizard stretching to meet the morning sun.

"Mr. Barnett, I happen to know my nephew didn't take drugs. He smoked spliffs, but that's it—no pills."

"How can you be so sure. People do lots of things we don't know about," I assured him gently.

"Even so," the giant's voice was deep and quiet now. "Let's for the sake of argument say that he had taken the pills, OK. Now the fact that he died from an overdose resulting from the pills mixed with alcohol was highly unlikely, because you see, Mr. Barnett, Lee was a diabetic and didn't drink at all. He had too much to lose. Knowing Lee as I did, suicide would have never entered his mind. He had everything to live for. As sure as we sit here, Mr. Barnett, my nephew was murdered."

"There's some shit in the game, that's for damn sure," Shelby agreed.

"Shelby thinks that you can get to the bottom of this business and find out why my nephew was really killed. I need to know the truth," Holmes said.

A thousand thoughts shot through my mind seemingly at the

speed of light, all converging to make one big mess in the center of my brain.

The men were dead. What difference would it make if I found out why? Did I really care enough?

"Money is not a problem for me, Mr. Barnett. I can pay what you ask," the giant told me.

Shelby hadn't moved a muscle. He just sat looking at me without blinking, waiting for my answer.

"I'll do what I can," I said.

Shelby nodded his appreciation.

"Name your price," Holmes said.

And I did.

"You might want to start with the manager of the group, J. T. Brown." Holmes handed me a business card. "This is the name and number of Oliver Reems, the entertainment lawyer I set Lee up with."

I pocketed the card.

"Thank you again, Mr. Barnett," Holmes said. "I feel a lot better now. Shelby said you are the best."

"What about the funeral arrangements?" I asked.

"I'm taking the body back to England tonight. I'll stay for the funeral and return here directly afterward."

We shook hands, I accepted the check and left.

The evening wind blew snowflakes across the street and into my face as I made my way back to the car with thoughts of two murders playing across my brain like a discordant Cecil Taylor piano solo. Two more black men dead in Harlem. Famous black men who would keep people hooping and hollering for a hot minute. But all too soon the voices of outrage and bereavement would grow faint and, famous or not, these two men would be absorbed into the great abyss of misfortune that regularly claimed the lives of young black men throughout the United States of America. Experience had taught me that they would soon be relegated to that very *un*famous category of black crime statistics. Black crime statistics that nobody seemed to care very much about. On my way back I listened to the evening news on the car radio. The news announcer said that the country was still in the midst of an economic boom and still flourishing, and that productivity was up and inflation was down. Maybe somewhere all of this economic good fortune was indeed taking place. But from where I sat, here in the middle of Harlem, most of the people I knew were still waiting to receive the good news. Here, it was still a matter of a few crumbs going to a small select group and a whole lot of nothing for the rest.

Back at the bar I called the travel agent to inquire about two tickets for the Bahamas, separated the bills from the other mail, and watched Christine manage the evening shift. Lonnie and Sarah looked as if they were working out fine.

My years with the CIA had taught me to consult the opinion of the experts when entering a field I knew nothing about, and the music business was one of them.

I picked up the phone again and called 411 and asked if there was a listing for a Doug Anderson living on Central Park West. The computerized voice came on and gave me the number. I called. Another computerized voice answered and asked if I wanted to leave a message.

"Hi, Doug. This is Devil Barnett, Ernie Barnett's son. Could you give me a call at the Be-Bop. It's kind of important. Thanks."

I hung up.

I hesitated before making the next call to Al Mack at the New York City Police Department.

"Detective Mack here," the familiar voice answered after the third ring.

"Mack, it's me. Dev."

"Hey baby, how it be?"

I could almost see Al Mack's round face grinning at the other end of the phone.

"I'm working on something that I could use your help on. Don't worry, it's nothing that would endanger your health like last time."

"Ha-ha," Mack's voice came loud and hearty from the other

end. "What happened happened. It could have been you as easy as me."

"How are you feeling?"

"Good. I get the occasional shortness of breath, but otherwise . . . My brother-in-law suggested I start doing yoga. You know what, I did and the problem is a lot better, almost gone," Mack said.

"I'm glad to hear it. Listen," I said, swinging into the reason I had called. "I'm working on a little problem for someone and I need to get the reports on this thing."

"Which thing?" Mack asked, lowering his voice.

"Two rappers found in an apartment up on 150th the other day."

"Those two English guys?" asked Mack.

"Yeah."

"You told me you really didn't ever plan to go into the detective business. What changed your mind?"

I thought about it for a moment, but didn't have an answer.

"I'll tell you the truth, I'm not sure myself. Seems this stuff just keeps happening."

Mack chuckled. "I know what you mean. Give me till tomorrow morning on the reports."

"Great, thanks. By the way, how is your comrade these days?" I inquired.

"You mean Varney? He's shitting bricks as usual, but these days he's trying to keep his head down so he don't lose his retirement. For my money, it's just a sham. He's still up to the same old game with Deke."

Mack hung up and my mind turned to Deke Robinson, the smooth-talking black Harlem politician with his hand in the drug game, who operated under the police protection of Captain Max Varney. We didn't like each other. In fact, we despised each other. I looked forward to bringing Deke's operation to an end. But that was another play for another day.

* * *

8:00 a.m. the following morning. A bleak and cold January day. Ate scrambled eggs, cereal, toast, and coffee, then headed downtown, The destination was the Brill Building, that famous music venue on Broadway near 49th Street.

The Brill Building gained its reputation during the late 1950s and '60s as a place that housed a lot of independent record companies that made some of the early classic rock-and-roll recordings. The building still boasted a couple recording studios and many music-related businesses like publishers and booking agencies. The office I sought was on the fifth floor.

A frosted glass door bore the words PATTERSON, REEMS AND HOLLIS, ATTORNEYS AT LAW.

Oliver Reems was in his thirties, of a slender build, with a light brown skin tone accented by reddish kinky hair. In fact, he looked a lot like Malcolm X. We sat opposite each other in his office discussing the late Lee Mainwaring.

"What about the terms of his contract—his uncle says he wasn't happy about it," I said.

"Lee didn't think they received the best deal because their English attorney who originally negotiated their contract wasn't an entertainment lawyer. Now that the group had produced millions of sales for the record company, he wanted to know if he could renegotiate because their contract had not anticipated the kind of success the group was to have."

"How does his manager fit in?" I inquired.

"J. T. Brown. Yes. In fact, that was one of the things Lee wanted to make sure of . . . that the manager would not be included in any new deals," Reems explained.

We talked for a while, Reems doing his best to give me a picture of his client. I finally thanked him for his time and candor and said that I would be in touch.

Just as I was leaving the room, I turned back. "Hey, has any one ever told you that you—" "Look like Malcolm X," he finished the sentence for me. "At least five times a week," he said, and smiled a familiar toothy grin.

I smiled back and walked out.

* * *

The surviving members of the Dancehall Dogz were rehearsing for an upcoming television show at The All-Star Rehearsal Studios in lower Manhattan, where I had arranged to meet Mack. From the outside, the place looked like just another warehouse in SoHo, but inside it was designed for comfort. In addition to five rehearsal rooms complete with state-of-the-art recording equipment, TV monitors, and a stage on the main floor, there was also a recreation room full of pinball machines, videos games, and a pool table. The top floor housed a gym with a small swimming pool, Jacuzzi, sauna, steam room, and weights room. First class all the way.

Mack flashed his badge at the two beefed-up men who searched me for weapons before directing us to rehearsal room three. Seated at the mixing desk were four technicians busily pressing and pushing buttons as if they were about to launch the Starship *Enterprise.*

"Rich, the mike on the left seems to be getting a lot of feedback. Click the switch on the stem to the 'off' position," the audio technician was saying to Filthy Rich when I entered the room.

We were immediately met by an overweight man wearing dreads, dark sunglasses, and a purple and green baseball jacket with the name DUNCAN written over the breast pocket.

"The guys are just finishing up. Take a seat," Duncan said gruffly in a distinctive East End English accent.

I did as I was told and watched the proceedings.

J. T. Brown, the group's manager, was onstage giving instructions.

J. T. was fat and bouncy—about five feet nine and near 290. He paced back and forth across the stage in short, waddling steps that made him look as if he'd descended from ducks. He wore a white warm-up suit with a purple and green baseball cap.

When they had finished rehearsing, I started asking questions. "First off, do any of you know of anyone who might have made any threats against anyone in the group?" I inquired.

"You mean like hate mail? When we were touring we got a telegram once from some white supremacy group saying we should all be castrated. And from time to time the record company get letters from parents of the fans saying our lyric is too bad and sexy, but other than that, nothin'," explained Wicked.

"That's standard, though. Anybody famous gone get dogged out by jealous-hearted fuckers," inserted Rebel.

"Can you identify the white supremacist group?" I asked.

"No, mon, dem just chatting shit. I never realize this country got so many mad people," Wicked stated, lighting a fat spliff.

"Did anyone in the group have a particular beef with Shogun or Man O War that someone else might have known about?"

"You mean did we fight among ourselves and get mad and shit with each other. Of course we did, but that was normal. We would blow off and that would be that." Rebel shrugged.

"There's a lot of pressure at this level," J. T. quickly inserted, and pulled a cigarette from a pack of Lucky Strikes. "Little arguments here and there, but nothing serious."

Goldfinger shot a glance in J. T.'s direction.

"Are we suspects?" Filthy Rich asked point-blank.

"I have not ruled anyone out at this point. I'm just gathering information. I will say this, though: I think whoever chopped Shogun's head off was someone he knew and felt comfortable with," Mack stated.

"Why do you say that?" Goldfinger spoke for the first time.

"I prefer not to go into that just now," Mack quipped.

The men exchanged furtive glances.

J. T. seemed quick to bring the meeting to a close.

"Well, it doesn't seem like we can be of much more help," he said, glancing at his Rolex. "Sorry chief, but we got to get ready for a TV show in Jersey," he said, puffing on his cigarette.

"If anything else comes up, give me a call," I said, passing out my business card:

DEVIL BARNETT. PRIVATE INQUIRIES. HARLEM USA.

Back inside my car I put *Q's Juke Joint,* by Quincy Jones, into the CD player and listened to the track "Stuff Like That." My body told me I needed a rest, so I stopped at the house to catch a few winks. I warmed up some pasta that Sonia had prepared and brought over. Then I drank some hot chocolate. It hit the spot. I set the alarm clock to wake me in an hour and I went out like a light. Exactly one hour and five minutes later I fitted my Beretta into the holster attached at the back of my pants and called the bar to check with Christine, who was running the night shift. She told me that Doug Anderson had called and left his number. I dialed and Doug's voice answered on the third ring.

"Hey, how are ya," he said in his native New York accent. "Everything OK at the bar? It's been, what, almost a year . . . since the funeral."

"A year next week."

"Goddamn shame what them fuckin' punks did to Ernie. I wish I had caught them. I would have paid someone to put them in the fuckin' ground. Ernie and I went back more than fifty years," he added. "I was still in high school and waiting tables at Minton's when I met your father. He was playing drums in the house band and then he started working behind the bar on the nights they had the be-boppers in there."

"Yeah, I know, he's told me the story. Tell me, Doug, how are you doing?" I asked.

"I'm doing good, thank God. I'm working. Most of the guys who came up around the time I did are either dead or out of the business. My health is still pretty good. I'm sixty-six years old and can still get my dick hard, that's the main thing." He laughed.

I laughed, too. Doug was always good for a funny saying or story to brighten up the mood. He had a wicked sense of humor. Dad has often said that Doug Anderson was the most honest man he knew, strictly no bullshit, honest right down to the bone. What you saw was what you got.

"Listen, Doug. I've got a problem related to the music business."

"What is it?"

"It's kind of detailed. Can we talk about it over dinner or lunch?"

"No problem, tell me when," he said.

We set a time for the next day.

My next stop was the apartment of Lee Mainwaring. I got the key from the office of Livingston Holmes.

The apartment building was located on 84th between Third and Second. A nice, respectable east side neighborhood. I flashed my fake I.D. to the doorman and was let upstairs.

Lee's apartment was done up nicely. The living room was decorated in black and gray. Lee's bedroom was deep blue, and the other room was cream colored. On the dresser was a photograph of Lee flanked by an attractive middle-aged black woman who resembled Livingston Holmes, and a young woman. Beside this was a photograph of the Dancehall Dogz signing their record deal with their manager looking on.

The place was neat and orderly. I looked through the dresser drawers in the bedroom and found nothing unusual. The other room was his studio. It was filled with digital recording equipment that included three piano keyboards, two drum machines, four samplers, two computers, and four speakers. There were wall posters of Stevie Wonder, Duke Ellington, Miles Davis, Jimmy Cliff, Bob Marley, and George Clinton, plus loads of vinyl and CDs. On the desk was a small woven basket filled with receipts, a Day-Glo Dry Cleaners ticket, an unsigned Sunoco credit card, three paper clips, two rubber bands, and a pack of Wrigley's chewing gum. In the trash can, an empty cigarette packet. Lucky Strikes—J. T's brand.

On the way out I showed the doorman the pic of J. T. at the signing of the Dogz record deal.

"Lotta people come and go, I can't be sure, my memory's not the best. Sorry."

He was in his late fifties, slightly bent over, with blond hair, and fair skin blotched by broken veins that showed through on his bulbous nose. His speech was accented by a slight Irish brogue.

I showed him the color of a hundred-dollar bill, which lifted the veil from his memory.

"Oh yeah, I remember now, it was on the day before the story hit the papers about Mr. Mainwaring's death."

"How long did he stay?"

"Not long, maybe thirty minutes," the doorman said.

"What time was it?"

"I'd say about, um, seven. Yeah, seven or eight."

"Did Mainwaring have any other visitors that day that you can remember?"

"Yeah, the other one."

"What other one?"

"The other one that was found dead. The one whose head got chopped off. Ugly business, huh?"

"When did he show up?"

"Maybe twenty minutes after the first guy came."

"So the two of them were here together?"

"Yeah, that's right."

"Did you see what time they left?"

"Nobody left on my shift," he said, shaking his head. "I work till eleven."

I handed the doorman the hundred-dollar bill and my card. Told him there was another hundred waiting for him to call me if anyone else turned up sniffing around.

My next stop was Shogun's crib. He had lived in a high-rise apartment building in a swanky east side neighborhood.

My "I.D." did the trick again.

Shogun lived in a luxury suite complete with all the trimmings and decorated in the group's colors—purple and green. Purple walls, green furniture, purple and green towels especially monogrammed with D.D. Purple bed, green silk sheets. Purple carpet, green curtains.

Whereas Lee's apartment was neat, Shogun's was messy. Dirty dishes, clothes strewn about, a Jacuzzi full of dirty water, and five empty champagne bottles was just part of it. I looked around for any signs that might tell me something about why his head had ended up flying off his shoulders in the middle of Harlem, but I didn't see anything that jumped out at me. The police had already been there, so some things had been removed. But not much. It was not the crime scene. On the dresser was a note with the words *CALL ME TONIGHT, C.*

The doorman was busy helping an old lady load packages into a cab when I went back down to the lobby. I asked him if he had seen anyone go up to Shogun's apartment on the day that he died.

"No bro, not me," he said.

His name was Roberto and he was Puerto Rican, about forty, with a clean-shaven face and a wide, ready grin. I pressed a hundred-dollar bill into his palm and continued my inquiry. Roberto looked around to make sure he wasn't being seen taking the money and winked at me.

"I need to know anything you might have seen unusual, in the last week or so," I said.

"Wasn't nothing unusual, bro."

"Did you ever see this big fat guy go up with Shogun?" I showed him the pic of J. T. and the boys.

"J. T. Sure, I know J.T," Roberto said.

"Has he been here recently?"

"No, I haven't seen J. T. in about a week or maybe, yeah at least a week. He came by to pick up Shogun sometimes," Roberto said.

"What about the day he was killed. Were you working that day?"

"Today is Tuesday, that would have been Sunday. Oh yeah, I did see him Sunday. Yeah."

"When?"

"Early afternoon, maybe one o'clock. He had two girls with him."

"Two girls?" I repeated. "Who?"

"Shogun. Yeah, that wasn't unusual, though, because he always partied," Roberto informed me.

"Did you ever hear of a girl called C?"

"Yeah. She came sometimes . . . know what I'm sayin?"

"What did she look like."

"Uh, let's see, about twenty-three, I guess. Black girl, nice chocolate flavor." Roberto showed me his wide grin again. "Long dark hair and a Coca-Cola body, know wha' I'm sayin? Pretty eyes, kind of like a cat's."

"What else?"

"That's about it, really." Roberto shrugged.

I nodded and gave him my card. "Find out where I can get hold of C, and that's two bills," I assured him.

Roberto lifted a clenched fist and smiled. Money talks and bullshit walks.

Back in my car I called J. T. Brown on his mobile. He answered on the first ring.

"Mr. Brown, I just came across some information that might be helpful. Can I meet you later today?"

"Man, I'm very busy, can't promise you." There was agitation in his voice.

"This won't take but a minute, and it could be important," I told him.

"I'll call you back in fifteen minutes," J. T. said, and hung up in my car.

Fifteen minutes later, no callback.

One hour, fifteen minutes later, still no callback. I was getting the picture.

My next appointment was with Max Hammill, president of Grooveline Music. Oliver Reems had arranged it. The offices were located in a building near Columbus Circle.

Max Hammill was a white man who looked about forty-five years old, stood about five foot nine, suffered from badly pockmocked skin, wore thick-lensed, wire-framed glasses and walked with a slight limp. The voice didn't go with the body and face. The voice was refined, with a northeastern accent. Maybe Vermont or Rhode Island. His features looked stained.

"Mr. Barnett, I'm very glad you've come to our aid in this matter," Max said as we sat in deep, comfortable chairs inside his large, plush office.

Max looked at me intently as we spoke.

"How long have the Dancehall Dogz been contracted to your company, Mr. Hammill?"

"About nine and a half months."

"And from what I understand, the group came here to live in America about four months ago."

"Yes, they came over and we did a three-month tour to support the record."

"I understand that on tour they received some hate mail from a white supremacy group, as well as some letters from disgruntled parents who felt that the group promoted behavior unbecoming to young people," I recounted.

"True in both cases," he said.

"Do you have any of the letters?"

"No, we don't keep that kind of thing. We don't want to clog the machinery up with that kind of negativity, so we just throw them away." Hammill scowled.

"You mean to say racist mail is common?" I asked.

"Sorry to say, but it's very normal. What isn't normal is people following up on their threats. In most cases, the artists don't even get to see these letters. Our publicity department takes care of it."

"How come the group members got to see one?"

"Oh, that one was delivered backstage at one of the performances, accompanied by a bunch of roses like it was from a female fan. I don't think the group ever saw any others."

"How long have you been in the business, Mr. Hammill?"

"Twelve years."

"And no doubt this is one of your biggest hit groups?"

"Are you kidding? This is the biggest hit group of the last ten years for the entire record business." He smiled proudly.

"How will the death of two members of the group affect things?" I asked.

"I wish I could answer that. We're still in shock about it. I'm not even thinking about myself, just mostly concerned about how the group is coping emotionally. None of us know which way to turn. I mean, we don't know if it's a wacko or what. Jesus Christ, as you can imagine, it's been terrible for everyone."

He rubbed his face, yawned, then got up and limped to the other side of the room.

"Why is the group still working? I saw them in rehearsal earlier today," I said.

"Some of the group wanted to call it off, but Wicked insisted that they continue working and make the TV show a tribute to Man O War and Shogun. Besides, the rights for that TV show have already been sold worldwide and each member of the group is making good money."

That answered the sentiment question. Dead men don't get paid.

"Any of the other group members showing special concern for their own safety?" I asked.

"If they have, nobody has said anything."

"Might the group move back to England?"

"Mr. Barnett, I don't even want to think about it. That would be a terrible move for all concerned."

"One last thing, Mr Hammill. I've tried to call J. T. but he doesn't seem to call me back. Can you help?"

Hammill picked up the phone on his desk.

"Monica, get J. T. in here right away. I'm sorry, Barnett, but J. T. is very protective of the group—you can understand that."

Three minutes later, J. T. Brown walked into the room.

"Sit down, J. T.," Hammill said.

The fat manager did as he was told without question or hesitation.

"Mr. Barnett says that he found—"

Just then Rebel walked into the room. "Yo Max—" He stopped when he saw me in the room.

"Feel free, we have no secrets here," Hammill said.

"It's very simple. I just wanted to ask J. T. if he knew a young lady who was hanging out with Shogun called C?"

"Uh-uh, never heard of no one called C," J.T said quickly.

Right away I knew he was lying.

"Why you want her—you think she might know something?"

J. T. asked sniffing and wiping his nose. He twisted nervously in his chair.

All the classic signs. J. T. Brown had a serious coke habit. Experience told me that where cokeheads were involved, anything was possible. Over the years I had found out that in the coke game, murder was just an appetizer on the menu in a world of sordid deeds. I had known men who'd had their skins peeled off while they were still alive and their entire families wiped out, from the ninety-five-year-old senile grandfather right down to the three-month-old in the crib. The world of coke was not a joke.

"Shogun had lots of girls around him all the time. I never knew they names though," J. T. spewed.

"What about Roachie?" Rebel quipped.

At the mention of the name, both Max and J. T. stiffened ever so slightly.

"Ah, that's n-n-nothing," Max stuttered.

"If you don't mind, could you tell me about this nothing?" I said.

"I'd rather not. It was just a personal matter that took place about a month back that had nothing to do with the group. Just an irate boyfriend jealous of his girlfriend's success. It happens all the time." Max smiled sickly.

"Did he threaten you or anyone in any way?"

Max looked to J. T. then to Rebel, then to me.

"Well, not threaten, but—" Max started to say.

"The fuckin' geezer said he would put you in the ground. You forget?" Rebel blurted, unaware that his well-meant input had tied a nervous knot in the pit of Max's stomach.

An invisible force had invaded the room. Whoever Roachie was, he was sending chills down Max Hammill's crooked spine.

CHAPTER 4

Roscoe Simmons's bloodshot eyes were popping out of their sockets, and his throat was burning hot like the Kalahari. Life as he had known it for the past thirty-one years was in the process of ending. The tightly wound wire around his neck had almost completely drained away his life. Another two seconds and he would be a memory, lost forever to the vague, darkened shadows of a lonely Harlem night. Roscoe had known the best of times. Big money, big cars, pretty women, fancy vacations to exotic places. He'd had it all, just for the asking. Those things were forever behind him now as the tightening wire around his neck cut off the supply of blood to his brain. Now he was dying. He was actually living out the words of that old Bible verse he had heard his grandmother read so many times in that storefront church in Harlem where she had spent all of her Sundays for over twenty years. Living by the sword and dying by the sword. Death was an unrepentant runaway locomotive moving at full speed. Unstoppable. If he could have spoken, with his last words he might have told his mother or his daughter that he loved her. But the anxious, unrelenting and voracious hand of death denied him such formalities. Instead of a dignified send-off that a man of his status felt he deserved or would have liked, Roscoe was helplessly writhing in uncontrollable agony in an undignified abandoned warehouse some-where in Harlem, with less than a half second to live. But still, something inside him fought against death. Understandably, because by nature, Roscoe was a fighter.

That was the quality that had aided and abetted his rise to the top of the heap in the dog-eat-dog world of the illegal narcotics business. But now he couldn't fight anymore. Roscoe's will gave way just a nanosecond before the very last thought went through his brain, which was the phrase "OH HOLY JESUS."

Roachie pulled with all his strength to tighten the wire around his victim's neck. Roscoe's body had stopped moving. His mouth gaped opened, and his breath was nonexistent. His eyes were perfectly still and bulging from their sockets like two brown cat's-eye marbles. Roscoe Simmons was a "Used-To-Be."

Roachie moved Roscoe's body into the trunk of the rented car and drove to the location where he placed the body into a Dumpster.

Roachie liked killing. He was good at it. When he realized it was something he actually liked, he wasn't sure how to feel about it. Naturally, everything he had been taught growing up was that killing was morally and categorically wrong. But those thoughts had eventually been replaced by other thoughts and, more importantly, other values.

He had been able to wash away his "sins" by justification of the cause. The cause was all-important. It offered him not only absolution, but also salvation. Roachie was a professional soldier in the army of "the cause."

He had honed his body to fit his profession. Martial arts, weight lifting, meditation, healthy diet—all geared to meet the needs and obligations of the cause. He was thirty years old, with a Bachelor of Arts in Computer Science and a bright future. Seven assignments he had been given, and seven assignments he had flawlessly completed.

The job was done and by now Roachie should have been able to relax, but instead his mind had turned to someone else he wanted to kill: Max Hammill. Often he would sit up nights thinking how he would take his revenge. Torture, slow slow torture. Make him wish he had never been born. Thinking about how he would take Max's crooked back and twist it into the shape of a pretzel until he begged to be put out of his misery. Every time he thought about Thelma, fresh thoughts about killing Max Hammill entered his mind. Until she'd met him, she had been his. All his. Now she belonged to . . . just the thought of it was too painful. The only reason Max was still able to walk on God's green earth was because Roachie was now a soldier and more dedicated to the cause than he was to his own emotional needs.

The phone rang. He recognized the voice at the other end. He took the information down slowly on a scrap of paper, making sure every detail was correct, then hung up.

Roachie sat down, committing the instructions to memory. He didn't know why he was supposed to do it. He didn't care. As a soldier for the cause, it was not his role to question. He looked down at the name he had written on the scrap of paper: DEVIL BARNETT.

CHAPTER 5

It was 9:45 a.m. The temperature had dropped six degrees from the day before, and my insides were chilled even though I was warmly dressed.

Duke walked over to where I was sitting at the end of the bar reading the morning paper and drinking a steaming hot cup of coffee. Duke always walked slowly because he had a bad case of bunions.

"Hey, boss man, how you coming along?" he said as he approached.

"OK, and you?" I looked up as he stopped next to me.

"I'm making it, you know." He smiled.

Duke Rodgers was fifty-seven years old, stood over six feet, with big, broad shoulders and a sharp ear connected directly to the underworld grapevine in Harlem. In a former life he had been both a numbers runner and a sergeant in the U.S. army during the Vietnam War.

Duke had worked part-time for my dad when he ran the bar. When I took over, Duke came on as a full-timer to run things during the day shift, to teach me the facts and figures part of the business, as well as to fill me in on the unspoken rules that you only get to learn from actually running a business in Harlem.

Dad and he had been good friends, and Duke extended that friendship to me.

"How's Mildred?" I asked.

Duke nodded his head in a positive gesture. "She's doing OK; the chemo seems to have worked. We went out last weekend to a birthday party and she really enjoyed herself. It was the first time in a long time that she didn't go out and come back real tired. So I would say that things are looking up." Duke smiled.

"That's good, I'm glad to hear it." I smiled back sincerely.

"By the way, I forgot to tell you when you came in, Sonia called about a half hour before you got here, said she would be in the office all morning." Duke raised his eyebrows, grinning.

"Thanks."

I went and called Sonia directly.

"Did you get a chance to check out the tickets to the Bahamas?" she asked me.

"Yeah, but the last week of February is as soon as we can go. Everything else is all booked up."

"That's cool. You coming to dinner tonight?"

"I'd like to, but I'm working on something and can't be sure."

I could hear the disappointment in her voice as she said good-bye and hung up. Who was I fooling? She liked parts of me even better than I did.

Doug Anderson arrived at the Be-Bop at ten o'clock sharp, dressed in his signature tan suede oxfords and looking twenty years younger. He also wore an expensive tan cashmere coat and a winter-white tailor-made tweed suit.

"Howzit goin'?" he greeted me.

We shook hands and sat down near the back of the bar, where we could talk without fear of being overheard.

I briefed him on the killings and what I had found out so far.

"Max Hammill?" he said as his face knitted itself into a scowl.

"You know him?"

"Coke dealer." Doug laughed and shook his head, then continued. "A bullshit coke dealer steps into horseshit and hits the jackpot. On the other hand, that's what's makes music such a great business. Anybody can come in and get lucky."

"Can you see him as the killer?"

"He's making so much money on the group, he would be crazy to do anything to jeopardize his gravy train. On the other hand, where coke is involved, all kinds of crazy shit can happen. You have to understand this is a very volatile business and the artists are a necessary evil. Ninety-nine percent of them are a pain in the ass. When they're hot, you have to kiss their ass, babysit them and do whatever the fuck it takes to keep them happy 'cause they're a fucking moneymaking machine. Artists easily go crazy, freak out, or turn up dead in their hotel rooms with a bullet hole in the head or an overdose. A smart manager knows that. If he has already put a lot of money into developing his artist, the manager will hedge his risk by taking out a key man insurance policy on the artist's life making himself the beneficiary. Who is the manager?" Doug looked at me inquisitively.

"A guy named J. T. Brown. Know him?"

"J. T. Brown." Doug laughed. "Yeah I know that scumbag. He's a cokehead who can barely manage to get his dick out of his pants to take a piss. Strictly small-time. Started out as a promotion guy on the scene back when disco was hot. How the hell did he get to manage these boys? It don't add up."

"What do you mean?"

"J. T. is a first-class asshole who wouldn't have the brains to manage Elvis if he came back from the dead. J. T. has to be fronting for someone. Probably Max is, too."

"If that's the case, you think J. T. is happy with the situation?"

"Happy as a horny faggot in a big dick factory. All the coke he can snort, all the broads he can screw, and more money than he's ever made in his miserable fuckin' life. Like I said, this thing goes deeper than that bullshit asshole." Doug said matter-of-factly.

I still didn't have a clue, but at least Doug had given me some insight into the music business as well as another path to follow. An hour later I called a man I believed could trace down any information in the world as long as it was on a computer.

"Hey Devil, how's it hanging?" Onion quipped.

Onion had worked for me as a freelance hacker during my days in the Agency. We had developed a friendship over the years. He spent his time confined to a wheelchair in a room full of computers in upstate New York with his wife, Jessie, who was devoted to him.

At around six that evening the phone rang in my office. I was surprised to hear the voice on the other end. It had an English accent."

"Mr. Barnett, this is Goldfinger from the Dancehall Dogz. Rebel said you was looking to find Shogun's girlfriend, yeah."

"You know her?" I asked.

"Yeah. She was Gun's personal freak. For threesomes and foursomes and all sorts. A first-class freak, yeah. Know what I mean?"

"Yeah, I know what you mean. What's her real name?"

"Chandra. Lives in New Jersey. Works in a beauty salon—The Braiding Factory. In Fort Lee. Listen, I want to get whoever is responsible for killing Gun and War. We've been close mates since we were at school. To be honest, we really shouldn't be working. We should be in a state of mourning. But Grooveline ain't givin' it the right kind of respect, sayin' we've got to promote the new record. See what I'm sayin'?"

"Yes I do. Thanks again. I'll be in touch," I told him.

Within five minutes I was in my car and headed to Jersey.

7:16 p.m. The Braiding Factory was still open. Still three women under the dryers. A lady with a lisp was taking money at the cash register. I flashed my phony I.D. and she called the manager, a middle-aged black woman about five foot seven with a dark, uneven complexion and a slim, shapeless build, who wore enough pancake on her face to feed a camp full of hungry lumberjacks.

"I'm Patty, step in my office," she said curtly, leading the way through the array of hair care products to the back of the shop, where she sat down behind a desk and lit a cigarette. She inhaled deeply and blew the smoke over her left shoulder through her thin, aquiline nose. The only thing that looked decent about her was her hair, cut short and fitted perfectly to her angular face. Otherwise she looked as if she had just rolled out of bed. The thin, cheap-looking purplish dress hung like a wet sack on her bony frame. The worn lines around her eyes told of too many late nights and long drinking sprees. As I sat opposite her desk I could smell whiskey on her breath.

"What can I do for you?"

"I'm looking for Chandra."

Patty looked at me for what seemed like a long time, then said, "About the death of that rapper she been keeping company with?"

I conceded that it was. She wrote down the address for me

without saying another word.

The white and yellow single-family house where Chandra lived was on a neat, tree-lined street in a nice part of town. The doorbell was mounted on an orange and white porcelain sign that read THE DORCUS FAMILY. A light was on inside.

I rang the bell. A dog barked and the porch light came on. Then the dark, pretty, flat face of a large, middle-aged woman appeared at the glass panel of the front door that had been fitted with a security grill, bulletproof glass panel, and intercom system.

"Yes?" she called through the intercom while sticking her face up to the glass panel in the locked door.

"I'm from the New York investigative unit of a law enforcement agency. I'm looking for Chandra Dorcus."

A look of hesitation mixed with confusion passed over her face and she disappeared. Two minutes later a man took the woman's place at the door. He was big and caramel colored with a scruffy beard and looked to be in his late twenties.

"What you want?" he inquired gruffly.

"I'm looking for Chandra," I repeated.

The man continued looking at me suspiciously. "She ain't here," he said.

"When is she coming back?" I asked. "She may be in danger."

At the word "danger," the expression on the face of the big man turned from distrust to concern. The woman came forward again.

"What kind of danger?" she wanted to know with deep concern in her voice.

"It involves murder, ma'am," was all I said, and left the statement hanging in the cold night air.

Through the security glass, the woman looked directly into my face as if she were trying to read my mind while she slowly started to undo a number of locks that secured the front door. "Come in," she said.

I stepped into the living room of the house and was greeted by the young caramel-colored man pointing a sawed-off shotgun in my direction. "I hope you're for real, mister," the man said.

From his expression I knew he was willing to back up his words.

"Now, what is all this about?" the flat-faced woman demanded.

"My name is Barnett. A friend of Chandra's has been murdered. We have reason to believe she might also be in danger. It's vital I speak to her."

"I see . . . uh sit down Mister . . .," the woman offered.

"Barnett," I said again.

I sat down on the beige sofa, and the big man kept his distance on the other side of the room with the shotgun still trained on me.

"You'll please forgive us, Mr. Barnett, for being cautious, but in these trying times you don't quite know who to trust," she apologized, then left the room.

The man looked at me with an impassive expression.

The living room was decorated in cool pastel colors. Pale blue walls with a cream-colored wall-to-wall carpet. The mantelpiece was peopled by six fat cherubs in various poses. Hanging above was a framed poster of a black Jesus and his twelve black apostles at the last supper. The apostles' faces were those of various black heroes, including Marcus Garvey, Malcolm X, and Martin Luther King. Resting next to the wide-screen TV was a rack full of family photographs. I recognized the photograph of the teenage boy as a younger version of the man holding the shotgun.

Ten minutes passed and there was a knock at the front door. The flat-faced woman of the house returned from the other room to answer it. A young woman in her early twenties entered. She was an older version of the teenage girl in the family photograph. Chandra pulled off her coat to reveal a beautiful body as she eyed me with suspicion from her catlike face.

"This is the man," flat-face said.

"Ma, I tol' ju, I 'on't know nothin' 'bout nothin'," Chandra cried defensively.

"At the least, you can see what the man has to say, girl, don't you think?" her mother advised in a calm tone that suggested a hammerlike fist inside the velvet glove.

A look passed between them. Unspoken but understood that

Chandra's mother had not been born yesterday, and also knew that where there was smoke there might be fire.

Chandra looked at me sourly and then at her brother, who still sat like a hungry guard dog clocking my every move. "What's he doing with that gun?" Chandra demanded.

"Bucky's doing what I told him to do. Don't worry 'bout him. You just talk to this man," her mother answered.

"OK," Chandra relented, then slumped across from me in one of the nearby chairs. "Who are you, anyway?" she asked, screwing up her face distastefully as if I were a newly discovered turd on her dinner plate among the steak and potatoes.

"I'm here to find out what really happened to Shogun."

"I knew Shogun, yeah, but," she inserted cautiously, "I don't know what happened. He just got kilt is all I know."

"Goldfinger said that you guys hung out."

Chandra batted her eyes as tiny alarm signals flashed inside her pupils. She took a long pause and then started to twitch nervously in the chair. She tweaked and fingered her hair, which hung shiny and shoulder length.

"I tol' ju, I 'on't know nothin'," she blurted, her voice rising almost an octave.

"Was Shogun dealing drugs?"

"Nah, it wasn't like that. Gun was deep into his music."

"Did J. T. and Shogun ever argue?"

"Yeah, once."

"What was it about?"

"Money, I guess. Listen, I wasn't involved. The only thing I knew was Gun told me he was getting some money and he was going to buy me a car," she said.

"A car?"

"Yeah, we was close. He really liked me more than people realized," she said. "What I heard was in pieces, you know, but I figured something out."

"What?"

"That there was some static."

"Within the group?"

"Yeah."

"Do you know what the deal was?"

"Not exactly. I tol' you that, but I think it must have had somethin' to do with Fuzzy and frees, that's what they kept talkin' about."

"Fuzzy?" I remarked with an obvious puzzled expression.

"Fuzzy Martin, the deejay," she exclaimed, and glared at me as if I were an alien from Mars not to have known who Fuzzy Martin was.

"I'm not exactly familiar with the pop music scene, so you'll have to be patient with me. Now explain to me exactly who Fuzzy Martin is," I said.

"He's the biggest hip-hop deejay in the world. He did the remix of 'What About the Bullshit,' which went number one in only four days after it came out. Plus, he's the program director for what is only the top hip-hop station in New York."

"What happened with Fuzzy, then?"

"Well, I heard War and Gun talking about Fuzzy getting fifty thousand cleans from J. T. but that they weren't getting nothing from them 'cause Fuzzy was getting them on the D.L."

"The D.L.?" I repeated.

"Yeah, the Down Low. You know, under cover."

"OK."

"Well, War was real upset 'cause he said Fuzzy told him that the cleans he was getting was a special order that they were doing just for a few deejays around the country. War kept sayin' he didn't like it 'cause he was losing on both ends. That's when Gun said he was losing on both ends, too, and tol' War he wanted to be brought in on the deal. I didn't really understand all of it but when J. T. came by the house, War and Gun was beefin' with him."

"Saying what?"

"War said that he was going to talk to the other members of the group. And then J. T. tol' him that if he kept quiet, he would talk to the man and cool him and Shogun out."

"You mean getting cooled out with money?"

"Yeah, I guess so."

"Who was the man he was talkin about?" I asked.

"They didn't say. J. T. just said 'the man.'"

"Do you have any idea of how much money was involved?"

"No, but Gun just kept sayin' he was going to buy me a new car 'cause the one I got keep messin' up."

"When did all this beefin' happen?"

"About a week, nah . . . about two weeks ago."

"What happened the last time you saw Shogun?"

"Nothin' really, we was just getting high and partyin'."

"You and Shogun?"

"Yeah. Me, Gun, and Peaches."

"Who is Peaches?" I inquired.

She sucked her even, white teeth in disgust, then looked over to her mother sheepishly. "She ain't nobody, just some hoochie always up in Gun's face," Chandra spat.

"Do you know where she lives?"

"No, why should I, she just a ho. I don't be hangin' around skeezers." Chandra scowled. "She wasn't nobody important. Just one of Gun's hoochies trying to get close, know what I'm sayin'?"

"Describe her."

"She got a cheap-ass set of extensions and a skinny, no-shape body, that's all I know." Chandra chuckled. "I didn't pay her that much attention."

"Just the three of you, huh?"

"Yeah," she mumbled.

When I left the house the cold night air was whipping around me and I felt the wind cutting into me like a hundred razor blades.

I drove back to Manhattan listening to Lisa Fisher and Lee Ritnour performing together on a tune called "Baltimore," and thinking about what I was going to say when I caught up with J. T. Brown, the punk cokehead record hustler who had gotten lucky with the hottest group of the decade. The same J. T. Brown whose luck was about to turn from sugar to shit.

I got home around midnight and turned up the heat. It felt good. My body was crying out for some TLC again, the love drug.

"Damn!" Suddenly I realized that I had forgotten to call Sonia. I dialed her number and waited.

"Hello," her sleepy voice came on the line.

"Hey, I'm sorry baby, I got hung up in Jersey."

"You couldn't have taken just two minutes out to call. I wasn't even that important to you?" she seethed angrily. "I waited to hear from you. I didn't know what had happened. I was worried."

"I know, I'm sorry."

"Why you got to be getting involved with other people's business, anyway?"

"Listen, I'm a little tired right now. Can I call you back tomorrow and straighten it out?"

"Now you don't even have time to talk, huh?"

"Sure, I've got time, but I just wanted to—"

"Listen, when are you going to get your priorities straight?" she barked. "You must have someone else over there—that's it, right?"

A tinge of anger had started to replace the irritation inside me. I could almost taste the poisonous venom of her words. "No," I retorted, trying to sound cool.

"Well, tell that bitch that she can have you, 'cause you don't mean that much to me. OK?"

I opened my mouth to tell her again that it wasn't true, but all I heard was a *click*.

I went into the bathroom and filled the Jacuzzi. I got in and tried to relax, but it wasn't that easy. The emotion stuck in my body like a monster trapped in a cave. I sat in the tub for almost twenty minutes, then I got out and played back my answering machine.

There were five messages. Three from Sonia, one from Honey Lavelle, and one from Onion. I finally felt relaxed enough to crawl into bed.

2:34 a.m. A blaring noise woke me. My doorbell. Instinctively, I slid my hand under the mattress until it connected with the steel of my Beretta. I held it by my side and walked the two flights down. The doorbell sounded again. On the other side of the glass door stood Sonia. Her face was pulled into a mask of anger and suspicion.

A gust of icy winter night pierced my silk pajamas as I opened the door. She stood staring at the gun.

"Come in," I growled sarcastically, then turned and headed back up the stairs after her.

Sonia entered my apartment with eyes darting around the place like the police on the lookout for a prowler. She sniffed the air for any alien perfumed scent.

"Feel free to look around," I said, slipping back into bed and pulling the covers over my head.

"I'm sorry," she said after she had finished her inspection and was satisfied that I didn't have some naked woman hidden in the fridge.

I remained sullenly silent and pretended I was asleep.

I heard her undressing. Within a few seconds she joined me in bed. Her smooth, soft skin sent a warm glow through my body as she wrapped herself around me like a hungry anaconda.

"I'm jealous and I know I shouldn't be, it doesn't make any sense, but I get like that sometimes. I hate myself for it," she whimpered.

Emotions clouded my thinking. As she squirmed and wriggled closer to me for comfort, I relaxed into the scent of her body and her inviting softness. "Listen, baby, I'm sorry I didn't call," I told her

"I know, let's forget about it," she said, and pushed her hand under my pajamas.

That was it. We made love for what seemed like an eternity, then I dropped off into a deep, deep sleep.

The telephone rang at seven. The voice belonged to Onion.

Sonia was still curled around me and I didn't want to wake her.

"Yeah," I said as quietly as possible. "What'd you come up with?"

"A million-dollar baby, actually, a five-million-dollar baby."

"Explain," I said and sat up.

Sonia stirred and looked up at me out of a half-closed eye.

"The record company had insurance policies on each of the rappers valued at two and a half million pounds with Lloyd's of London. The record company is the policyholder, but the beneficiary is the Ultimate Management Company, at a London address. I checked them out, but all I got was an answering machine," Onion reported.

"OK, thanks. If you get anything else, give me a call," I said and hung up.

"Everything OK?" asked Sonia.

"Yeah, just business," I said, and kissed her gently on the forehead as she snuggled up closer.

The studio was on the eighth floor. A three-dimensional sign outside the elevator announced FRONTROOM STUDIOS. I introduced myself to the young secretary, who was wearing a blue sweater and matching hair that was sectioned off by what seemed like a minefield of various colored rubber bands holding up clumps of hair on different points of her head. She directed me to a sitting room and offered me a coffee. While I waited, I read through the latest edition of *Billboard* magazine. The Dancehall Dogz had had the number one album for the last twelve weeks on the rap charts and for the past ten weeks on the dance charts. On the pop charts they were listed at number three behind Madonna and somebody else whose name I didn't remember.

Fuzzy Martin rounded the corner with his hand extended and a fake smile plastered on his face. Fuzzy was a white man in his late twenties and stood about five feet five. He might have weighed 140 pounds soaking wet. His hair was cut so close that you could see his scalp, and he wore a silver hoop through his left eyebrow. His face was smooth and hairless.

"Hey, what's up, Mr. Barnett," he greeted me in a thin, nasal-tinged voice that made one think of a cat meowing. "Would you mind following me inside the studio."

There was another white man inside. He had long hair, thick glasses, and wore jeans and a black T-shirt. As he worked twisting knobs on an amplifier he smoked a joint that dangled from the corner of his mouth.

The room was dimly lit. On one side of the recording studio were three keyboards flanked by two metal racks that held a combination of amplifiers, samplers, drum machines, and other whatnots that made music without the benefit or talent of real musicians.

"This is Mace," Fuzzy Martin said, nodding in the long-haired man's direction. Mace nodded back, took the joint from his mouth, and offered me a hit.

"Thanks, I'm cool," I said, declining the weed.

Martin led the way deeper into the studio to a soundproof room that had a real drum kit set up in one corner. "So you wanted to talk?"

"I understand you did some business with Man O War before he died," I said, jumping right in, not knowing where I was going to land.

"What kind of business?" he asked suspiciously.

"Record business. You mixed their latest hit record, didn't you?"

"I did the remix, sure, but I didn't work with War specifically. In fact, part of my deal with any record company that I work for is that I have total creative control. The last thing any remix producer wants is to have the producer of the original tracks around when you're doing a remix. Egos tend to fly, artistic differences, you know—it's only natural," Martin explained cautiously.

"What was your deal with them?"

"Uh, my deal?" He swallowed hard and suddenly paled a bit.

"Yes, how did you get paid for your services?"

"They paid me like they usually do," he said, squirming uncomfortably on the stool.

"And how was that?"

"Uh . . ." He looked down and paused, then looked back up at me a bit defiant. "I thought this meeting was about the deaths, not how I get paid for what I do? Anyway, I could call my lawyer and end all of this bullshit right now."

"Listen, Mr. Martin, as an important potential witness I can arrange to have the police pick you up for questioning. I can also arrange to have my police friends put you in a cell with some very bad men who would appreciate a nice young sweet-assed virgin like yourself. All I have to do is make a phone call. Am I making myself clear?"

He didn't know whether to shit or go blind. Fuzzy Martin had been used to dealing with people who were in awe of his status. But I wasn't in the club. I just wanted to find out who had killed who.

Fuzzy Martin sighed heavily and looked around as if to make sure nobody could hear what he was about to say.

"In most cases when I do a mix, I get a fee and a percentage of the sales."

"How much?"

He hesitated and rolled his tongue nervously around in his mouth.

"How much?" I reiterated.

"Uh . . ." He hesitated again. "Thirty thousand a remix plus three percent of the sales profits."

The figure startled me for an instant.

"Thirty thousand dollars for *one* remix?" Wanting to make sure I was getting this right.

"Yeah," he confirmed matter-of-factly.

I realized I must have been gawking.

"OK, so how did Grooveline pay you?" I asked, regaining composure.

"With cleans."

"Cleans?"

"Yeah, cleans are copies of CDs that don't go through the company's accounting system but can be used by the company for promotion purposes. In reality, the cleans get sold to record stores at a discount."

"Like the black market, huh?"

Fuzzy shrugged.

How much are the cleans sold for?"

"About ten percent less than wholesale as an incentive to the retailer."

"And how many cleans did you get for your part of the deal?"

He hesitated again. "Fifty thousand," he managed weakly.

"How much would that have amounted to after sales?"

"About two hundred thousand."

"Why would they give you so many cleans if your fee was only thirty thousand?"

"I don't know." He blinked. "I just take my cut and give the rest of the money to J. T."

Suddenly I felt like hitting Mr. cooler-than-cool Fuzzy Martin in the mouth for lying to me, but for some reason I didn't. Besides, I knew I could always pay him another little visit, one that wouldn't be so friendly.

My next stop was Grooveline Music.

"Mr. Brown's not here at the moment," the receptionist informed me. "Is there something I can help you with?" She smiled flirtatiously.

"I need to see him, but if Max is here, I can see him instead," I said meeting her beautiful gaze.

She shook her head and blinked her almond-shaped eyes seductively.

"Uh-uh, Max is traveling and won't be back for a few days. In fact, he's gone to England for the funerals."

"Isn't J. T. going?"

She leaned forward over her desk and dropped the level of volume of her voice. "It's a damn shame, isn't it, that he's not even letting the group go back for their friends' funerals. I heard that they all wanted to go, but Max had J. T talk them into staying and completing some TV program. Talking about they'll have a special memorial service instead. That's some cold-blooded bullshit, ain't it?" she confided.

"It is," I agreed.

"If it was my friends, I would just have to say later for what the record company is talking about. But these artists don't know their rights. I've seen you before," she said, changing the subject in midstream.

"You have? When?"

"I was at an office lunch party for a friend of mine a few months ago at a place called the Be-Bop Tavern and you were working there."

"That's right." I smiled back.

"You still work there?"

"Yeah."

"Then what you doing here? I thought Max said you were some kind of detective."

"I'm just helping out a friend trying to get a few things straight—you know for the family type thing."

"Oh." She nodded, eyeing me up and down in an approving fashion, letting me know in no uncertain terms that if I wanted it, all I had to do was ask.

"The best time to catch J. T. would be around seven in the evening."

"Seven o'clock, but you'll be gone by then?" I said.

"Sometimes I am, but sometimes I'm here until late." She winked.

"Tell me something."

"What, you want my telephone number?" She grinned.

"No, uh . . . no, but I was . . ." I hesitated. Her directness had caught me off guard. She realized it, too, and started to laugh.

"Sorry, I have a bad habit of doing that," she admitted.

"You know you should develop a mind-reading act," I told her.

She laughed out loud. "By the way, my name is Monica." She smiled.

"Oh, OK, tell me something, Monica."

"Uh-huh," she said, licking her lips. "Tell you what?" She straightened up in her chair so that her breasts stood at full attention. She had turned the flirting machine up full blast.

"Tell me . . . um, do you think there's a chance you'll be in when J. T comes in tonight?"

"If you need me to be here I will."

"Thank you. Will you call me when he comes?" I asked, giving her my best smile.

"I will," she said, smiling sweetly in return.

I gave her my card, and that was that.

"By the way, do you know a girl who hangs out with the Dancehall Dogz named Peaches?" I asked.

"The way these hoochie mommas throw themselves at those poor boys, you think I can keep up with the names of every one they come in here with?" Monica stated.

"Just asking," I apologized.

"Don't worry 'bout it, baby, ask me anything you want." She smiled, licked her lips again, and giggled.

Monica was the kind of woman who knew how to turn up the flame, and if a fellow wasn't careful he would find himself up to his neck in boiling hot water.

It was almost two o clock when I returned to the bar. The lunchtime crowd was just winding down. Benny Sweetmeat had started to put away the cold cuts when an attractive, well-dressed woman who appeared to be in her early fifties walked over to the counter. At first she just stood at a distance away from the counter and stared at Benny as if she couldn't believe her eyes.

"Sheila, Sheila, it's him," she said in a loud, excited tone.

"It couldn't be," Sheila exclaimed and stretched her neck in the direction of Benny Sweetmeat, who was oblivious to the two women checking him out.

"Yes, it is, too," the attractive lady assured Sheila. "Let's go say hello."

"Oh, Mary Ann, I couldn't. I would be too embarrassed," Sheila exclaimed girlishly.

"Come on, girl, just say hello for old time's sake," Mary Ann said.

The two women approached the counter gingerly as if

creeping up on a deer so as not to frighten it away. All the time their eyes were glued to Benny Sweetmeat, who was making a ham on rye with pickles for a customer.

"Girl, you're right, it is him," Sheila said, the excitement rising in her voice.

Po Boy, who had been following their conversation and hoping for an opening to make his move, saw the perfect moment and chimed in with the precision of a percussionist in a symphony orchestra.

"It surely is, ladies, in live and living color," Po Boy said, donning his most flirtatious grin which more closely resembled the lecherous, shiny-eyed leer of a carnival barker selling a pair of Siamese twins doing a striptease act.

Goose Jones, his partner, just sat by taking it all in, saying nothing as he usually did.

"You know him too?" Sheila inquired joyfully.

"Know him—why, I practically managed him back when he was performing. He's the original sugar dick daddy with the candy nuts." Po Boy grinned and winked lecherously at the women.

"Sho is," Goose threw in enthusiastically. Just in case something developed, he wanted to have a nickel in this quarter that had just dropped from heaven.

"Do you think we could say hello?" Sheila asked demurely.

"Sure. I'll arrange everything, ladies. My name is Po Boy, and this here is Goose."

Goose tipped his hat in their direction.

"How do you know Benny?" asked Goose, curiosity finally getting the better of him.

"Well, uh, we . . .," Sheila started, then hesitated shyly.

"Fans, huh?" Po Boy interjected, and grinned wide enough to show all of his dental work for the past thirty years.

"Well yes, we are that," Mary Ann mused coquettishly.

"Sit down here and I'll give you ladies a special introduction. Might even be able to get you an autograph," Po Boy added, pouring it on thicker.

"You ladies live up here in Harlem?" asked Goose, thereby pretty much using up his whole repertoire of pickup lines. He had been married for fifty of his seventy-two years, so he was somewhat out of practice.

"Yes," Mary Ann crooned sweetly.

Goose swallowed hard and batted his weak eyes behind thick, smoke-tinted lenses.

"What y'all drinking?" inquired Po Boy.

"Nothing, thank you, we just had lunch," Sheila told him.

The two ladies took seats at the bar.

Benny looked up and noticed the ladies smiling at him. "May I get you ladies a sandwich?" he asked.

"Are you . . . are you . . .," Mary Ann almost swooned, "Benny Sweetmeat, the film actor?"

Benny's brows suddenly furrowed together, and his thick bottom lip tightened into a straight line. His expression seemed frozen in a mask of permanent distress. He was caught smack dab between time zones of who he was now and who he used to be.

Now he was Benjamin Eldridge Johnson, grandfather, husband, solid citizen, congenial server of sandwiches, an upstanding member of the Harlem masons as well as a junior deacon in good standing at the Mount Moriah Greater Baptist Church of Harlem. But who he used to be was Benny Sweetmeat Johnson, "The Longest Dickingest Stud That the World Had Ever Seen." That's how he used to be billed on the hundreds of live stage performances and countless pornographic movies in which he had appeared in his youth.

According to local legend as well as his publicity, Benny had a thirteen-inch penis that could keep a permanent hard-on. Or, as one advertisement had put it: THE LEAD IN HIS PENCIL WILL NOT BEND OR BREAK.

"Sure, that's him, live and in living color," quipped Po Boy proudly. "The one and only Benny Sweetmeat. Did you see him in *The Plumber*. He was laying pipe from coast to coast. He was the best in his day. Better than all these porno studs around now. I know, 'cause I rents them all from the video store."

Mary Ann cooed, then turned to Benny and smiled sweetly. "Remember me, Benny? I played the part of Little Sally Walker in that movie you was in, *Nasty Boys in the Nursery*."

Benny's skin was a deep shade of brown, but his complexion had turned almost purple from embarrassment.

"*Nasty Boys in the Nursery,* yeah, I remember that one," mused Po Boy, going back in time.

"And I was your partner once at a stag night, over in Brooklyn. You probably don't remember, but that night you took on five girls and wore us all out." Sheila blushed. "Do you still do live performances?"

Then, with eyes flashing and talking a mile a minute, Mary Ann jumped in with both feet.

"When I came in here last week and saw you behind that counter, I could hardly believe it. It was like I was reliving my days as a young girl. And then I got to thinking that if it really was you when I came in here this week, I was going to ask you a special favor. See, my sister is getting married next month and we wanted to do something a little different, so we thought that we could get you to perform like you used to do. It will just be me and Sheila and my friend Betty and—"

Before she could finish, Po Boy was off the barstool and up on his feet, drooling.

"Sure, that would be a dandy idea. Can I come?"

"But this is a hen party. Only women are allowed," Mary Ann interjected.

"Well, I'd come as his manager," Po Boy said, looking over at Benny's frozen face and then turning back to wink at Mary Ann with his one good eye.

"Me too," Goose put in, just in case things went forward on a positive note. His daddy had always told him "Better get the getting while the getting is good," and he didn't see how it could get much gooder than this. Three women all buck naked as jay-birds in one room. Lawd have mercy. Goose could feel himself starting to sweat.

Sheila smiled up at Benny. "Well, what about it?"

Po Boy, Goose, Mary Ann, and Sheila were all turned to Benny Sweetmeat with bright anticipation written on their faces. The way they looked, you might have thought they were all standing in the stable awaiting the birth of the baby Jesus.

Benny didn't know quite what to say. "Listen, the devil had me by the neck in them days, but I've gotten myself free and I'm thankful for it, so I'd appreciate it if you'd let the dead stay buried."

Having said his piece, Benny Sweetmeat then turned, picked up a stack of dishes from the sandwich board, and stomped off into the kitchen. The two women looked dejected, but Po Boy was quick to not let a golden opportunity go down the drain. "Don't worry. Like I say, I was practically his manager. I'll bring him around."

"Do you think you can really talk him into it?" Sheila asked hopefully, allowing a soft whisper into her tone.

"Sho, I can," Po Boy assured, purposely deepening his voice to give it what he interpreted as a confident tone.

"He can talk most folks into anything," added Goose.

"We'll pay him five hundred dollars," Mary Ann said.

"If I don't get him, I'll get someone else, younger," said Po Boy, covering his position from all sides.

"Somebody else," Mary Ann almost exploded. "Ain't nobody else can compare with Benny Sweetmeat, you said that yourself."

"Yeah, but uh . . .," Po Boy stammered.

"If we can't get Benny Sweetmeat, we'll just forget it," Mary Ann exclaimed matter-of-factly.

Sheila nodded in agreement as they both walked out.

"Damn," was all that Po Boy could say as he watched the women leave.

"Damn," echoed Goose.

CHAPTER 6

When I walked into Doug Anderson's office, it was almost 5:30 p.m. He was sitting behind a large oak desk smoking a huge cigar.

"Sit down," he said, motioning me to an oversize chair in front of his desk.

He then offered me a cigar, which I declined.

"So you fucking around in the music business, huh?" He grinned.

I explained to him about my meeting earlier with Fuzzy Martin.

Doug shook his head in awe and laughed. "Can you image a little cocksucker like that will make over a million bucks a year all because he goes into the studio and takes what someone else has produced and puts a club mix to it? Incredible."

"A million—he told me he gets thirty grand a remix," I said.

"Yeah, but gotta figure he does four or five a month, that plus what he makes on the side for pushing certain records."

"But isn't that illegal?"

"So is drugs and prostitution, but people still getting rich from it, ain't they?" He scowled, then continued. "Airplay is still essential for most hit records. Sometimes there are exceptions with underground rap, but the majority depend on airplay like a newborn calf depends on its mother's tit. The major record companies spend millions on promotion to make sure cocksuckers like Fuzzy Martin play their records. That's how Martin got to be big in the remix business, because he controls what gets played on a major New York radio station."

When I left his office I looked at my watch. 7:32 p.m. I felt hungry and was stopping to eat at a Chinese joint when my phone rang. It was Monica with the news I was hoping for.

It took me all of thirty minutes to make it to Grooveline Music.

"Thanks." I smiled at Monica and eased a rolled-up hundred-dollar bill into her hand.

"He's got someone in there now."

"I'll wait." I smiled and took a seat in the waiting area near her desk.

"If you want, I'll tell him you're here." She smiled back.

"If it's all the same, I'd prefer it be a surprise," I said.

"You something else," she said, lowering her eyes in a sexual gesture. "Anyway, I'm going, J. T.," she said into the intercom, and winked at me.

"See you soon, Mr. Fine." Monica giggled and headed toward the elevator with the kind of wiggle in her walk that made you realize that poor old Adam never had a chance against Eve.

I waited patiently for twenty minutes until a slender blond man wearing a dark cashmere coat came from the direction of J. T.'s office and stepped onto the elevator. When J. T. looked up from sniffing a line of coke on his desk, he saw me standing in his doorway.

"How did you get in here?" he scowled.

"Just walked in," I responded.

"Take a seat," he said, issuing a fake smile.

"I won't need to take up much of your time, just a couple more questions. I met with Fuzzy Martin today," I said calmly, deciding to cut the bullshit. "I hear that you're basically a bagman for drug dealers, so I need to know who the real boss is."

His face contorted in rage, J. T. exploded as if an atom bomb had gone off inside him. "You jive bullshit nigga, I'm the fucking boss. Who the fuck you think you talking to? Now get the fuck out of here before I kick your black ass," he screamed, and stood up behind his desk.

I stood up quickly in response to his threat and took three steps in the direction of the door as my hand went into the small of my back. I swiveled toward him and in one deft motion brought out my snub-nosed .32 caliber revolver. I crashed the gun into the bridge of his nose, felt the bone crack as I made contact. He fell backward and his eyes rolled up into his head. I hit him again. He gasped for air, but it didn't help. I stopped beating him just long enough that he didn't pass out, then I beat him some more. By this time, his mind had gotten the message to his mouth that it had made a serious error.

"Don't kill me, please don't kill me," he pleaded.

"Who's your boss?" was all I said.

He hesitated. "But I—"

I cut him off and hit him in the face again, three times in rapid succession. *Bam! Bam! Bam!*

He coughed and spat and struggled for breath. I leaned him forward to keep him from choking on his own blood and hit him again. He was as limp as a rag doll. I placed my knee in his chest and opened the chamber of my revolver, took out the bullets and held them inside my hand. I then held one bullet in front of J. T.'s face and placed it back into the chamber. "This one has your name on it," I said.

Before he could protest, I forced the gun barrel inside his mouth and pulled the trigger. His eyes blew up as big as saucers. He tried to mutter something. It came out garbled. I took out the gun barrel just enough to let him have his say.

"I'll tell, don't kill me, I'll tell, please don't." He was one big black nervous twitch. "The Reverend. It all belongs to the Reverend Jennings—he set everything up. He da boss," J. T. managed breathlessly.

"Does Max work for him, too?"

"Don't know," he gasped. "They got somethin' goin' but I don't know exactly what."

I replaced the gun inside his mouth and pulled the trigger again.

J. T. closed his eyes and trembled with fear. "Oh Lord, I swear. I swear, I'm telling you all I know," he begged as tears rolled down his fat face.

"Where can I find this Reverend Jennings?"

"At God's Holy Tabernacle, on 137th Street."

"Who killed those two rappers?" I demanded.

"I don't know. I swear I don't," J. T. blubbered.

"Why was Lee Mainwaring mad about you giving Fuzzy Martin the cleans?"

"'Cause War said he wasn't getting no royalties on them. He was mad and he said he was going to tell the group."

"Who offered him money?"

"Money, what?"

I put the gun into his mouth again and pulled the trigger.

"Ahhhh," he let out a long, wailing moan. "Reverend Jennings told me to offer them money. Twenty thousand each. I swear before God, that's all I know."

"What else?" I demanded.

"I don't know know nothing else. The Reverend takes care of things."

"Does the group know the Reverend is the man behind things?"

J. T. shook his big bulldog head vigorously. "No, only War knew. Not even Shogun, just War."

"What were you and him arguing about?"

"War started threatening me that he was going to tell the group I was ripping them off, and I told the Reverend and the Reverend told me to bring War to him."

"Did Shogun see the Reverend also?"

"I don't know, I only took War. That's all I know."

"Who is Peaches?"

"Peaches? I don't know no Peaches," J. T. said through bruised lips.

I hit him in the face a few more times until he nearly passed out, then I stood up and kicked him squarely in the groin. He doubled over in pain and wallowed on the floor, holding his nuts.

"Next time you call me a nigger, you're a dead man," I promised.

CHAPTER 7

God's Holy Tabernacle was located in a huge building that took up almost the entire block between 6th and 7th Avenue on 137th Street. All of the windows facing the street were made of stained glass. In the building's foyer were two huge murals. Painted on one wall was a black Jesus leading a flock of sheep, and on the other there was a middle-aged black man smiling with his arms spread, standing among the heavenly stars. I waited for five minutes in an immaculate reception area painted in white with matching furniture.

Suddenly a middle-aged dwarf with light brown skin and a long, pointy head wearing what looked like a purple and yellow priest's robe walked through the door. He saw me sitting there and nodded without speaking.

"Mabel, have the leaflets for the weekend retreat come back from the printer yet?" he said to someone behind him that I couldn't see.

"Yes, Reverend, they came in this morning," a middle-aged woman wearing a gray business suit and carrying a notebook answered dutifully as she came into view walking behind the dwarf, who smiled at her.

"Good, then we can get them out right away," he said, and walked back out.

The woman stayed behind, writing in her notebook. She then turned her attention to me.

"Is that the Reverend Jennings?" I asked.

"Oh no." She chuckled. "That's our assistant pastor, the Reverend Waldorf."

"Oh, I see," was all I said.

Three minutes later a clean-shaven young man in his late twenties to early thirties with an effeminate manner and sad eyes dressed in a conservative black business suit appeared in the office.

"Hello, Mr. Barnett. I'm Wendell Somes, secretary to the Reverend Jennings. He's expecting you."

I followed Wendell through a maze of corridors until we came to the stairs at the end of a long hallway and then to a small chapel. Inside were about fifteen women all gathered around a man standing at a podium. Brown-skinned, in his mid-forties, dressed in a purple robe identical to the one worn by the dwarf except that the collar and the cuffs of the sleeves were made from African kente cloth.

"Reverend Jennings is just finishing off a service with the prayer warriors," Wendell told me.

"May I watch?" I asked.

"Sure." Wendell smiled.

The Reverend was sweating profusely and preaching to the assembly of women, who all seemed spellbound by his delivery.

"We all are walking in the wonderful light of God, walking in and talking in and living in that wonderful light that has touched us in our sinful state," the man preached.

"Amen, yes Jesus. Oh, Father God, God is soooo good," the women chanted and moaned as the preacher poured his words over them.

One large woman weighing at least 250pounds walked right up to the podium and suddenly let out a deep moan, then collapsed to the floor. To my surprise, no one seemed to take any notice. The woman lay still on the floor for almost five minutes before one of the other women reached over and covered her with a banner that was hanging on the railing of the altar. There was a golden cross emblazoned on the banner. Then another woman dipped her finger in a large jar that rested on a table near the altar and wiped the forehead of the woman lying on the floor with a sign of the cross. As the Reverend continued to preach about walking into the wonderful light, three more women moaned and fainted. And just as was done with the first woman, each fainted woman was covered by a banner and was crossed with something from the jar.

The women still standing took up the words of the song.

"Walking in
Talking in
Living in and Loving in
Walking in the Wonderful Light"

And then. one by one, each fainted woman woke up and joined in the song.

When the service was over, Wendell ushered me into a large room that seemed more like the penthouse of a high-class hotel than an office. Ten minutes later I was introduced to the man whose face appeared on the wall in the foyer opposite black Jesus, and had just mesmerized the prayer warrior women, the Reverend Trevor Jennings himself.

The Reverend Jennings seemed smaller up close with his smooth, clean-shaven face. His salt and pepper colored hair was neatly cropped close to his head. He wore an exquisitely tailored tan double-breasted suit, a beige hand-stitched shirt, brown alligator loafers, and a gold watch.

The room was decorated in purple and yellow. We shook hands, and I took a seat on one of two canary yellow straight-backed chairs in front of the Reverend's deep purple wooden desk as he walked over to a table and poured himself an orange juice from a crystal glass pitcher. "Freshly squeezed," he offered.

"Thank you," I said.

"Welcome to God's Holy Tabernacle. So, I'm told you have been asked to look into our unfortunate occurrence," he said as he poured a glass for me.

"I was told that you were in fact the real manager of the Dancehall Dogz," I said, getting right to the point.

"Are you a private detective, Mr. Barnett?" the preacher inquired coolly without batting an eye.

"In a manner of speaking," I replied.

"The deaths of both Alan and Lee are very regrettable indeed, two talented young men taken from us by the Lord in their prime. But like so many things, it is beyond our understanding," he replied with the tinge of an upper-class British accent running through his speech.

"Are you so sure that it was the Lord?" I posed, looking him directly in the eye.

He raised his eyebrows and took a seat behind the large purple desk and flashed a patented well-practiced grin that he must have used at least ten thousand times before.

"In my profession, Mr. Barnett, we believe that the Lord is not the direct cause of our earthly misfortunes and we also accept as fact that when a terrible tragedy ends someone's life on this earth, the soul of that unfortunate one always goes back to He that gave it. We live in the hope that God will guide them to a better place. So you see, certain things are not for me to question. I just accept it as part of the Lord's work."

"And there are some who will profit handsomely from the Lord's work," I responded sarcastically.

"I'm afraid I don't quite follow you," he said calmly.

"The insurance policies that were written on the lives of the deceased men, by Lloyd's of London."

"Oh, I see what you mean." He sighed heavily. "My attorneys advised when I got involved with the group to take out a life insurance policy on each of the young men involved, due to the high-risk nature of the entertainment business. Which is what I did. In fact, I was warned that anything could happen, and as a way of protecting my—or shall I say the church's—investment, insurance was a necessary evil. Well, unfortunately something did happen."

"You say the church?" I queried.

"When I say the church, let me clarify. The money that went into developing this group came directly from the church. I got involved for two reasons. Firstly, the kind of music that they are performing is extremely popular here in Harlem. Almost every young person and his brother wants to be a rap artist. Secondly, I got involved because I figured that even if I made a moderate go of it, I could use the money to help build our new church as well as fund some of our more controversial programs that we haven't been able to get funding for."

"How much is your new church costing, if I may ask?"

"Eight million, it's no secret. Our new tabernacle development will take up two city blocks."

"And right now, the church is five million dollars closer to getting built because two men are dead," I said.

"Unfortunately, that's true," he said.

"What other programs did you plan to fund?"

"For instance, there is a program we had been trying without success to get funded that we call Gear for Homeys, which would involve young people from the Harlem community running their own clothing store. Our traditional funding sources thought this idea sounded ridiculous because they reasoned that a group of teenagers and young adults from Harlem with no experience or business training in retail could never run a clothing store. I begged to differ. Not only do I think the young people know what other young people want to buy in the way of clothes, I also think that the young people around here will develop some of the very best creative marketing and sales ideas for these products. If you are aware of the advertisements on TV now, many of them are filled with the language that started off as ghetto slang just a few years ago. So my involvement with the Dancehall Dogz was an alternative way of creating funding for projects like these. I never dreamed, however, that the group would become as successful as it has," the preached related.

"What interests me is why did you work so hard to stay in the background? From what I understand, even the group members don't know that you're the power behind the throne," I told him.

He pondered the question for a moment and then started judiciously, as if measuring each word. "As you probably know, Mr. Barnett, church people in America can be among the most politically conservative people around. I have a board of directors I must report to. Can you image what some of them would say if they knew I was investing the church's funds into a group that gave concerts where they held their private parts and used profanity on stage? For that reason alone I have found it prudent to keep a low profile. Mind you, no one on the board will complain because the money the church is making from its investment in the group will make us one of the richest churches in the country, but it's just not the kind of thing that my board members would want to get around." He smiled benevolently.

"Does keeping a low profile also have something to do with the fact that you chose two drug dealers within the music industry to be your representatives?" I asked.

He played it cool, but I could tell the question made him uneasy. He sighed deeply, stood up, and walked to the other side of the room.

"I knew that Max was a former addict and dealer, but he assured me that it was a part of his past that he wanted nothing further to do with. I know what you're probably thinking, Mr. Barnett, that I must be out of my mind to take the word of a former junkie. But you have to remember what my business is. I believe totally in the redemption of man. Remember Mary Magdalene, who turned out to be one of Jesus' staunchest followers, was once a prostitute."

I stood up to leave. "When you get Gear for Homeys together, let me know. I'll be one of your first customers."

"Better than that, we've already got a lease for a store on 125th. I'll send you an invitation to our grand opening party," the Reverend said, beaming proudly.

Shelby Green, who was very well connected in Harlem, had given me the name of a woman who worked in the accounting department of the church and saw the Reverend on a daily basis.

Her name was Irma Madison. She looked to be in her late thirties with a bronze complexion, soft brown eyes, and a firm, shapely body that boasted a pair of oversize breasts that would make a man's mouth water. The day I met, her she was dressed in a dark green and sunshine yellow tight-fitting dress that made her breasts look like two torpedoes ready for launch.

"So you're Shelby's friend, huh?" she mused as I entered her ground-floor apartment. "He said you was going to be coming by. You know I'm only doing this 'cause I owe Shelby a favor. I usually don't get into folks' business."

"I understand," I assured her sympathetically.

The room I entered was the kitchen. It was neatly done up in yellow and green, which I assumed were Irma's favorite colors. The smell of pig feet hung in the air like a thick fog.

I took a seat at the kitchen table. I could tell by the way Irma walked and accentuated every gesture that she was one of those women who had an overwhelming need to be noticed. She could have worn a flashing neon sign reading PLEASE PAY ATTENTION TO ME.

"Would you like some pig feet, Mr. Barnett?" she crooned.

"No, thank you."

"Shelby says you own the Be-Bop Tavern. Ain't that somethin'." She grinned, showing off her cheap dental work. "They used to have singers in there a few years back."

"Yes, my father owned it for fifteen years before I took it over."

"Oh yeah, he got—" She broke off her sentence and glanced up at me sympathetically.

"Killed in a holdup," I said, completing her sentence.

"What a shame, what a shame. Harlem is gone to the dogs, you know. I grew up here and the stuff going on now is just madness. Drugs everywhere, kids killing kids for nothing. Madness pure madness. Sure you don't want no pig feet? I just cooked 'em," she assured.

"No thank you, I'm not hungry," I lied. I just didn't want to eat her pig feet or anyone's else's pig feet, for that matter.

"What about something to drink? Folks don't have any kind of manners no more, do they. When I was growing up, people would come into your house and you would offer something to drink even if it wasn't nothing but a glass of water. Manners. That's the way I was raised. But nowadays you can sit up all day in somebody's house and it could be ninety degrees outside and they won't even offer you a glass of water. No manners. Like I said,

Harlem is gone to the dogs. I used to sing. Did Shelby tell you?" she said, pouring me out a glass of Kool-Aid.

"No he didn't."

"I could have been another Tina Turner, but Stokley held me back. That's my husband. He got jealous of my success 'cause I was getting too much attention. I hate a jealous-ass man. You probably seen Stokley around. He cruises all the bars around Harlem." She got up and went into the other room. Within seconds she had returned with a photograph of herself and a smiling man sitting in a nightclub. Both of them looked like they were having a good time.

"That's Stokley, damn fool. He from the country, you know. Alabama. That's why I cook all these pig feet and stuff."

Stokley looked to be in his early forties, with a stocky build and jet-black skin.

"You probably know him if you see him in person. He can play drums, too. He's very talented. I tell him all the time he should have stuck with his music, but he didn't listen. Now he's working as a janitor, damn fool. We could have been like Ike and Tina Turner. Everybody say I sing just like Tina Turner—power, you know," Irma said.

Without warning, she stood up and hit a series of loud, shrill off-key notes that made my teeth hurt.

"*What's love got to do, got to do with it,* she shrieked. Then she looked at me for an approving reaction.

I didn't disappoint her, I forced a smile.

"Just like Tina, huh?" she said.

I nodded blankly and hoped like hell that she would spare me the torture of trying to sing again.

"Shelby tells me that you keep all the church's accounts?" I said, steering the conversation to what I had come for. "What kind of person would you say the Reverend is?"

"Like most men, I guess."

"You know someone he's been involved with?" I inquired.

She thought about the question and wrinkled up her nose.

"No, not really. He's too slick to let his cat out of the bag, you know what I'm saying, otherwise them sisters would drag his name through the mud. You know how our people do each other. Whoever he's doing he's doing on the Q.T." She grinned and winked.

"How about his business dealings generally?"

"Good. I mean, he gets an awful lot done. And even though I ain't no fan of his like a lot of these Harlem women are who think he walks on water, I still got to give him his due. He does a lot of good and he knows the right buttons to press to get things done."

"How long have you been working for the church?" I wanted to know.

"Three years. First I started working in reception, then I moved to the accounting department after I got my associate's degree."

"So the Reverend is honest, generally?"

"In business, yeah, as far as I know. I mean, he's honest, I guess, but that don't always make him always right, if you know what I mean."

"Not exactly. What do you mean?"

"Well, he looks out for his own, like anybody is supposed to. I ain't saying he's crooked. I'm just saying I don't always approve of the way he does certain things," she said sourly.

"What certain things?"

"I ain't spreadin' no dirt on nobody, 'cause what goes round comes round—you know that, don't you?"

I said that I did.

"One thing that really sticks out in my mind was last year there was an opening at the church for a janitor 'cause the one we had, old Mr. Budrow, retired. I got Stokley to apply for the job. Stokley can fix anything. He can paint, lay floors, hang paper, plumbing—anything in a building, Stokley can do it because he come from a long line of fix-it men. His granddaddy back in Alabama had a fix-it business and Stokley started working with him when he was just a boy, so he knows his stuff," Irma said proudly, sticking out her torpedo chest with pride.

"I believe you," I said.

"But the Reverend said he turned Stokley down because he was not a member in good standing with the church. And he chose a man who ain't half as good as Stokley and he only been a church member for less than a year. I didn't think that was right, and when I asked the Reverend Waldorf about it, he said the church member thing was just part of it. He told me that the other part was that Reverend Jennings had got word that Stokley liked to smoke weed on the job, and that might not go down too well with some of the church members. I said so what, everybody smokes weed nowadays. And so what if he smokes a little weed on the job. We're just talking about a janitor in a Harlem church, not the official greeter at the White House, for God's sake. You can walk down the street here in Harlem every day and see people lighting up joints like they cigarettes. Some of the police be smoking joints, too. I ain't saying it's right, but I do think it's right to give a man a chance," she stated.

"I see. I take it you are a church member."

"Oh yeah, me and my mother and two sisters. I told Stokley when I joined the church that he should join, too, because you never know when a good church membership can come in handy, but do you think he listened to me? Nope, damn fool."

"What about the assistant pastor, Reverend Waldorf—does he work closely with the Reverend Jennings?"

"Who, midget man?" She threw her head back and laughed loudly. "Now him I could tell you a few stories about—that little sex-crazy, perverted devil—that would make a deaf, dumb, and blind man sit up and take notice. I ain't never seen nobody so hot for women as much as he is. And he got the nerve to think he's cute and sexy, too. He hits on anything in a skirt."

"Does that kind of behavior get back to the Reverend?"

"Of course, but the Reverend turns a blind eye to it 'cause midget man and him been working together forever. You know what he had the nerve to do last week, I was getting something from the cupboard at work and I had my back turned, so I didn't see him come in and when I straightened up he was standing right underneath me and my breasts went right into his face. And I know he meant to do it, talking 'bout 'Excuse me, Sister Madison, I didn't see you.' The nasty little devil." Irma laughed. "He's all right, just nasty. Only one person there that gets on my last nerve, and that's Mother Hinton."

"Who's she?

"She's the head mother of the church. She's in charge of administration. Old maid. Ain't got nothing but the church in her life. Walking around acting like she so high and mighty with her old West Indian self, but she just a po ass nigger like the rest of us," Irma said chuckling sourly.

"Is she close to the Reverend?" I asked.

"Loves his dirty drawers. And he believes anything she says. I wouldn't trust her far as I could throw her, but that's just my opinion. We don't particularly see eye to eye. But that's personal, so I won't go into it. Like I say, I don't generally like spreading dirt on folks 'cause I wouldn't want nobody bad-mouthing me," she said.

I left feeling a bit sorry for Stokley that he had to come home to Irma's big mouth every night. The picture being painted of the Reverend and his operation was all too smooth and perfect. The feeling I was experiencing reminded me of a story my grand-mother used to tell about a woman down south who would go to buy a dime's worth of sugar from the general store but she would always come home with a quarter's worth. Her husband, not being naive, figured out eventually that there was something going on between his wife and the storekeeper but he could never prove it. But just so she wouldn't think he was a damn fool, when-ever she would come back home with the groceries, he'd simply say, "Hey baby, that's too much sugar for a dime." That's exactly how I was feeling now.

I decided to stop in at Walter Dixon's Soul Food spot. I drove there and parked a block away. I got out of the car and started walking toward the restaurant when suddenly I felt something hard being stuck into the small of my back. It was an all too familiar feeling. Unmistakably a gun barrel.

"Just keep walking, Mr. Barnett," the voice behind the gun told me.

CHAPTER 8

I couldn't see anything because my head was inside of a cloth bag. The car drove for what seemed about an hour and came to a stop. I was ushered out. My legs ached and my head hurt. I realized I was being taken into a house.

I was led to a chair and the bag was removed from my head. For the first time I got a look at the man who had abducted me.

He was about six feet two, in his late twenties or early thirties, and black, with a block-shaped head and deep-set brown eyes.

"Relax, everything's cool," was all he said, and he left the room.

The room was neatly decorated in a utilitarian manner. Three oversize brown chairs with a matching brown couch, a simple desk with a telephone, cream-colored walls adorned with paintings of nature scenes. Nondescript but comfortable.

Within a few minutes a thinish black man who looked to be in his late thirties entered the room. He was dressed in a casual black pullover sweater and brown khaki pants. He wore glasses and smoked a pipe. I watched him as he crossed the room toward me. He stopped about a foot from my chair and extended his hand.

"I'm sorry about how we brought you here, Mr. Barnett, but we had to do it that way for security reasons. You are in no danger, so please relax. You were brought here at the recommendation of a mutual friend who thinks that we may be of help to each other. My name is Malik," he said.

I shook his hand reluctantly, and he smiled politely in response.

"Please have something to drink. Coffee, tea, milk, juice, beer," he offered.

"Coffee," I said.

Malik rang a bell that was on the nearby desk and within seconds a young man in a white servant's jacket appeared.

"Please bring our guest a coffee and myself a tea along with something to eat," Malik requested in a firm manner like he was used to giving commands. "Mr. Barnett, I am part of a very special kind of organization dedicated to saving ourselves from self-destruction," he said.

"Ourselves?" I must have scowled without realizing it.

"I know how it must sound, but after you hear me out, I'm sure you'll find we probably have more in common than you now think. Firstly, we are not a cult or a religious group. We are strictly a civic and paramilitary organization dedicated to stopping the things that destroy the black communities in this country. If you decided to label us, I guess you could say our organization would be similar to what Mao Tse-tung built in China during the cultural revolution. In fact, we find a lot of parallels in the conditions of the black community now and how China was prior to their cultural revolution. A select few preying on the many, causing the terrible conditions in which black people have to live."

"The sixties and the Black Panthers revisited," I said sarcastically.

Malik smiled indulgently and drew on his pipe.

"There are those I'm sure who would take that point of view, but there are others who take the point of view that unless we as black people start dealing with the destruction of the black community, then we are truly lost and doomed to second-class citizenship forever. We may even be looking at the eventual return of legal segregation. What we have done as an organization is take responsibility for what goes on in our communities through a combination of approaches that include prevention, education, and elimination. Our main focus at the moment is the drug epidemic that has found roots in our communities across the country. The way in which we deal with it is quite simple. We take junkies off the street and try to make them kick the habit, then we re-educate them and develop them as soldiers for our organization."

"What if the cure doesn't take?" I asked.

"They are offered a choice: Either they go back into the community and try to help some other unfortunate souls or, if they go back into drugs, we see that they disappear from the community into a forced labor situation."

"Forced labor camps?"

Malik paused "Yes, exactly. On the surface, it may sound harsh, but you know yourself, Mr. Barnett, that our government is generally in no great hurry to stop the drug problem in our communities."

"The junkies are only part of the problem," I reminded him.

"I was coming to that," he said. "Remember, I said that we had three approaches to our program. There are the prevention and re-education elements that we offer to the addicts. But to the pushers, we offer only elimination. We send the word to the bosses to stop selling drugs in our community, and if they don't, we eliminate them."

"Eliminate as in assassinate," I clarified.

"Precisely. It's a question of sacrificing a few to save the many, or accepting the alternative of eventual genocide from within. As it says in the Bible, a house that is divided against itself cannot stand."

"You take the Bible as a reference source then?" I asked, raising an eyebrow.

Malik smiled. "In certain instances, yes; in others no. We are not unlike any other organization; we have areas where policy may conflict with certain moral positions. But like any organization, we must be willing to turn a blind eye to certain things in order to get other, more important things done. You know as well as I do, Mr. Barnett, that black people make up twelve percent of the population, yet fifty-two percent of the prison inmates in this country are black. Of that prison population, eighty percent are there for drug-related crimes. We also both know that prisons are big business now. There are more prisons being built than schools in this country. There's money in it, so the aim is to get more people inside. More black people, which further leads us along the road to self-destruction. We see these as desperate times, Mr. Barnett, and as the saying goes, desperate times call for desperate measures."

"I'm sure you'll do just fine," I said.

"In places like Singapore, the penalty for drug dealing is

death, pure and simple," he continued as if I hadn't spoken. "Pre–Communist China was rife with opium addicts, but after the revolution it stopped. Do you know why? Quite simply because Mao Tse-tung had a strict policy: death to all drug dealers. But drugs is not the only heinous crime being carried out in our community. Rape, for example, is punishable by castration."

"I still don't see how I fit in," I told him, knowing fully well where he was heading.

Malik took a deep breath just as the young man reappeared with a tray of coffee, tea, buttered toast, and blueberry muffins.

"I think we could do each other a lot of good," Malik said. "We've checked you out thoroughly. We know that you were a first-rate assassin with the CIA, the best man in your field, and that the reason you left the Agency had to do with the racism within the department that prevented you from promotion."

I was surprised. Not many people knew the real reason that I had left the Agency.

"You see, we didn't just get your name from the yellow pages. You come highly recommended," Malik said.

"By who?" But I knew his answer before I asked the question.

"That information is classified, as you would expect it to be." He smiled again. "But be assured that the person is part of our organization and believes that we can help you in your work as well as you can help us. We believe that nothing short of a major social and cultural reawakening is going to save black people in this country. The progress that we have made in the past three decades has been a double-edged sword. We as black people have been fooled into believing America accepts us. And you know as well as I do, we are a separate nation within a nation. And even though many have fought and died for the political, economic, and social progress that has come our way, we as a people are still institutionally discriminated against by the major institutions that run this country. We're not saying we plan to overthrow the government or any nonsense like that, we are just dedicated to giving the next generation a real chance to continue the progress that our parents' generation started. But with the proliferation of drugs in the ghettos, that's guaranteed not to happen. That's why we have decided that we have to police our own communities," he said.

"It's all been said and tried before and nothing has worked," I reminded him.

"True, what we are doing is not a new concept, but it is one that has been put into practice in a unique way," Malik stated.

"What about the bigger problem of large drug traffickers who never show their faces in the ghetto? How do you reach them?" I countered.

"Oh, we know," he said, and began walking around the room. "They have started to react already because we have hurt their businesses, but we're ready for them as well. We are well financed and organized. And we have learned from past mistakes. For example, as an organization we don't have a name or an identifiable leader who can be made into an easy target like a Martin Luther King or Malcolm X. When they were eliminated, the work of their organizations came to a halt. Our system of leadership is designed so that no one person is so vital that if they disappeared it would stop our work. And our punishment for any leader who is caught giving information to any unauthorized person is death. Not only to that person, but the death warrant also extends to members of their family."

"I see," was all I said. The man was making sense. At least they had set the organization up the way real revolutionaries do. I respected that.

"We don't plan to lose this war, Mr. Barnett. We can't afford to. Black people have to start caring and working on behalf of one another as a political strategy, otherwise we can't guarantee our own individual survival in this country. Crack, welfare and miseducation has fast-forwarded black America back into slavery. If not for our huge purchasing power, black people would be expendable."

I couldn't argue with the man. What he was saying was a fact.

"After you've conquered the drugs, then what?" I put the question to him.

"Then we start building institutions. Banks. That is vital to the growth of our community," Malik explained intensely.

"I'm going to level with you. If you are in fact doing what you say you're doing, it appeals to my beliefs. But I've spent a long time in the trenches, too long living on the edge of sanity. I'm not prepared emotionally to live like that again. The individual price is just too high. I don't mean to sound selfish or apathetic, it's just that I've got a new life now and I want to live it the way I want to."

Malik bit into a slice of toast and offered me a muffin.

"Let me show you something," he said, then stood up. He led me upstairs to the top floor of the house. We entered a huge room with a polished, bare wooden floor. One side of the room was empty except for a chair that sat in front of a window. The other side of the room was full of video and recording equipment and computers that sat on four desks all lined up side to side. Malik opened one of the desk drawers and took out two pairs of high-powered binoculars. I followed him over to the window, where he pulled up another chair. He motioned me to sit down and handed me a pair of binoculars.

With the help of the binoculars I could see across a stretch of grass twice the size of a football field. The house we watched was strategically tucked away in a corner of the grounds. I could see about twenty people dressed in karate suits practicing martial arts.

"This is our camp where we train our new recruits. We have ex-addicts as young as fifteen to grandfathers in their seventies. We are on a mission, Mr. Barnett."

"I hope you get there," I said honestly.

"Will you at least consider what I've said?"

"Insofar as being a part of your cause?"

"Yes, but there is no pressure whatsoever. You are not the first person who has respect for what we do but does not want to play an active part. No matter, there still may be things and ways in which we can help each other," he assured me confidently.

"Such as?" I was curious.

"Such as there may be something more than meets the eye with the investigation you're working on. The Reverend Trevor Jennings, for example."

"From what I get, he's on the up and up," I said, playing my hand close to the vest.

"Is that what you really think, or is that what you want me to think you think?" Malik queried.

"I'm not sure exactly what to think. Everything seems OK on the surface, but my instincts tell me differently," I admitted. "For the time being and for the sake of argument, let's go with *your* instincts."

"I've got a feeling that in the not too distant future you may get some information that will bear out your suspicions," Malik said.

"You can pass me information, if you like, but that doesn't mean I'll be in your debt," I told him flatly.

"Not at all. Whatever we do will be as much for ourselves as for you. By the way, you frightened the life out of J. T. Brown. The word on the street is that he's making a move to Miami."

"Good riddance," I stated.

"I'll drink to that." Malik smiled and finished off his tea.

After watching the training session for a few more minutes, Malik ordered dinner. We had fish, potatoes, gravy, and salad.

The trip back was more comfortable. It was in a limousine. The side and back windows as well as the window divider between the front seat and backseat had been blackened so that it was not possible to see out. The way in which Malik's group had set themselves up was very smart.

I spoke the truth when I told Malik that I liked their ideas and I was truly sympathetic to their cause. But I also spoke the truth when I said that I wasn't ready to relive my past all over again.

CHAPTER 9

Roachie pulled the limousine to the curb and jumped out. He opened the door and watched the man named Devil Barnett climb out of the limousine and walk toward a bar in Harlem called the Be-Bop Tavern. Bringing the man up to the training camp and now delivering him back had been his assignment, and that's exactly what he had done. He felt good. It felt a world away from the way he used to feel as a kid growing up in Harlem, when people would laugh at him and call him the son of a fag daddy. The thought of the children's taunts still made him burn with shame. He used to pray to God that he could change who he was, at least change who his father was.

Roachie's father, Carl Herbert Linstrom, had been a jive, fast-talking pretty boy hustler in his youth, who gambled and stole for a living. He had met and married Roachie's mother when she was still just seventeen, working at the lunch counter in Woolworth's. But like all nickel-and-dime hustlers, Carl's luck ran out and he was sent to jail, where he was turned out. In jail his pretty boy features acted as a magnet to some of the real tough convicts who made him into their girlfriend. He went in Carl and came out Carletta. Ain't that a bitch.

Whenever Roachie's mother would force him to go down to the barbershop where his father worked to pick up his monthly support check, he would damned near die from embarrassment as he saw his father switching and prancing around like he had a lit firecracker stuck up his ass.

He hadn't seen or spoken to his father in years. And he had no plans to change that. Carletta was a part of his past as was his image of a loving and innocent Thelma, whom he had loved almost as much as he had hated his father. In a funny way, he still loved Thelma and deep in his heart he knew he always would, no matter what she had become.

Thelma and Roachie had met and fallen in love almost five years ago. They had gone out steadily for two years and had planned to get married as soon as Roachie finished his Computer Science degree. Thelma was attending dance classes all over the city and planned to be a professional *dancer. She had even been invited to try out for Alvin Ailey. She was great. Roachie used to love watching the way her naturally beautiful supple body would bend itself effortlessly this way and that in response to a drum beat or a flute melody. And everything was going fine until she met Max Hammill and he got her to start dancing in music videos. At first, it was the constant rehearsing and working and never being around. Next was the constant hanging out with the music crowd, running from this city to that city, staying up all night working for days on end without rest or sleep. Then came the cocaine habit. Thelma's behavior became so erratic that he couldn't even talk to her. Inevitably it led to their breakup. Then came the crack. When one of his friends had told him he had seen Thelma cruising for tricks under the train on 5th Avenue and 125th, Street he couldn't believe it. He remembered wanting to kill the man just for saying it.*

Thelma sucking dicks for a three-dollar crack beam-up. Just the thought of it almost wilted his heart and exploded his brain. Deep in his heart he knew it was true. His Thelma, his beautiful precious Thelma, how he loved her. When he saw for himself what she had become, it nearly broke his spirit.

Thelma and her street life went on for a while until she miraculously found religion. For some reason she got involved with God's Holy Tabernacle. At least it got her off the crack. But by that time she wasn't the Thelma he knew anymore. In her newfound salvation, Thelma would dress up in strange clothes and wigs and talk in strange voices almost as if she were acting a part from a movie. Most of the talk was about God and saving souls. She wasn't the Thelma that he knew anymore, but deep in his heart he still loved her. Missed her more than he even knew it was possible to miss somebody. Missed her as much as he hated Max Hammill. And one day when he got the chance he promised himself that he would pay Max back for what he did to Thelma. But that would come in time. Right now he had to concentrate on the matters at hand. Because he was a soldier for the cause.

CHAPTER 10

It was after 1:00 a.m. when I got back to Harlem. I was dog tired but I called Sonia, anyway.

"I thought I'd hear from you earlier. The girls were hoping to see you tonight. You disappointed them," she complained.

"I had an incident today that took me away from the city," I explained.

"'An incident'?" she echoed.

"Yeah."

"What kind of incident?"

"It wasn't a big deal—just a little something that I hadn't planned on."

"I guess that you couldn't have been considerate enough to make a phone call?" she said, sounding distant.

"Actually, I couldn't," I responded.

"Whatever," she said angrily.

"Listen, can we get together and talk tomorrow, lunch?"

There was a long pause.

"We'll see," she said in a dispirited tone.

"OK, good night," I said.

I had a hard time getting to sleep. Malik's words kept ringing in my ears. The Reverend's grin kept playing on my mind.

I drifted off eventually and began to dream. I was on a dark street somewhere in Europe waiting and watching. For whom or what I didn't know, but I was waiting and watching in the same way that I had waited and watched for so many years. Sometimes it was waiting on an unsuspecting victim who was a target for a bullet from my gun; other times it was waiting for someone to leave their apartment so that I could break in and plant a listening device. Always waiting and watching.

The phone jarred me back to reality.

The clock at my bed read 7:13. The voice belonged to Al Mack.

"Hey, baby." Al's voice sounded like a bullhorn in my sleep.

"Hey," was about as much as I could manage in response.

"There's been another attack on one of your English rappers," he told me.

Like someone had injected my brain with a shot of adrenaline, the layers of sleep evaporated and I was suddenly wide awake. "Another one?" I said.

"Yeah, I just got into the office. It happened about three this morning. This one is still breathing. He was knocked out by someone as he walked into his apartment."

"Where is he now?"

"Roosevelt Hospital. Want me to meet you there?"

"Yeah. Which one was it, by the way?"

"Maxie Waxie."

I made the drive south and pulled up in front of Roosevelt Hospital on 10th Avenue and 57th Street. Exactly thirty-seven minutes after I had hung up the phone. Al Mack arrived five minutes later.

The duty nurse directed us to a room on the third floor.

Maxie Waxie was walking around his hospital room nervously wearing a hospital gown and a bandage wrapped around his head.

He recognized us from our meeting at the rehearsal studio.

"They killed Gun and War. Well now they're trying to kill me, too, yeah. You got a spliff? Me need a spliff, mon."

As Maxie paced he peeped nervously out of the window.

"What happened?" Al Mack asked.

"I came into my flat and as soon as I walked into the door, something hit me. *Bam!* That's all I remember. That's all I remember," Maxie repeated. "I not going back there, mon, they try to kill me again. I gon' stay with my mates. Safety in numbers, ya know, now we don't know who's next yeah?"

"We don't. either," I said. "Did you get a look at the person who hit you?"

"No, I just walk in and *bam!*" Maxie said, shaking his head.

Then he paused and seemed to search his mind for something. "I can't remember nothin', ya know . . . and my head is causing me a misery. I need a spliff," he reiterated.

"You have a concussion," Mack said. "They want to keep you here under observation."

"No no, I not staying here. Where can I get somebody to look after me? J. T. is out of town and Max, nobody can't find him. Shit, man. This country is fucked, yeah. People killing each other all over the bloody place," Maxie complained. "Yeah, that's what I need, somebody to protect me. You know somebody?"

"I'll give a few people a call," Mack assured him.

"Cheers, mate."

"Let's get back to last night's attack. Did you have any arguments with anyone recently?" I asked.

"Naw, I'm a man of peace, everybody know dat."

"Do you know anything about why Shogun and Man O War were killed? If you do, now is the time to tell," Mack said.

"No, I don't know nothin'."

"Maybe they were involved in something they shouldn't have been?" I said.

"Don't know, don't know. My head is killing me, yeah." Maxie shook his head again and frowned.

"Do you know a woman Shogun hung around named Peaches?" I inquired.

"Peaches? Naw, don't think so."

At that moment a male nurse walked in.

"You shouldn't be walking around, you have a concussion. You should be lying down," he said to Maxie, shaking his head.

"No, I can't stay here. I'm going somewhere safe," Maxie said defiantly.

The male nurse looked at Al Mack and me, hoping we had the influence to back his recommendation. "You tell him," he said.

We returned his strained look for our assistance impassively and shrugged. The nurse only shook his head again and sighed heavily.

"Well, if you insist, we can't hold you against your will," he told Maxie.

"Can you give me something for my head? It hurts badly."

"I'll see if I can get you some painkillers," the nurse told the rapper. "But if you're not going to stay here, you had better go home and take it easy for the next couple days. And if you have any more pain, then call us and come back in right away. OK?"

"Yeah, I will. I got to get out of here," Maxie said. "As soon as you can, have someone call me, yeah. I don't want to leave here unless I'm protected."

"Yeah, sure thing. Give me an hour," Mack said as we left the room.

"Think he's hiding anything?" I asked Mack as we walked through the sliding doors back out onto the street.

"I think he's scared shitless. If he knew anything, I think we'd have to put a muzzle on him to stop him from talking now," Mack said.

It was still early and New York City was just getting into its morning groove. People were spilling out of the surrounding apartment buildings and heading for work, school, and wherever else. A brigade of yellow taxis rolled up and down 57th Street as residents popped in and out of their doors. Steam poured out of the underground pipes, and storekeepers opened their places to do battle once again for the almighty dollar. A sign in a shoe repair shop said it all: IN GOD WE TRUST, ALL OTHERS PAY CASH.

"Man, I could go for a nice hot cup of coffee and some glazed doughnuts," Mack muttered as his teeth chattered against the morning cold.

"Sounds good to me." I smiled as we walked out of the cold and into the warmth of a small corner coffee shop.

It was almost 10:00 a.m. when I got back uptown. I parked in front of the bar and met Cowboy coming out with Gerald as I was going inside.

"Man, these peoples is a bitch. They want everything and don't want to give nothin' back," he hollered in my direction.

"I know just what you mean," I responded.

With Cowboy, one didn't necessarily have to try to make sense of what he said. Just the recognition of him having spoken to you was usually enough.

"If it wasn't for Gerald I would have killed me some niggas long time ago, know what I mean?"

"Yes, I do," I said, moving past him. I was halfway inside the door when I heard his words. They hit me like an arrow in the back of the neck.

"Muthafucka said he was going to put out a hit on you, but I said I had your back," Cowboy said.

I turned to face him. Cowboy stood behind the baby carriage, leaning onto its handles and chewing on a piece of a red plastic stirrer.

"Who said it?" I inquired carefully. I knew Cowboy was crazy, but I also knew that he was nobody's fool. He pushed the baby carriage closer to where I was standing and spoke almost in a whisper.

"That ass wipe that you pistol-whipped—J. T. Brown. I heard him talking over at Johnny Ray's place last night. He asked Johnny did he know anybody who would do it, but Johnny told him that you was all right. When he got outside, I told him I was going to put out a hit on *him*. I told him that I had your back. Jive muthafucka. I would have killed him long time ago if I didn't have Gerald to worry about." Cowboy frowned up at the sky, coughed, and spat a mouthful of thick yellow phlegm out toward the street. "Don't worry about nothin'. I got your back, Devil." Cowboy turned abruptly and walked briskly down the street and disappeared around the corner.

Now I had something else to think about. I'd have to watch my back or else go back and visit J. T. again. But I knew the answer to that one even before it had passed through my brain. If I did pay him another visit, J. T. would never be able to draw breath again. For now I just had to wait and see how J. T. decided to play his hand.

Inside the bar, Duke was hard at work serving customers,

Goose and Po Boy were at their usual perches watching the TV, which was tuned to ESPN and highlights from last week's basketball games. Benny Sweetmeat was as busy as a beaver preparing for the lunchtime crowd.

"Sonia called," Duke told me.

"Any message?"

"Nope, just said to tell you she called. Sounded like she was breathing fire, though." Duke grinned.

"I know that's right," I chuckled.

I worked through the rush hour until 3:00 p.m. when Christine's shift took over, then I went into my office for a little relaxation. I put on a CD by Bob James and let his tickling of the ivories wash over me until I lost myself in the melodies. I switched off the phone and the light, then lay down on the couch and drifted off to sleep. It was an hour later when I woke with a strange urgent feeling. I took out my notebook and called a number from it. After five rings, Maxie Waxie came on the line thick and lazy. I asked him to do something for me and he agreed.

At 5:05 p.m. I pulled up to the apartment house on 102nd Street just off Central Park West, where Maxie Waxie had been attacked. The first man I talked to was Henry Bowers, a retired accountant who lived in the apartment next door. Henry was in his early sixties and lived with his girlfriend, a tall, platinum blonde whom he called Kitten. Kitten looked to be in her early forties and had a pair of long, showgirl-type legs that seemed to extend from the floor right up to her chin. While I talked to Henry, Kitten sat in a nearby chair with her legs curled up, drinking a martini and making goo goo eyes when Henry wasn't paying attention.

"I'm an insomniac, so I was up watching CNN. I heard someone scream and I called the police."

"Did you see anyone?"

"How could I see anyone. I was inside the apartment. This is New York City, mister. You don't go poking your nose too far out or you might get it cut off. Know what I mean?"

I couldn't argue with that.

I turned to Kitten, who was eyeing me with the enthusiasm of a kid watching a magic act. She was waiting her turn to be questioned.

"Did you happen to see or hear anything?" I asked her.

But Henry stole her spotlight and answered for her.

"She was out like a light. She wouldn't have heard an atom bomb."

"Yeah, out like a light," Kitten giggled drunkenly.

The next couple I talked to, the Farrows, were both in their thirties, with one small child. She looked oxlike and seemed as gentle as a lamb, and he looked birdlike and seemed as mean as a snake. Their four-year-old daughter played with a Barbie doll as I spoke to the parents in the living room.

"The scream woke us both," the wife told me.

"I didn't know what the hell was going on, so I got my baseball bat just in case. I was ready to crack a few heads, I'll tell ya." Jake Farrow said with a smirk.

Maria Farrow picked up the conversation. "A few minutes later Amy came into our room saying she had seen someone climbing the building outside her bedroom window. You see, her room is next to the fire escape," she told me.

"Someone—yeah, tell what she says she saw, though," Jake Farrow taunted his wife.

Maria Farrow sighed. "Well, she says she saw a big, big teddy bear man in a green cape."

"How about that, huh?" Farrow remarked. "The only thing that could have been was a nightmare caused by too much of these crappy TV programs and video games that she watches, that's what I say," he spat.

"Is that all she said? A big teddy bear man in a green cape?" I asked.

"No, correction, a big, *big* teddy bear man." Jake Farrow smirked again. He shook his head with laughter, then pulled open the fridge and extracted a can of Budweiser.

"Amy, come here for a moment, darling," the child's mother called to her daughter.

Amy came from the living room clutching her doll, took one look at me, and walked over to her mother for protection.

"Can you remember anything else about the big, big teddy bear man with the green cape you saw climbing the walls?" the mother asked gently.

"He was scared," Amy told her mother matter-of-factly.

"Ooh, now we've a scared, big, big teddy bear man," Farrow chided.

I felt like hitting him in the mouth.

"Why do you think he was scared?" her mother asked calmly.

"I don't know, he just was," Amy responded.

"Was he climbing up or down?" I asked.

"Up," Amy stated, looking into my face.

I gave the Farrows my card and asked them to call if anything new developed.

"Were you around when Maxie rented this apartment?" I asked the super as we entered the elevator for the ride back down to the street level.

"Yes, I was the one who told them it was going to be available when the old man died that lived in it before."

"Told who?"

"The Reverend Jennings."

My mind was suddenly twisted and confused. "How does the Reverend Jennings have anything to do with it?" I asked.

"The church owns the building; when I first took this job, the Reverend Jennings asked me to look around and let him know if anything should come up. We have another one living here, too. The one named Rebel. He lives on the tenth floor. I used to be the janitor over at the church, too, until I retired a few months ago, "cause it got to be too much. Now I just take care of things around here," he explained to me slowly as if I were a person with a learning disability.

"Then your name is Budrow?" I asked.

"That's right, Wallace Franklin Budrow at your service," the big super grinned proudly.

* * *

When I reached the bar again I called Sonia, but she wasn't in. I checked my answering machine. She had left a message. She said she was going out to dance salsa and would be back late. Chandra had called and asked that I call her back. I called the hair shop and was told she was out and would be back within the hour. I left my number.

Christine was talking to an elderly couple at the end booth as the two people she had hired were filling orders at the bar.

I considered going up to the place where I knew Sonia would be. It was a club called Julio's in Spanish Harlem, where they played salsa and meringue music six nights a week. Sonia was a great dancer. She had even been in contests. I had tried salsa a couple times but I just didn't have the knack. Whenever I had gone to Julio's with her in the past, I would wind up standing around watching other people dance, so I decided against it. Instead, I joined some of my regular customers who were watching the basketball game between the Knicks and Boston.

Then Chandra called.

"Hey." Her voice was full of anticipation. "Anything yet?"

"Anything like what?" I asked.

"You said you would check to see if Gun had hooked it up so I could still get my car. I told you he had said he would get me a car."

"I still have to get to his legal people. But the deal was, as I remember it, that you would see if you could come up with anything, then I would see what I could do."

"I remember," she said, "that's why I called. I found out something."

"Something like what?" I asked skeptically.

"I know why Gun and War was having all those meetings alone away from the other group members. Why they was always on the phone with each other. I found out what they was doing."

"OK."

"They was doing a special project. Like some secret recording sessions."

"How do you know this?" I wanted to know.

"I got my ways," she assured me confidently. "Now, you going to try to help me get my car or what?"

I sighed deeply. "If what you got is worthwhile, I'll talk to his lawyer."

"OK, I'm going to trust you. OK."

"OK."

"This brotha I know with a studio named Bobby P, I saw him yesterday 'cause his hoochie be comin' into the shop to get her hair done and he came with her and he ask me what's going to happen to the tracks that him, Gun, and War hooked up now that they dead. Like I'm supposed to know. He said they hooked up a whole album that War was supposed to take to get a sweet deal on," Chandra said.

"Can I get in touch with this Bobby P?"

She paused. "You ain't going to try to swindle me, are you. I've dealt with you slick ass New York brothas from Harlem before," she reminded me. "You seem honest, so I'm going to give you a shot, but if you fuck me, I'm going to get you back, believe that," she threatened. "I'll call you later tonight 'cause I got to find out exactly where he lives."

I disconnected from Chandra and called Doug Anderson. His answering machine came on, but as I was leaving my message, he picked up the phone.

"Yeah, how you doing?" Doug said.

"OK, I need a little more education about your business. I'm getting new information, but I don't know how to translate it," I explained.

"No problem. Lots of shit to this business. What you got?" Doug chuckled. "I was going to call you yesterday."

"Yeah?"

"My man called me today and confirmed something that I suspected. Are you around tomorrow?"

"Sure, no problem," I said.

"Plan on going over to Jersey in the morning with me, I'll pick you up at the bar. Is that good?" he asked.

"See you then," I said, and hung up.

The rest of the evening went by slowly. I made arrangements with Christine to lock up and I headed home early.

I put my key into the lock and let myself in. I jumped into the Jacuzzi to try to ease the aching muscles that had been caused by the strain of the past few days. From the open window I could hear rap music pouring from a boom box someone had turned up full blast. The lyrics chanted out something about bass in your face, and rock in your sock. It made me think about the two dead rappers and the media-made images of the gangster rap fantasy world they had created and how it paled against reality. For Shogun and Man O War there was no more bass in your face, rock in your sock, or baby let's get funky tonight. Now it was just the plain damp earth of a cold and lonely grave. I also started to think about Malik and his dedication to their cause. His organization had apparently brought a lot of diverse elements together to try to fight what seemed like an undefeatable giant. Nevertheless, Malik and his organization had proven a theory I'd always believed about human nature: Sometimes, to fight the good fight takes saints as well as sinners. People who normally would never have anything to do with each other could be brought together by a common interest. It's like how people in New York City were mobilized to respond against the four white policemen who murdered an innocent young African named Amadou Diallo by shooting at him forty-one times. People turned out en masse to protest the police action as well as the mayoral policy that sanctioned a group of public servants functioning outside of the very law they were hired to enforce. People who never even saw themselves as part of the same society were brought together in spirit because they were all outraged by the sheer brutality of a single event.

Sonia didn't call me and I didn't call her. Bad sign. But I tried not to let it bother me. Chandra phoned back and left an address for Bobby P.

Doug Anderson drove a new Mercedes, which we rode in over to

Paterson, New Jersey. On the way I recapped the conversation that I had had with Chandra. Doug didn't say much. He just listened.

In Paterson, Doug drove to an industrial area along a row of warehouses and stopped at the end where a number of large trucks waited outside a back entrance. Over the loading dock was a sign that read DISC-O-RAMA VINYL AND CD MANUFACTURING. We parked on the side of the building and walked in through the back entrance. Doug led the way into a room with large presses, where vinyl was being shot out in big black globs and put onto another machine that smoothed the glob out into the shape of a record album disc. Through a glass partition there was another room filled with computers and stacks of CDs.

We were met by a tall, thin white man with a bald head who walked with a springy step.

"Hi," he addressed us, smiling. "I haven't seen you in ages, Doug. How're you keeping? Still in the game?"

"Jerry, sometimes I wish I knew another game to get into, but I don't," Doug bantered. "How are your boys? They still work with you?"

"Yeah, they mostly do the weekends or the evenings when we get busy. Eddie's making me take time off, says I work too hard." He winked.

"Dev, this is Jerry Gohanran. Him and his brother Eddie own this place."

"Hiya," Jerry said, and shook my hand. For a man who looked in his sixties, Jerry's grip was surprisingly powerful.

"I'll call ahead, tell Eddie you're on your way," Jerry told us.

"Thanks," Doug said.

"One helluva nice guy," Doug informed me as we walked down a long corridor.

"I didn't know they still made vinyl albums," I said.

"Not for general public consumption anymore, but they're essential for deejays in the clubs. For people like your man Fuzzy Martin," Doug said.

At the end of the corridor there was a locked door with an intercom on the side of the wall. Doug pressed a button on the wall and announced, "Doug Anderson and Devil Barnett for Eddie."

The man who came out to receive us was also in his sixties and sported a full white beard. His lively eyes twinkled as he and Doug shook hands warmly.

"Devil, this is my good friend Eddie Gohanran," Doug said.

Eddie and I shook hands, then we followed him down another long corridor into a large office. The furnishings were comfortable but not expensive. The wall was lined with gold and platinum discs encased in glass frames.

"Don't let Eddie's low-key profile fool you, he's a rich mutha-fucker but he's one of those cheap rich muthafuckers. He wouldn't give you two nickels for a dime," Doug teased.

Eddie laughed heartily and offered us coffee from the pot that sat in the corner of his office.

"Eddie, Devil is looking into the killings of those English rappers. I want you to tell him what you told me yesterday," Doug said.

Eddie sat behind his desk and relaxed back into his chair with a knitted brow.

"I'm not quite sure where to start," Eddie began. "So let me start by explaining how things work. The music business is a very unique business in that nobody actually knows what makes an artist or a record successful. And when I say nobody, I mean nobody. Big companies spend millions all the time on what they think is a hot act or the top singers, musicians, songwriters, studios, top-of-the-line everything. And they make record after record and nothing happens. People don't buy the record, and the artist's career goes into decline. Then up comes some kid from Bum Fuck, Texas, with a sound that people like, and he outsells everything in the market and sets the world on its ear. It's happened again and again. Elvis Presley, the Beatles, Smokey, the Spice Girls—all examples of a nothing growing into a huge some-thing. Now, when an artist is hot, they are a virtual gold mine for almost anyone associated with them. The record company makes money, the booking agency, the publisher, the producer, the writers, the disc jockeys—everybody makes money hand over fist until the artist gets cold. The only problem is, nobody knows when that's going to be. It could take twenty years or it could take six months. So what professionals do is try to milk every moment of a hot artist, because they've seen enough to know that today's overnight success could very well be tomorrow's afternoon flop.

A lot of record companies are under the gun right now because with the Internet and new technology on the scene, the profits in the music business are threatened and they aren't sure how to deal with it. At this stage the major phone companies, which are the major Internet carriers, won't get in bed with the record companies to enforce copyright protection by trying to stop people downloading their music. And the scientists haven't come up with a way to put out a music product for public consumption that can't be copied. That's not to say that it's a bad thing in the long run, but it's just to say that the major companies that are responsible for the distribution of ninety percent of the hit records you hear on the radio are not in a growth pattern. These are public companies that are responsible to stockholders. And stockholders keep pressure on any public company to sustain a growth pattern, otherwise they sell their stocks and move on to something that they feel is a growth industry. Because the big companies are running scared, the executives look to take advantage of anything they can to survive because they know in the next minute they could easily be out on their asses. So one of the things they do to make sure they don't wind up in the cold is bootleg their own records. By that, I mean they press and sell the records and CDs of their artists for cash. That way, they don't pay out any royalties to the artist or their distribution company, especially if they have a large company who will take up to a third of the wholesale price as a distribution fee and even more if promotion and publicity is involved."

"Not to mention Uncle Sam," Doug chimed in.

Eddie continued. "When an executive in the record company does this, it can amount to a big bundle in a short period. When I say bundle, I mean if the record is hot enough you can make a few million in weeks—cash."

"Damn," I said.

"There's more, much more," Doug said. "Go on, Eddie."

"About three weeks ago I got a call from Max Hammill, who wanted to set up a meeting right away," Eddie continued. "I knew Max had this hot rap group from England, so I'm interested, right, because as I said, a hot group like he has generates money for anyone associated with them. At the meeting, Max tells me he wants to set up a pressing deal to make some promotional copies for deejays. Right away I know what he's doing. I'm not one to lose money, so I take the order and look the other way. He orders five hundred thousand copies of the CD and pays me three quarters in cash before I start and the other quarter on delivery. He gives me all the negatives from the original artwork and everything, so when the job is finished, the product I made will be indistinguishable from the ones made by Global's pressing plants. I finish the job, and he immediately puts in another order. Now of course I'm thinking that it's the same record, but I was wrong, this is another record. He gives me some different artwork."

Eddie stood up and went over to a cabinet and picked up a folder. Inside the folder was an envelope, which he handed to me. "Open it," Eddie directed me.

Inside the envelope were CD covers bearing the photographs of Shogun and Man O War.

The title on the front of the CD cover simply bore the title Brainstorm, with the names of Man O War and Shogun, but nothing else; no writers, no producer credits, no record company.

I passed the CD covers over to Doug, who looked at them quickly with an expert eye and handed them back to me.

"The way I figure it, Max Hammill's contract with Global would cover the group as a unit as well as individually, but he wants to do an end run, so he's putting these out and will make up a story to say either the tapes were stolen or lost and then bootlegged by someone else once Global got wise, but by then he would have probably pocketed a few million," Eddie said.

"And with these two rappers being dead, it's almost guaranteed these CDs are going to sell faster than a hot pussy on a cold ship at sea," Doug added.

"So that's it in a nutshell," Eddie said.

"Eddie, where did you ship the records to?" Doug wanted to know.

"Some place in England, just outside of London, a place called Milton something . . . let me see."

Eddie looked through a packet of shipping slips on his desk.

"Milton Keynes. No client of record. Officially, these records don't exist. It's a cash deal all the way, with no questions asked," Eddie explained.

Doug and I thanked Eddie for his time and then we left. Back in the car, Doug started to let me in on his thoughts.

"You said this Reverend was from England. If that's where the records are going, then you can bet your ass he's in the middle of it. Like I said before, I knew Max Hammill as a dope dealer, not as a record man."

"So you think that the Reverend is behind all of the bootlegging?" I asked.

"I don't know exactly what to think, but I do know that this Reverend understands the music business a lot better than he pretended to you," Doug stated confidently.

I agreed. The Reverend had tried to play me for a chump. But he never figured that I had a few aces up my sleeve. Aces like Doug and Chandra.

The address that Chandra had given me for Bobby P was in Teaneck, New Jersey, the place made famous by the Isley Brothers. Bobby P's house was a small affair on the edge of town, located in a cul-de-sac.

"I'm representing the interests of the estates of Man O War and Shogun. I'd like to talk to you about the tracks you did together before they died," I said when he came to the door.

"Come in," the man invited, and we stepped out of the cold into the warmth of the house.

"You Bobby P?"

"You from the record company?" Bobby P asked in return.

"Not exactly. My name is Barnett. This is Doug Anderson."

Bobby looked to be in his early thirties. He was tall and lanky, with a yellowish complexion. His hair was cut close in a zig-zagging pattern, and he was wearing a wrinkled nylon warm-up suit. He held a cigarette in the corner of his mouth, which burned with a long ash.

"What kind of interests did you say you represent?" he asked, twisting up his face and lighting a fresh cigarette.

"The interests of the dead men's estates," I said.

"You did some tracks together, right?" Doug said.

"Yeah, some fat tracks, too, but . . ." he shook his head and shrugged his shoulders. "But now what? They dead, and the tracks is with the record company. Truth is, I don't even know what the deal is. I don't know what the hell is going on. What I need to do is get the rights to the tracks back, if I could."

"Tell me, how did the making of these tracks come about?" I asked.

"The making of them? Well, uh, you know, War came to me and said he was going to start doing some more productions with different people, and then he asked me if I wanted to be down with him," Bobby P explained. "I did one of the remixes on their album, the second single, 'Butter Butt'. Do you mind if we go downstairs? I got to finish something by this evening."

He led the way through a door that led downstairs, and we followed. We emerged into a recording studio complete with a multi-keyboard setup, amplification racks, two computers, a mixing board, and a vocal booth. It was clearly state-of-the-art equipment in a room that was as clean as a whistle. Only a large ashtray overflowing with cigarette butts marred the otherwise spotless studio.

"You're good to go," I said, looking around.

"Yeah, I'm doing OK. After damn near eight years mixing for this one and that one, last year I hit it right," Bobby P said.

"So when did you guys start working on the project?" Doug

asked, looking around, obviously impressed at what he saw.

"About a month ago."

"Who was the main man?" Doug asked again.

"War was. He made sure all the business was taken care of. You know, set up the deal and everything."

"You mean the business as in who paid you?" I interjected.

"As in who paid for everything. Studio time, singers—we have a few live musicians on the tracks guitars and horns, too. He said he was getting the money from a Reverend. That's the funny part; 'cause I asked him what the fuck was a Reverend doing giving up money for a project with lyrics talking about puttin' niggas in body bags and eating pussy and shit. I thought that was strange, but he said don't worry about it, so I didn't."

"Obviously all the bills were paid," Doug put in.

"Yeah, paid in cash and in full. No problem there. The problem is that I own a piece of the project, and now that everybody got kilt, I ain't got nothing to show or prove that a third of the project belongs to me."

"Didn't you sign something?" Doug asked.

Bobby P dropped his head again, then sighed deeply and looked back up at us woefully.

"Naw man, I didn't get nothin'. War said he was waiting to get his company set up with his lawyer. then he could hire me through his production company. And I trusted him 'cause he always came through before. If I knew he was going to go and get himself kilt I definitely would have gotten something on paper. When War started riffin' about the percentages or something, I should have signed somethin' then."

Bobby P smoked nervously as he talked. "I trusted War to do the right thing 'cause I knew he was a good brotha. Plus, I mean, how can you press somebody that you just made over seventy-five grand with."

"Seventy-five grand," Doug echoed.

"Yeah, the 'Butter Butt' remix went platinum and I got some nice points on it."

"Who was he riffin' with?" I asked.

"I guess it was that Reverend dude. 'Cause once we finished the tracks, I know War wanted to get a different kind of deal than he had. I heard him and Gun talking about it, but I don't like to get into people's business if they don't invite me in, know what I'm saying? You lose clients like that. But I do remember War saying to Gun that this Reverend dude could kiss his ass 'cause he had other places to go with the project. Like I said, I didn't get too much into it 'cause War always delivered with me, so I didn't feel I needed to put the full court press on him, know what I'm saying. But now looks like I'm fucked, know what I'm saying. So, you going to help me?" Bobby asked.

"Maybe," Doug said. "You've got the master tapes, right?"

"Oh yeah, I got a copy of the masters, but I ain't got nothing on paper protecting me."

We thanked Bobby P and said we would look into how we could help him. On the way back to New York, Doug and I hardly talked at all. I didn't have all of the answers, but I did have enough to know that the net was closing in on the Reverend.

"Do you think Man O War and Shogun's disagreement over percentages could have been enough for the Reverend to have them killed?"

"I know people who have gotten killed for a lot less," Doug answered.

"Me too," I remarked, and thought back to that time in Berlin when I had been ordered to assassinate the editor of an anti-American newsletter who had started an affair with a U.S. Army general's wife. A man whose dick betrayed him.

About halfway home Doug turned to me. "I've got an idea," he said.

CHAPTER 11

I was about eight feet away from the front door of God's Holy Tabernacle when I heard a series of shouts that held my attention. A man wearing nothing but what the good Lord gave him on the day he was born bolted out of the front entrance looking and breathing like a Thoroughbred heading for the Kentucky Derby finish line. His eyes were wide with fear, and his face was desperate with the notion of escape. Close behind him was a screaming trio consisting of the dwarf Reverend Waldorf, the sad-eyed Wendell, and an elderly lady with a headwrap. Both men held pieces of wood in their hands, threatening the air as they ran in hot pursuit. The buck naked man ran out into the middle of the street filled with afternoon traffic and just narrowly missed being killed. He didn't get away clean, however. One car bumped him hard enough to send him sprawling onto the hard, cold ground. The driver had to slam on his brakes so hard that it caused his car to skid and sent him into a 180-degree spin directly into a moving van that was coming up behind.

As the naked man struggled to regain his footing, the dwarf raised the piece of wood high above his head, but as he steadied his arm to strike, his foot slid and his tiny body went sliding. The dwarf lost his balance and hit the ground. This mishap gave the naked man just enough time to jump up and scamper across the hood of a stopped car to the other side of the street.

"Goddamnit shit," the little minister cursed as Wendell helped him back to his feet.

The little minister got up slowly, but the frustration in his face told the real story. His moment of sweet revenge had literally slid away and disappeared from view.

The trio returned to the tabernacle, and I followed them.

Inside, things were in an uproar as voices poured out of the reception office, each seeming more excited than the other.

"He was holding his nasty old penis in his hand and he

pointed it straight at me," a woman's voice said with a distinctive West Indian accent.

The voice belonged to the elderly woman who had accompanied the dwarf Reverend and the sad-eyed Wendell in pursuit of the naked man. She was speaking to a woman in a white cook's cap and apron. Also in the room watching the scene was a woman in her twenties accompanied by a little girl about four or five years old.

"Mother Hinton, I don't see how that man got into the sanctuary," the woman wearing the apron said.

"I don't know, either," Mother Hinton blurted angrily, and stamped her foot to emphasize her statement.

"Mommy, what's a 'nasty old penis'?" the child asked her mother innocently. The mother of the child didn't answer, she just shifted from one foot to another and looked nervous.

"Mary, if you can't handle responsibility, I'll have to find someone who can. I'm not going to put up with that kind of nastiness in this tabernacle—not today, not tomorrow, not ever," Mother Hinton spat adamantly.

"But the only one who could have let him in was Thelma. She was the only one with the sanctuary key," Mary defended herself firmly.

"It was your responsibility as head of the food program not to let her have the key. You know Thelma's history. And you have to accept certain facts. God gives us all crosses to bear, and I have accepted that Thelma is our cross," Mother Hinton said.

"Mommy, what's a 'nasty old penis'?" the child inquired again, in a louder voice this time.

"But it wasn't my fault," Mary protested.

Mother Hinton turned to the mother and child.

"Bernice, for goodness' sake, would you take that child home. There are certain things her ears should not hear."

"Yes, Mother Hinton," Bernice answered meekly, and began buttoning up the child's coat.

"Mother, I . . . ," Mary began again, but Mother Hinton didn't respond. Instead, she turned on her heel and angrily stormed out of the office and down the corridor in a such a huff that I wouldn't have been surprised if a visible trail of dust had materialized behind her.

Since no one was available to show me up to Reverend Jennings, I made my way there alone. From outside I could hear the Reverend's voice raised in anger.

"I don't give a damn what he promised you, you were not supposed to let that man in. You know that. I promise you, as God is my judge, I will send you away from here to someplace where you can be watched twenty-four/seven. You're too damned old for this. You're supposed to be the assistant administrator, but you don't do fuck all. And what's worse, every one here is affected by your bullshit. It's just a load of bollocks, is what it is. For fuck's sake, why can't you get it right just once."

I knocked on the closed door but was met by the sad-eyed Wendell, who suggested that I wait for a moment in order to let the Reverend know I had arrived.

A few minutes later, Wendell returned.

"I hope you can appreciate that we have had some major problems here this morning and the Reverend is not in the best way to receive you. He asked me to extend his sincerest apologies and asked if you could call and make an appointment for some time in the future," Wendell said in a subdued voice.

I told him I would, and left.

I couldn't see the Reverend, so I figured I would try the next best thing. I called Grooveline Records.

Monica's voice answered.

"Hello, this is Devil Barnett. I need another favor."

"OK." Her voice was soft and purring into the receiver.

"I need you to tell me where I can find your boss."

"You are too much. I'm going to do this for you because I like you, but on one condition," she said.

"What's that?"

"You take me out to dinner soon, someplace romantic."

"Romantic?" I repeated.

"You heard me," she said.

"Romantic, huh. OK, but it has to be in a restaurant, none of this 'I'll cook for you at my place' stuff."

"Of course." She laughed.

"OK, I owe you a date," I said.

"Max is at Global. He went into a big meeting there about a half hour ago. He's expected to finish in about two hours," she said.

"Thank you." I smiled into the phone and hung up, then headed for the A train.

Global Music Distribution was located in a new building on 8th Avenue, between 54th and 55th. Across the street was a parking garage.

That's where I decided to wait.

Max came into view about forty minutes later. Carrying a briefcase. Accompanied by a large black man.

I waited until Max and the bodyguard entered the garage before I made my move. They were side by side as they walked toward their car. When the bodyguard went to the driver's side, I walked directly up to Max, and the big man made a move to step in between us. I dropped to the ground and sent a straight leg into his left knee, which buckled the bodyguard like he was made out of cardboard. I moved forward and hit him hard in the solar plexus, and he hit the ground. I took his large shaven head into my hands and banged it hard twice on the cement floor. He went out like a light. Max stood gawking like he had just witnessed the Second Coming, but as I turned my attention toward him he made a move to reach for something concealed under his jacket. I used my leg like a scythe against his ankles in a neat sweeping motion that sent his head in one direction and his body in the other. After his head banged against the ground I grabbed him by the collar and relieved him of the gun and dragged him to his car. "Get in," I said.

Max obeyed. He unlocked the car. I pushed him into the passenger seat, then picked up the keys from the floor of the garage and started the car.

"I'm a rich man, don't kill me. I can pay you," Hammill pleaded.

"Get down on the floor," I ordered, pointing the gun at his head.

Again he obeyed without resistance. It was only then that he recognized me as the man who had visited him earlier.

"I thought you were a detective. I thought . . .," he said.

"Shut up," I said roughly, and drove the car out in the direction of the West Side Highway. I found a place to park and quickly pulled in.

"Why are you doing this?" he asked out of breath from fear.

"'Cause I'm sick and tired of the bullshit," I said. "Now I'm going to give you one chance to tell me what I want to know. Otherwise, what I did to your boy J. T. is going to seem like a picnic."

"What do you want, anything, just tell me?" Max seemed more than willing to cooperate.

"The truth—remember, one chance is all you get. Who's bootlegging the records in Jersey, and where are you sending them?"

"I . . . I am, but . . ."

"But what?"

"I am. We're sending them to London."

"Who is 'we'?"

"Reverend Jennings and myself."

"What about the new record with Shogun and Man O War?"

"The Reverend got it from Man O War. It was an independent project, but they couldn't come to an agreement. They were supposed to be working out a deal, though. That's what they were doing when Man O War was killed."

I went for the gusto. "Who killed them?"

"I swear I didn't have anything to do with it, and I don't know who did it. I've been trying to find out, and so has the Reverend."

"Is he your partner right down the line? Does he really own the record company or what?"

"I . . . I . . .," Max stammered.

"I see, he must be worth dying for," I said as I pulled back out into traffic.

"Don't kill me, please. Jennings is the owner, but I front it for him. My deal is only twenty-five percent, but he owns the rest of it. But I swear that I don't know who killed those two boys . . . I mean men." He stopped himself, almost swallowing his tongue for having called a black man a "boy" in my presence. "I didn't mean any offense, please."

"Keep talking," I said. "Tell me the whole story of how the Reverend got involved in this deal."

By the time I arrived back in Harlem, I had found out that the Reverend had not only been the brains and the money behind the bootlegging operation, , he was the financing source behind Max Hammill's drug-dealing operation as well. But how was I going to prove it? I called Al Mack and asked him to meet me at a seedy diner under the bridge at 125th Street on the West Side Highway. Ten minutes later he showed up looking as cool as a cucumber dressed in a black double-breasted pinstripe suit and a gray fedora.

"Got your cuffs?" I asked.

"Sure." Mack eyed me suspiciously and complied by reaching in the leather pouch on his side where he kept them.

I took his cuffs and secured Max Hammill to the steering wheel of his BMW, then I dropped the keys to Max's car in my pocket and walked with Mack into the diner. I told Mack what Hammill had told me.

"Do you think you can help me close in on the Reverend?" I asked.

Mack thought about it a moment. "Yeah, I think so. I ain't no lawyer, but I think if we use Hammill as a material witness and the bootlegging operation to back it up, there might be enough at least to get a grand jury interested—no promises, but just maybe. But you know the situation as well as I do. If we do manage to get an indictment, the Reverend will bring in the kind of lawyers who will twist the law until he walks free. But if you want to go ahead on a maybe, I'm with you."

"I'll take the maybe. It beats a blank."

"OK, first let's get Hammill over to the station."

"Where are you guys taking me?" Max Hammill asked nervously as we returned to the car.

"You're going to be a witness for the Empire State, my man."
Mack grinned as he stood beside the car, looking down at the
captive.

"For what? You aren't arresting me, are you? I can't be a witness," Max cried.

"Either that or you get arrested for making a drug sale to a
police officer," I said.

"But I never did that!" Max interjected.

"Of course you did, and I'm the officer you made the sale to."
Mack smiled.

"Oh, God. Oh . . ." Max Hammill burst into tears. "If I testify,
I'm a dead man, a dead man. Believe me, I'll do anything, but
don't make me testify."

"Don't worry, you'll be safe." Mack smiled congenially.

Mack arranged a private room in the Harlem police precinct,
where a woman from the D.A.'s office listened as Max Hammill
told the tape recorder what he had already told me.

"OK, let's go to church," Mack said as we left the precinct and
headed for God's Holy Tabernacle. Along for the ride were two
uniformed officers.

Outside the entrance to the tabernacle, Mack directed the two
uniforms to the side and back entrances of the building just in case
the Reverend suddenly got itchy feet. Thelma was at the reception
desk, and things looked normal again when we entered.

"I'm Detective Mack, from the Harlem police precinct. We
need to see Reverend Jennings on an urgent matter."

Thelma eyed us suspiciously, then made a call.

"You can sit down if you want," she said, playing with the
braids in her hair.

"We'll stand," Mack responded, looking around the room.

A few minutes later, sad-eyed Wendell Soames led us down to
a small office.

"In here, please." We followed him inside. The place was
neatly furnished with a small wooden desk and four chairs placed
in a semicircle. "I didn't want to say this where we could be heard,
so I thought we had better come in here where we could talk."

Mack and I looked at each other.

"I'm sorry, but the Reverend is not here," he said in his usual apologetic tone.

"Where is he and when will he be back? This is urgent police business," Mack told him with the threat of injury in his tone.

"That's just the thing. He left suddenly, and when I asked him where he was going, he told me that he didn't know. In fact, he said the strangest thing. He said he may not be back for a long time. And that if anybody asks for him, to say that he had to go out of town on urgent business," Wendell explained.

"Long time as in a day, week, month?" I asked.

"He didn't say. But him going out of town now is very strange because we have a board meeting tomorrow where some important matters have to be settled. I know he wouldn't have just left if it wasn't a very serious matter. That's why I'm concerned that he might be in some kind of danger."

"When did all this happen?" Mack asked.

"About an hour ago," Wendell admitted. "He got a phone call, then left. That's all I know."

Something about Wendell had changed. I couldn't put my finger on it, but I could feel it. My first impression of him was that he was an effeminate minion, the kind I'd seen around black churches all my life, but somehow that label didn't fit so well anymore. He was being as polite and deferential as ever, but something behind the smile and manner was different.

"If you hear from the Reverend, give us an urgent call," Mack said, handing Wendell his police business card, and we left.

"Looks like the good Reverend got his hat," Mack said.

"Where exactly does that leave us, then?" I asked.

"Smack in the middle of nowheresville. Without someone to prosecute, we don't have a case."

I called Sonia at home around 8:00 p.m. but no one answered. I left a message on the answering machine and made a mental note to call again later.

The phone rang.

"Hello, Mr. Barnett, it's Malik."

He was the last person I expected.

"Remember me saying that we worked to help people we felt were helping us," Malik continued.

"I remember," I responded dryly.

"Well, Reverend Jennings flew out earlier today, destination London. Just thought you might want to know," he said.

"Thanks," I said, and hung up with the sound of Malik's voice still ringing in my head. How did he know the Reverend had flown the coop?

The clock at the side of my bed read 12:13 a.m. when the phone rang. The voice at the other end belonged to Sonia.

"Yeah, baby," I said, fighting sleepiness.

"This is going nowhere. You know that, don't you?" She was agitated and breathing heavily.

"Sonia, believe me, I have been thinking about you. I called and left a message but—"

"Listen, Devil," she said, cutting me off, "I've heard sob story after sob story for too long. I'm just calling to say I'm sick and tired of it and I deserve better. Let's just forget it. Go and put your time and interest into something you care about."

She hung up.

Now I was fully awake again. Damn. Maybe Sonia was right, maybe she did deserve better.

My thoughts drifted back to the Reverend Jennings. I made two overseas telephone calls, one to a man named Dave and the other to a man named Munir. Somewhere between my conversation with Sonia and all of the thinking I had done, a decision had emerged. The feeling that drove me now was an almost insatiable urgency combined with an unmistakable adrenaline rush that I had known many times before.

The Reverend was the prey and I was the hunter. At the top of my things to-do-list, I wrote the words "airline ticket" because tomorrow I knew I had a plane to catch.

CHAPTER 12

London.

The Rover drove steadily along the M1, the highway that ran from the south to the north of England. As the Rover passed Junction 12, the man in the passenger seat glanced at his gold Rolex, then looked over at the driver. Nothing was spoken, but the driver could feel the tension.

"Don't worry, we soon reach," the driver reassured him.

The words seemed to calm the edginess of the passenger, and he relaxed. The passenger smoothed his dreadlocks, lit a spliff, and peered out of the window into the darkness. He moved his hand to the middle of his stomach and felt the hardness of the Glock pistol that rested there.

"Bush," the driver spoke again, "this one gon' be the lick, mon."

"Yeah," was all that Bush said.

He wasn't much of a talker, never had been. His strength had always been his ability to execute. To make sure others carried through to get the job done and to impose his will on those weaker than himself. His business was moving product. Stolen car parts, counterfeit money, contraband cigarettes. But now he was into bigger things. He was into the moving cocaine product business. Over the past two years he and his posse, The Burning Bush Posse, had broken through the jungle of the UK drug trade and now they were going to be real players. On the backseat of the car rested a black canvas bag containing packs of banknotes totalling a half million pounds. Another man sat in the back of the Rover guarding the bag. His name was Marga and he was so tall that he had to sit sideways to allow room enough for his long legs to stretch. Marga worked for Bush. Marga's job was to back up Bush with the Uzi he carried in case anything went wrong. Eight minutes later the Rover pulled off the M1 into the lane for the exit to Milton Keynes, following a National Express bus that pulled into the bus station just ahead of them.

The station consisted of a road in, a parking lot, and a road out. On the road out where buses stopped to load and unload passengers was a twenty-four hour café with two toilets, a ticket window, and a news-agent's shop. Only the shining light in the café window broke up the monotony of the dull, cloudy night. The parking lot was almost empty except for a few cars. Mostly there were empty spaces. It was past midnight. The driver of the Rover was called Punch.

He pulled the Rover into an empty space with the nose of the car facing out in case he had to make a speedy exit. Bush checked his watch again. It read ten past midnight. They waited another five minutes and Bush gave Punch the OK to make the signal.

Punch flashed his lights twice. Then, from the other side of the parking lot, Punch's signal was answered by another flash of lights.

Bush and Marga climbed out of the car and headed toward the café. Bush went in, but Marga positioned himself hidden from view in the shadows of the night, standing ready for action.

The Burning Bush ordered a coffee from the middle-aged woman working the shift on her own. He sat down in a booth with the canvas bag next to him and sipped the hot liquid, looking through the window until he saw a white man wearing a business suit walk toward the toilet. Bush finished his coffee and followed the man into the toilet. The white man's name was George. He was an Englishman from up north near Lancashire, and they had been doing good business for over a year. George always gave him good product. The Burning Bush liked doing business with George because George, like himself, was not a talker. George just did the business and never indulged in idle chat to either cover up the nervousness of the moment or try to become buddy buddy. Both men were professionals. Bush and George did the business, and that was that.

Bush tested the product as always.

The narcotic rush gave him a quick ringing in his ears, proof that the product was what George had said it was. Bush gave George the canvas bag, took the plastic package of cocaine and dropped it into a pocket inside his loose-fitting jacket, and left the toilet first.

Marga joined Bush back at the car.

"Ready?" Punch asked after Marga had gotten back into the car.

"Yeah mon, everyting cool."

Punch started up the Rover and drove it out of the Milton Keynes bus station and off into the murky night.

The thought of becoming a drug kingpin, mixed with the cocaine dancing in his brain, gave The Burning Bush a momentary sense of elation. As a way of private celebration, he passed a giant spliff over to Marga and Punch and then lit one himself. Bush was a stern man. He never attached himself to anyone, especially not those who worked for him. That way if he ever had to eliminate them, it would never pose an emotional problem. He was even stern with himself. He believed only in the power of money, his own abilities, and the inevitability and necessity of mankind's corruption.

He even had a woman and two children, but he didn't love them. How could he, when he did not believe in love.

Bush relaxed back into the seat and thought about his future. With the sale of the drugs he had just bought, he would step into another league. Then suddenly the melodious feeling of elation struck a sour note as it snagged on the thought of Mr. Patel. The mysterious Mr. Patel was Bush's only obstacle to becoming the drug kingpin he dreamed of time and time again. Mr. Patel ran an Asian gang that operated in London, Birmingham, and Manchester. They controlled huge amounts of cocaine and heroin that came into the UK from Pakistan.

Like any self-respecting drug dealer worth his salt, The Burning Bush often dreamed of knocking Mr. Patel off and taking over his business. He'd often thought that maybe one day he would have the chance. Now Bush believed that the deal he had just made brought him a lot closer to that day. The Rover passed roundabout after roundabout in the road until it came to an industrial estate. The large sign at the entrance announced a number of buildings and businesses contained therein. Included was the simple nondescript listing for warehouse number 16.

The Rover turned and headed for the location. Bush was feeling good again. His deal had just gone well and he was going to meet the man. The man, as in the key figure who was largely responsible for the growth of his organization over the past year. The man had made it all possible with his contacts and money. Bush had only met the man twice before.

The Rover stopped at warehouse number 16. The trio walked to the entrance of the building, where Bush rang the bell. A voice answered and the security buzzer sounded, allowing the trio to enter. The Burning Bush, Punch, and Marga met the two security guards who waited by the door as they entered. One of the guards spoke into a walkie-talkie. When a voice answered, he waved the trio onward. Another security guard met them and told The Burning Bush to go up to the second office on the left at the top of the stairs. He said that Marga and Punch would wait downstairs with him.

Bush admired the way the man had set up his security. As he entered the office, the man was sitting at a desk. He had his back to the door, talking on the phone. When Bush entered, the man turned around, acknowledged his presence with a simple nod, and continued with his phone conversation.

"Yes, that will be just fine, I'll await your call," the man said into the phone as he puffed on a huge cigar. The man hung up the phone and stood up. He extended his hand and shook the Bush's hand.

"Good to see you again, Reverend," The Burning Bush said.

"Yes, how did everything go?" Jennings asked.

"Right on schedule, like you said."

Bush liked the Reverend's style. He was dressed neatly in a brown silk business suit, pale yellow shirt, and a maroon tie with matching maroon alligator shoes.

The Reverend motioned Bush to a seat in front of the desk and poured them both a drink from a bottle of Johnnie Walker Black.

The man got right to the point. Bush liked that about the man.

"Bush, I'd like to outline a few changes that will be taking place here. I'll be located in the UK for the next few months. I've decided that in order to make certain moves in the way they need to be made, I should be present."

"Will that include knocking off Patel?" Bush wanted to know.

"All in good time," the Reverend said confidently.

Bush nodded his understanding and acceptance. Yes, with the Reverend, The Burning Bush felt he could realize his dreams. The Reverend had vision, and he had what it took to help the Reverend realize his vision. The Reverend was a thinker and an organizer, and he was an executer. Together they would each get what they wanted.

Yes, The Burning Bush envisioned himself as a drug kingpin with the beautiful cars, the piles of banknotes and the glamorous lifestyle, just like Al Pacino in the movie Scarface, up from the bottom of the gutter to the top of the world.

CHAPTER 13

As the wheels of the airplane touched down on the runway of Heathrow Airport in London, I woke up.

I got through passport check and customs quickly, then entered the airport terminal in search of a familiar face. Among a crowd of people waiting at the arrivals gate, I saw my friend Dave Roberts. We embraced warmly and exchanged grins.

"So you finally came back, eh?" Dave quipped in his native Jamaican accent.

"Finally." I laughed.

Dave and I had been friends for over ten years, since I lived in London during my early days in the Agency.

"I took care of those things you called about," Dave said as we walked toward the terminal exit.

I knew I could depend on Dave. He was a first-rate human being. He was also a first-rate detective in his own right. He made his living as an entrepreneur with a few businesses. There was a record shop, a driving school, and a pub. Because of his many contacts in these different areas, Dave became invaluable as a man who had his ear to the street. If there was something taking place in London and Dave didn't know about it, he could always put his hand on someone who did.

I exchanged an American hundred-dollar bill at the airport currency exchange counter and got back fifty-nine English pounds and sixty pence.

"I parked at the underground station because at this time of day, traffic is very busy," Dave told me.

"OK," I said as we headed toward the Piccadilly line at the Heathrow Airport Underground station.

As we arrived at the station and stood on the platform waiting for the train, I remembered some of the things I had always liked about England. Things like the Underground train service. It was a stark contrast to the subways in New York City. Not only were

English subways clean and orderly, they had cushioned seats in every car. I could only imagine what would happen if they tried that in New York City. Within a week, most of them would be stolen by junkies and sold as cushions for outdoor concerts at Central Park. That or vandalized by graffiti artists.

"I got you set up in Shepherd's Bush, your old stomping grounds." Dave smiled.

"Ah yes." I laughed, remembering some of the times we used to have in the Shepherd's Bush area.

"Guess who asked about you last week? And when I told her I had heard from you, she told me to make sure you got in touch."

"Don't tell me," I said.

"Yeah." Dave grinned.

Rhea, my old flame. A beautiful, intelligent Guyanese woman with whom I had had a long, torrid affair when I lived in London. In some ways we were great together and in other ways not so great, but it had always been fun.

As we exited the Underground station at Acton Town, we were hit by a pelting of rain. It wasn't coming down hard, just steady. The English weather was one of the things that I didn't miss.

Dave drove east for twenty minutes toward Shepherd's Bush, along the Acton High Street, then turned into a road called Potter's Lane. It was located in between two Underground stations both carrying the name Shepherd's Bush.

"We're here," Dave said as he parked the car. "Simon, a friend of mine, owns this place, so you'll be all right," he assured me.

The house was a large, prewar structure with three floors.

"My friend is in Spain this month, but he left the key. Anything you need, just ask the neighbor next door. His name is Ian, and he's acting as the caretaker while Simon is away," Dave explained, handing me the keys to the house.

My room was on the middle floor. It was large, furnished and faced the street. There was a shared bathroom and another toilet on the top floor.

The notion of sharing a bathroom was something I had to get

used to living in Europe. That as well as driving on the other side of the road and having the steering wheel on what I had always known as the passenger's side of the car.

In my room was a bed, a chest of drawers, a wardrobe, a small oven with double hot plates, and a small refrigerator. It was all I needed.

I put my bags down and we headed out again.

The next stop was the telephone shop, which was located around the corner. Forty minutes later I had a mobile telephone.

"About our friend . . ."

"Yeah?" Dave grinned over at me from behind the wheel of the car as we drove toward the Thames River.

"How is she?"

"She seemed good," Dave said, trying like hell to keep a straight face.

I thought back to one night when Dave, myself, and a few friends were all out at the pub and Rhea, who had had too much to drink, decided to tell me off. We had been going though a rough time in our relationship because I wouldn't commit to an engagement. She had kept on and on about it until it had erupted into a huge argument. She just kept drinking and drinking until she got drunk. Not falling down, but definitely over the limit.

Then Rhea quietly went over to the bar and ordered a pitcher of beer. She walked back to the table as nice as you please and poured it down the front of my clothes and called me a heartless American bastard. Dave and Ronnie, who were at the table with us, got so tickled that they fell off their chairs with laughter. After I had recovered from the initial shock, I joined them and we were all laughing like fools.

"I'm not looking to repeat that night in the pub," I said.

"I think she's more calmed down these days. I hear she was going out with some guy in the army but it didn't work out. I see her about once a month, when she comes into the pub. She always asks about you," Dave explained.

"I see."

I had enough complications without adding any more.

Dave was a reggae music lover, so as we made our way toward Brixton we listened to the music of Buju Banton on the car CD player.

The pub Dave owned was the called the Red Lion and it was located within shouting distance of the famous Electric Avenue that Eddie Grant sang about.

The Red Lion wasn't large, but it wasn't small, either. It was respectable and well kept. It was still early evening when we arrived, so people were just starting to drift in after work. In a corner of the pub, a youngish man in a baseball cap waved to Dave.

"That's the man you need to see," Dave told me.

We ordered two pints and joined the man.

"This is Andrew," Dave said, introducing the man. "He runs my record shop operation. Does all the buying in. He knows what's happening on that end of things, yeah."

Andrew and I shook hands. He looked young, but the experience in his eyes told me he had been around.

"I checked on what you asked me about, and I think I might have found something," Andrew said, looking at me and then at Dave. "I put it to a mate of mine with a shop here in Brixton who I know deals in hot and rare records. I told him I was looking to shift any hot product he could come across, and he said he might know where he can put his hands on some really hot product by the Dancehall Dogz. He just needs a little while to suss it out," Andrew informed us.

"Good," I said.

"He's out and about now, but he said he would get back to me tonight. Cash only."

"Sounds dodgy enough, yeah." Dave smiled over at me.

"I'd say so," I remarked.

For the rest of the evening I tried to relax and enjoy my return to England. It had been almost two years since I had been here.

Last night I slept like a baby. I turned on the radio next to my bed and tuned in to Jazz FM 102.2. The announcer told me it was

8:30 a.m. and minor harmonies of Take Six singing "Waiting for Me" splashed over me like water from a Sunday baptism.

My first call of the day was to Munir Ahmed, another friend of mine from when I lived in London.

"Sorry I couldn't meet you at the airport, but I was chakka yesterday," he apologized.

"No problem. Dave got me fixed up," I told him.

"I've set time aside today, so whenever you want, just let me know."

"What about lunch?" I suggested.

"Sounds good. One o'clock?"

"Yeah. What about I meet you in Piccadilly Circus?"

"See you then," he said, and hung up the phone.

Outside, it was still raining.

I bought two newspapers to get a feeling of what was going on, the *Guardian* and the *Times*.

I decided to try one of the many breakfast cafés I had seen in Shepherds Bush. The one I chose was a small, five-table affair and was serviced by two middle-aged women and a man with dark hair and eyes. He spoke to the women in rapid Turkish.

After breakfast, I bought some undershirts and returned to my room. It was almost 10:30. The telephone rang. It was Dave.

"I got something from Andrew this morning. He said his friend can meet you tonight."

"OK, we're moving. When?"

"I'll set it up for ten—is that OK? By the way, I have someone with me who wants to say hello," Dave said.

I held my breath and waited to hear Rhea's voice.

"Hello . . . welcome back stranger." It was a male voice and one I recognized. It belonged to Dave's cousin Ronnie.

"Hey man, how're you doing," I said, beaming into the phone.

"Good. Dave told me you were back in town. We've got to do some traveling, yeah," Ronnie said, and chuckled.

Munir was in his late forties and looked like a Bollywood matinee idol. The tall, dark, and handsome type with dark olive skin and sharp features. His parents were from India and Afghanistan, but he was born in Birmingham, England.

We walked over to The Union, in Soho, a members-only club that served lunch and had a reputation for being frequented by people who worked in the entertainment business. Munir was a journalist and knew where all the best places to eat were located. That was just one of his talents. His other outstanding one was the gathering of information. When he wasn't busy gathering materials for news or magazine stories, he was busy gathering information for MI6, England's equivalent to the CIA.

"So you're a detective now, huh Mr. Barnett?" Munir said, looking at me over his plate of prawns and rice.

"I guess I am at that," I said.

"That name you faxed me from the States—the Ultimate Management Company—I managed to trace to an address in Harlesden, a house which, by the way, is owned by a woman named Stella Jennings. . . ."

I smiled my approval across the table. "Nice work."

"Why don't we go have a word with her," Munir said, lighting up his after-meal cigarette.

Stella Jennings's house was located in a poor, working-class neighborhood in a section of West London called Harlesden that had seen better days. The road she lived on was colorless and drab, and most of the houses could have benefited from a coat of paint.

We found her address and rang the bell. We rang again and again, but no one answered. Munir looked through the window and saw someone moving around inside. We rang the bell again. This time, we scored. The woman who answered the door looked to be in her seventies.

"Yes," she said as she opened the door just enough to peek out at us.

"We're looking for Stella Jennings," Munir said. "I'm from the newspaper. We're writers."

"Stella?"

"Yes, do you know her?" Munir inquired in his most polite tone.

"Oh yes, I know her," she responded enthusiastically with the lilt of a Jamaican accent in her speech.

"Do you know where she is, or how we can contact her?

"I do," was all that she said, and she blinked at us a few times with bright, vacant eyes.

"Is she at home. Is this where she lives?" I asked.

The old lady looked at me strangely and grinned.

"I know Stella very well, I do." She grinned. "I know her, yes."

I exchanged looks with Munir. Either the old lady was senile, or we had come to the wrong place. As I gathered my thoughts for another approach, the woman suddenly opened the door.

"Come in, gentlemen it's cold out," she said.

The inside of the house matched the outside. It was poorly furnished and decorated, but not dirty. Just a combination of cheap furniture and poor taste. There were a number of empty beer cans on a small coffee table that sat in front of the television, accompanied by an empty, grease-stained wrapping that once contained fish and chips.

"Sit down, gentlemen. Would you like a cup of tea?" she asked.

We took the seats on the sofa but declined the tea.

"We are looking for Mrs. Stella Jennings because we would like to talk to her about an article I'm doing about her son Trevor."

At the mention of the name Trevor, she screwed up her prune-like face.

At that moment there was the sound of a key turning in the lock of the door. A few seconds later, a tall, middle-aged black man entered the room. His appearance was disheveled, and he was in need of a shave. His eyes were two burning cinders as they blazed in our direction.

"Who are you and how did you get in here—what do you want? Leave now or I'm calling the police," he blurted, looking from us to the old lady.

"She let us in, we're from the newspaper, I'm a writer," Munir explained.

The man ignored Munir's comment and looked at the old woman.

"Bloody hell, Auntie. I told you about letting strangers in here."

"They not strangers. They said they were looking for Stella Jennings. I know Stella Jennings, don't I? If they are friends of Stella, then they are friends of mine." She smiled.

The man sighed and looked at us. Some of the anger in his face had dissipated. For the first time, he focused on us with discernment. "Listen, I don't mean to be rude, but she's not well," he told us.

"We don't mean her any harm. We just wanted to find Stella Jennings and she told us she knew her, that's all," I said.

"She does, because she *is* Stella Jennings," the man informed us.

Munir and I looked at each other again.

"Now there. As you can see, she's past it, mate," the man explained.

"Sorry," Munir said.

Curiosity suddenly replaced the scorn in his expression.

"What newspaper you say you're from?"

"I didn't," explained Munir. "I'm a freelance journalist."

"What you want to see my aunt Stella about?" he added curiously.

"We wanted to talk to her about her son, the Reverend Trevor Jennings. We want to do an article on him," Munir said.

The man laughed. "About what—what a tosser he is?"

"Excuse me?" Munir said.

"That's right. That's Trevor's mother there, and you see how she's living. He's loaded with dosh, and she gets fuck-all. He doesn't even take care of her. If it wasn't for me, mum and me, she would be in an old folks' home. We take care of her, not him, and he's loaded with dosh. Big bloody church and all in America," he said angrily. He then looked at me directly. "You're from America too, yeah, with that accent."

"Yes, I am."

"Listen, I'll give you enough for a book on Trevor Jennings, but it won't be what his congregation wants to hear. I'll tell you the truth, and I know it, too. I'm his own blood. I'm his cousin," the man said.

"I'm willing to pay for the story," I said.

At the word "pay," the man started to look interested. "Cash?" he asked, and focused his gaze on me.

"Sure," I answered.

"How much?"

"Say, a hundred pounds," I told him.

"OK, maybe we can have a chat, then," the man said.

"Are you hungry? I'm dying for something to eat," I said quickly, seeing the advantage of taking another tack.

The man nodded. "Yeah, I'm a bit peckish."

"What would you suggest?" I asked.

"There's a chippy at the end of the road," he said.

"OK, I'll be right back," I said, shooting a sideways glance at Munir. "Does Mrs. Jennings eat fish and chips, too?"

"Fancy some fish and chips, Auntie?" the man said to the old woman, who had walked off into the adjoining room.

"That would be lovely," Stella said to her nephew.

Munir had picked up on my signal.

"By the way, my name is Munir Ahmed," he said as he extended his hand in the man's direction.

"I'm Neville, Neville Turner." The man shook Munir's hand.

"My name is Marcus Barnett," I said.

Neville nodded his response.

Twenty-five minutes later I was walking back through the door of the house, loaded down with two orders of fish and chips, three meat pies, two sausage rolls, a large box of orange juice, six cans of Tenants beer, and a hundred pounds in cash that I had just gotten from the bank's cash machine with my credit card.

As the four of us sat around the table eating and talking about the illustrious life of Trevor Jennings, the sounds of Bob Marley poured in faintly from somewhere outside.

"Trevor was a vicar here once, but he got sacked because he was on the fiddle," Neville explained to us.

The old woman seemed to be in another world, oblivious to our conversation. All of her attention was focused on her steak and kidney pie. Every now and again she would look up smiling and say, "Nice, very nice, this."

"Yes, it is," Neville responded dutifully, and then she would delve back into her food.

"You say he was on the fiddle," Munir asked, writing notes into his reporter's notebook.

"Um," Neville nodded. "This was about twenty-five years ago. He set up a charity for children and went about collecting for it, but then it comes out that the money was going straight into Trevor's pocket. A first-class thief he is, and smart too. An educated thief is the worst kind, harder to catch," Neville observed, finishing off his third can of beer.

"After he was sacked . . .?" Munir said, leaving the question open ended for Neville to respond.

"That was just part of it. The other part was the women. He made a couple of them from the congregation pregnant, and there was a row one night at the church. A brother, I think, of one of the pregnant women went after Trevor with a machete," Neville said, smiling at the thought.

"Sounds like a nice chap," Munir added sarcastically.

"A first-class bastard, Trevor is. Shortly after that, he moved to America."

Neville continued to supply us with other bits and pieces on the good Reverend as he worked his way through two more cans. Lunch was finished, and Stella had drifted off and was quietly snoring on the sofa with an expression of contentment on her face.

"Anytime you want more on that bastard, you know where to come,"Neville said. "Write it all down, mate."

"Thank you. I think we have what we need. You've been very helpful," Munir said, and passed Neville his card.

"If you hear from him, let us know, but keep it on the quiet," I said. "This little meeting never took place."

"No worries, mate." Neville winked at me and started to rise from his chair only to find wobbly feet.

"We'll find our way out, don't worry, relax," Munir said.

Neville raised his hand in gratitude and plopped back down in the chair.

"Cheers," Neville said as we left the house.

As we got into the car and made our way back toward Brixton, I was feeling hopeful. I hadn't located my prey yet, but I knew enough to know that all rats eventually had to come out of their holes. And when this one did, I would be there waiting.

Munir had another appointment for the evening, so I went to see Dave alone. He was working behind the bar and reading the results of the football games played the day before.

"I have to go with Manchester United for the Premier Championship," he told one of his customers, who was a short, wiry man with gray hair and a red nose.

"At Chelsea, the lads are better and the coach is steady. He knows the game inside out," the customer countered.

"My dosh stays with Man U," Dave reiterated confidently.

"Devil Barnett." Someone called my name from the middle of the room, and I looked back to see Ronnie standing there with a grin the size of the Grand Canyon spread across his face. Ronnie reminded me of a great brown bear as he stood six three and weighing about 280 pounds.

I rose off the stool and embraced him warmly.

"You look like you've been keeping well," Ronnie said.

"I'm OK," I remarked.

Ronnie ordered us two pints of Guinness Stout and lead me to a corner table. Not only was Ronnie Dave's cousin but he was also his business partner and closest friend. Ronnie lived in Nottingham with his wife, Prudence, and their three kids.

"What brings you down?" I asked.

Ronnie looked at me for a while without answering, then sighed. "Me and Prudence have been going through a bad patch, so we decided to take some time away from each other."

"Is it serious?" I asked. I knew Prudence and I liked her. She was a very nice woman, warm and very clever. She was also from an upper-class English family with old money but very down-to-earth.

"Seems like it happens every five years or so," Ronnie mused thoughtfully. "We have a go at each other and then I go off a week or so and when I go back home, then it's OK again. She called last night and asked when I was coming back. But I'm not quite ready yet. I want to give myself some time to sort out how to change our lives."

"What do you mean?" I asked.

"Now that the children have grown up, I think we need a bit of change in the way we've been living our lives, the both of us. She's been a good wife to me for over twenty years, and I want to do something special for her now, the kinds of things I could never do before because I was always building up my businesses. It's just something I've been feeling lately. Maybe it's that middle-aged crisis thing that you Americans go on about," Ronnie confessed.

"I'm glad to hear it's nothing serious." I smiled.

Ronnie was always full of laughs as well as philosophy. Full of theories about everything under the sun.

"Hey, geezer," a voice came from behind us. It belonged to Andrew.

"Hey, spar," Ronnie greeted him in return.

Andrew came toward the table with a man in tow. He was clean shaven, wore his hair in long dreadlocks, and donned a black leather jacket.

"This is my mate Brian," Andrew introduced the man.

We shook hands all around, and Brian joined us at the table.

"This is the man I was telling you about." Andrew nodded toward me, then looked at his friend

"Tell him what you sussed out, yeah," Andrew said to Brian.

"Like I told Andy, I was just offered a very sweet deal. Five thousand pieces of an unreleased record from the Dancehall Dogz. Cash deal," Brian said, looking from me to Ronnie and then back to me again.

"And the seller is?" I asked.

Brian smiled a wide, toothy smile full of gold caps.

"A bloke called Punch," Brian said.

"Punch? He's a driver, used to work for one of them mini cabs down the bottom, used to meet up and play dominoes by the patty shop, hates to lose, I remember him," Ronnie said.

"Yeah, that's him," Brian nodded.

"Did he say where he's getting them from?" I inquired.

"No, but he said that as soon as I shift those, I can get more," Brian told us.

"Wonder what connection Punch got that he can get as many as a man can shift?" Andrew remarked, scratching his thin beard thoughtfully.

"Don't know, but it must be rather strong," Ronnie said.

"Do you plan to buy any in?" asked Andrew.

"Yeah, I'm calling him tomorrow. I'm a businessman. If these CDs are as hot as I think they are, then I will make the same profit in two months as I made all last year," Brian said.

I looked up to see Rhea walk through the door. She was accompanied by a woman about her age with long blond hair and platform shoes. Rhea was dressed in a hot pink top that showed her perfectly shaped breasts, and black skintight pants with long black thigh-high boots that accentuated every curve the good Lord gave her. Her hair hung loosely around her shoulders and her makeup was perfect. She could have given any model a run for her money.

She locked eyes with me as the pair walked toward the table. Ronnie did a double take, then looked over at me and grinned widely.

"Hello, Mr. Devil Barnett," Rhea said without smiling.

"Rhea Warwick," I returned.

"I heard you were in town. Weren't you going to call me?"

"I had planned to, yes, but I needed to get some other business taken care of first," I responded, looking her in the eyes.

"I guess I believe you." She licked her lips sensually, then smiled. "This is my friend Clair," Rhea said.

"Hi Clair," I said.

"Hiya."

"Have a seat ladies. Can I get you somethin'?" Ronnie asked.

"A gin and tonic for me," said Clair.

"A gin and water," said Rhea.

"Still drinking the same thing," I chortled.

"I'm the same person, why not," Rhea countered, flirting with her beautiful eyes.

"I guess you've got a point there," I returned.

"Oh-oh." Ronnie laughed as he left with the other guys to get their drinks.

"So how has the world been treating you?" she asked.

"Not bad. I'm out of my old job and into a new one."

"I'm told you own a pub."

"Well, sort of, it's a bar."

"Where?"

"In Harlem, where I grew up. It was my dad's place, but he was killed in a holdup and I took it over."

"Oh, I'm sorry," she said. "It *has* been a long time hasn't it?" she reminded me.

"Yeah, almost two and a half years," I responded.

"Two and a half years too long," she said, looking straight at me and licking her lips again.

Clair, who was looking with keen fascination at Rhea's flirting, took the lull in our conversation as her cue. "So is New York as rough as they say it is?"

"I don't know how rough they say it is," I responded.

"Very rough. They also say everything is bigger, but they say the people are very friendly, though. My friend went last year and she says they give you really big portions of food when you go out for a meal. Is it true?" Her enthusiasm was almost childlike.

"I guess in comparison to England, yeah the portions are larger—in fact a lot of things are bigger there," I told her.

"I would love to go to New York." Clair smiled.

"Well, don't hold your breath if you think Mr. Devil Barnett is going to offer," Rhea chimed in.

"You know that's not fair," I protested.

"Well, you did promise to take me, didn't you?" she maintained.

"Well, yes, but you know as well as I do that was a long time ago. Plus, I promised to take you only if you promised to be on your good behavior, which as I remember you never were," I said.

"You're still as cheeky as ever, I see." She smiled, then crossed her long legs and lit a cigarette.

"To quote you, I'm the same person, so why shouldn't I be." I grinned back, enjoying the banter.

"As far as I'm concerned, a promise is still a promise," she cooed.

Ronnie returned alone with drinks.

"So what you got on for tonight?" Ronnie said, looking at me slyly.

"Oh, Mr. Devil Barnett is probably just going home and right to bed. You know how health conscious he is," Rhea answered coquette-like.

I didn't answer. I just looked blankly as if I hadn't heard either the question or Rhea's response. She had always loved winding me up. She threw her head back and laughed with pleasurable abandon. As I watched her I remembered the feeling she used to give me just watching her laugh, especially when we were in bed.

"How are you getting home tonight, Mr. Devil Barnett?" Rhea asked.

"By mini cab," I said.

"If you don't mind my driving, I'll take you home. I have to drop Clair in Ealing Broadway, anyway. Shepherd's Bush is on the way," she said.

"Sure, thanks," I said.

"Enjoy yourselves, come again soon yeah." Dave called and smiled to us as we left the pub.

"We'll talk in the morning," I called over my shoulder. Dave just smiled and nodded.

So we drove north from Brixton across the Thames River and headed west toward Ealing listening to Ella Fitzgerald, Gilberto Gill, Gabriella Anders, and Sergio Mendes.

"Naturally I'm dropping Clair off first, as she has to go to work early tomorrow early," Rhea said as she passed the sign that pointed toward Shepherd's Bush.

"Naturally," I said, pretending not to pick up on her hidden meaning.

She just looked at me and smiled.

We pulled up to Clair's house ten minutes later, and she jumped out.

Without another word, Rhea pulled the late-model Mercedes into traffic and headed toward Shepherd's Bush.

I opened the door and allowed Rhea to enter the house first.

"Cozy," she said as she looked around my room. "How long you here for?"

"Not sure. I've got some business to take care of. I haven't thought much past that, honestly."

"Oh, right," she said, and reached down inside her large black purse and retrieved a bottle of good white wine. "This still suits you, does it not?" she smiled.

"It does." I smiled back.

She found two glasses and poured us each a half glass, then she pulled off her boots and sat on the bed.

I sat in the chair.

"So what are you doing for a love life these days?"

"Um, well, just before I came over here I broke up with someone."

"Someone you loved?"

"Someone I care a lot about, yes," I said.

"I can understand that," she said, sipping the wine.

"What about you?" I asked.

"There was someone I got involved with seriously after us, but that ended when he went back to his wife."

"I'm sorry to hear that. You're a wonderful woman. You deserve real happiness," I told her.

We kept talking and kept drinking until we were in each other's arms. As Rhea snuggled under the covers, I felt her warm nakedness next to me. It heated and absorbed all of the dampness that I had felt since being in England. It comforted and filled in all of those empty spaces that I had been trying to deny existed. She touched me all over and started to kiss my chest. She had remembered all the things that I liked, as well as exactly which buttons to push to make all of the right things happen.

The more she did, the more excited I became. I was ready to burst when she passed me a condom. I quickly pulled it on and entered her waiting body. We made love slowly, then quickly, smoothly, then roughly . . . again and again and again and again, until we were both empty of physical passion.

"It was always this good, wasn't it?" she cooed, snuggling up to me.

"Yes, it was."

Within a few minutes I felt her warm breath on my neck. She was sleeping like a baby. I pulled the covers up over her shoulders and gently kissed her face. As she lay in my arms, I thought about the last time I had felt this way. It was like a scene from a movie. This moment with Rhea blurred and dissolved into sweet memories and soft, misty images of Sonia. I drifted somewhere between experiencing a heightened sense of emotional bliss and drifting toward a beckoning void. I relaxed into the darkness of the room and breathed in the scent of sex mixed with perfume emanating from Rhea's body, and I melted into a place inside my head where only the emotion of my spirit could fully understand the conversation.

CHAPTER 14

5:30 p.m. and it was already dark as Munir and I drove toward Brian's record shop in Brixton.

"Word came back on that Ultimate Management company that I checked. Even though the address is at a furnished office, they do have a bank account that is registered at an offshore bank," Munir said. "My people hacked into it and found there was about five thousand pounds going through the account each month until six months ago. Then it jumped to over five hundred thousand per month, thanks to Grooveline Records."

We reached our destination with about twenty minutes to spare. Munir went in wired.

"Listen, I'm making lots of money on this—you're not going to foul things up for me, are you?" Brain said.

"You're still going to make your money. We just need to know who is who," Munir assured him.

"Make sure you don't, because the only reason I'm doing this is that I owe Andy lots of favors," Brian said.

"No worries, mate," I heard Munir say through the receiver in the car as I waited for Punch to arrive.

We didn't have to wait long. At 7:10 p.m. a green van pulled up in front of the record shop. A large white man jumped from the driver's seat and entered the store.

"I'm here to deliver something for Punch," the driver's voice came through the portable receiver.

"Yeah, where's Punch, then?" Brian inquired.

"On his way. He called me from Stockwell a few minutes ago. Can I start loading?"

"Yeah, why not," Brian said.

Four minutes later a Rover pulled up and a youngish black man wearing a red baseball cap entered the store.

"I see everything's cool, yeah?" Punch said.

"Yeah, it's all there."

"I'll just do a quick count—not that I don't trust you, yeah, but I have to answer to someone else."

"Seen." Brian nodded.

I listened as Punch counted the money and the driver finished loading in the last of the boxes.

"If you need more, just ring, yeah?" Punch said.

"Safe," Brian answered.

A few minutes later, Munir returned to the car.

"Everything OK? he asked.

"Yeah, fine," I said.

Punch came out of the store and drove away. Munir pulled his car into traffic and followed the Rover at a safe distance. Punch followed the van to another store on Middlesex. After the delivery was made, the van went one way and Punch another. We decided to stay with Punch.

We followed the Rover as Punch drove to Hackney.

The Rover stopped at Kingsland Road. Punch got out and went into a place with a brown and orange hand-lettered sign that simply read HACKNEY GRILL CAFÉ.

We waited in the car for another fifteen minutes and Munir went inside and ordered a prawn sandwich with a cup of tea. Twenty minutes later he came back with a tuna and sweet corn sandwich and a cup of tea for me.

"Nothing, no sign of him. There's a doorway leading to the back, which is where he must have gone," Munir remarked.

I ate my sandwich as we continued to wait and watch the Rover parked outside.

The café closed at 8:00 p.m. and two hours later Punch emerged. He was with another man who wore his hair in dreadlocks. I snapped photographs of the two men using a tele-photo night vision lens and a special, super-fast film with an ASA that allowed one to take pictures in almost no light. This camera and film belonged to Munir and were part of the equipment he used when working as an agent for MI6.

The Rover drove to an address in Hackney, and the dread-locked man got out and disappeared inside a house. Then the

Rover quickly pulled off into traffic and returned to Brixton.

Munir made a call and spoke in the Urdu language that is spoken in Pakistan and parts of India.

"I can put surveillance on the café and I've got someone whose going to ring me back within the hour with the name of someone who might be helpful to us. Meanwhile, let's develop these photos," he told me after he had finished the call.

We drove back to Munir's house in Richmond. He lived with his wife and two daughters in a dwelling that had three floors. It was almost midnight when we arrived, and everyone was asleep.

We stopped in the kitchen and picked up some food from the fridge and made our way to the top floor, where Munir had his office and photographic lab.

The office consisted of two desks, two computers, a fax machine, two telephones, shelves lined with books on journalism, and a wall full of university degrees, community awards, and photographs.

Munir had been a journalist for over twenty years and was well known and respected in the Asian community, which is why he made such a good agent. He could go anyplace seeking out all kinds of information naturally as part of his job.

We had become friends when we both worked on an assignment involving a mole, an Asian civil servant who worked in the diplomatic service passing sensitive materials about a joint British and American undercover operation to Iraq. As a result, six out of eight British and American agents working on the joint operation were killed. Munir's job was to find out who the mole was, and my job was to eliminate him. We completed the assignment successfully.

Next to Munir's office was a darkroom. We quickly developed the film and made two prints. Then Munir made another call and again he spoke in Urdu. Munir hung up the phone and looked at me.

"Looks like we may be in for a long night, my friend," he said.

As we drove back to Hackney, Munir filled me in on the character we were about to visit.

The place was a mini cab shop with a sign out front that read At Your Service Mini Cab Open 24 Hours. When we entered, it was 2:05 a.m. and the mini cab shop was the only thing open in sight.

There were three men inside. One man sat at the window talking on the telephone and peeping over a pair of reading glasses at the sports pages of the newspaper and two other men who were apparently drivers sat in the lobby area waiting for calls. As we walked in, all heads turned.

"Where you going?" the man with the reading glasses asked.

"We'd like to see Zubin," Munir said.

"Just a moment," he said, looking at us curiously.

He got up and walked to the back of the lobby and opened a door. A few seconds later, a thin little man came out of the office. When he saw us, a nervous, worried look passed across his drawn features, but he quickly replaced it with a fake smile.

"Hello, my friend. I am glad to see you again," the thin little man said to Munir with a pronounced Indian accent. "It is very late for you to be out, isn't it?"

"Let's go somewhere we can talk, Zubin," Munir said.

"In my office," Zubin said, and led the way back.

His office was a small, cluttered dingy affair with an old worn, steel desk, two hard-backed chairs, and puke-colored walls.

"Hello, I am Zubin," the little man said pushing his hand out to shake mine. I returned the gesture but didn't give my name.

Munir took one of the photographs we had developed from the inside of his jacket pocket and gave it to Zubin.

"This man came out of the Hackney Grill Café down the road from here a few hours ago. Any idea of who he is?"

Zubin started to squint at the picture and shake his head.

"I don't recall ever seeing him before," Zubin said.

"If you insist on lying to me, I will see what I can do about closing this place down. And I think that can be done, especially if the police knew you use it as a place to sell drugs and prostitutes. So don't faff around with me, I'm not in the mood, yeah," Munir stated.

Zubin looked back up at Munir, whose face was set in a firm, no-nonsense expression.

Zubin started speaking in Urdu.

"No, English please, I want my friend here to know exactly what kind of snake you are," insisted Munir.

Zubin sighed deeply and looked humiliated.

"If I am caught giving you this information, it could go very bad for me. This man would kill me, he's that type."

"Let's just hope it won't go any further than this room, then," Munir stated.

"You have to promise me," Zubin insisted.

"Go ahead, Zubin, tell me. My patience is wearing thin," Munir countered.

"The man with the dreadlocks is known as 'The Burning Bush.' He is a dealer in certain substances," Zubin said, lowering his voice.

"The same kind you deal in?" Munir put in.

"Y-Y-Yes," Zubin eventually stammered. "The same exactly."

"Have you ever done any business with this man?"

"No," Zubin said, shaking his head emphatically. "I couldn't— I have my own people. In fact, my people and he are rivals, you might say."

"Your people as in Patel's people?" Munir said.

At the mention of the name Patel, Zubin began to fidget nervously. "Please don't use names, please. The walls have ears, you see," he said.

"So tell us, what goes on in the Hackney Grill Café?" Munir inquired.

Zubin looked around the room suspiciously, as if checking to see whether the invisible people he feared were within eavesdropping range.

"Ah . . . the Bush's people operate from there. From out of the back offices," Zubin said, lowing his voice to almost a whisper.

"Have you been there?" I asked.

"No, not me," he said, shaking his balding head.

"You know someone who works for him?" Munir asked.

"Used to work for him, but not now," Zubin answered. "I haven't seen him for a long time," he said nervously.

"What's his name?" Munir asked.

"Vennie."

"What else do you know about this Burning Bush?" I said.

"He's been around for years as a small operator—mostly stolen goods—but he just got bigger in the past year. Rumors are that he has financing behind him now," Zubin said.

"Who told you that?" I inquired.

"Vennie, of course."

"If we find you've lied to us, it's not going to go easy for you," Munir reminded him.

"I'm not lying. I'm telling you what I know."

"No mon, that's the price," Bush said into his mobile phone. "It's a good price for a good product, nah?"

The frustration was building up inside The Burning Bush like a bitter wind in a hurricane. But it was suppressed and took expression in the form of a frown that appeared across his dark features. He put down the telephone and started walking up and down the room. Walking was his habit. It always seemed to help, especially when he was upset like now. Maybe it was a throwback to his days as a boy in Trenchtown, Jamaica, when things were bad at home; his father drinking and beating up his mother, and no food to eat. He would often go for long walks to try to escape. Sometimes he would stay out all night walking and come home in the morning. He was never missed, not with ten children in the house. Even back then he dreamed of big money and big success. Now that he was standing on the brink, now that he could smell it and taste it, he had a problem.

Some of his best customers were starting to complain about prices. They were telling him that they could get the same product from Mr. Patel for a better price than he offered.

Even though the Reverend had said they were now concentrating on another part of the market, the thought of losing customers that he had cultivated still did not sit well with him. It was more than just money. It was a matter of pride and respect.

The Burning Bush was not the kind of man who allowed anyone to steal from him. Not if he could help it. Besides, what credibility would he have in the underworld if word got out that Patel could steal his customers right in his own backyard. As a boy in Trenchtown, when he was bullied by the bigger boys he had stood and fought, even if it meant taking a beating. He had never let anyone take anything from him.

Bush formulated a plan of action. He called a number that he knew by heart.

Marga's voice answered.

"We're moving tonight, so bring the tools, yeah?"

"Yeah, no problem," Marga said.

"And bring Dennis, too?"

"Yeah, what time?" Marga asked his boss.

"Meet me at 10:00 here," Bush told his worker.

"Seen," Marga confirmed.

Bush hung up the phone and lit a spliff. His watch told him he had three hours and ten minutes before Marga arrived. He spent the time going over the plan in his head again and again and again.

As the BMW made its way along the small, tree-lined country road, Bush looked into the night straight ahead. The clouds had covered the sky for most of the day, and now there was no moon, only darkness. Up ahead was the destination. It was a small nightclub called Henry's located on the outskirts of London.

As the BMW rolled up in front of the nightclub, Bush stretched his neck left and right to see what he could see. But it was mostly quiet.

Bush and Marga got out of the car. A sign above the door read 70s AND 80s MUSIC NIGHT. They made their way to the bar.

"What can I get you?" one barman asked the pair in an Australian accent.

"Looking for the manager, Vennie," Bush said.

"He's in the office now. He's busy."

"This is important—he'll see me, I'm sure." Bush was insistent but polite.

"I'll see. Just a minute, mate. What's your name?" the Aussie said.

"A friend of Mr. Patel's."

The barman walked up the stairs.

Bush watched the Aussie disappear. As soon as he was out of sight, Bush climbed the stairs quickly, taking three steps at a time. He heard the Aussie talking to someone in the office. Bush walked softly up to the door of the office.

"What did he look like?" Bush heard Vennie's voice inquire.

"He was a tallish black bloke, with dreads and . . ."

"And a beautiful smile, yeah," Bush said, stepping into the room.

Vennie almost swallowed his tongue. "Hello, Bush," he said nervously.

The Australian looked at Vennie, who smiled sheepishly.

"It's OK, Paul, I know him," Vennie said.

"OK," the barman said, and bounded out of the room.

Bush and Vennie locked gazes.

Vennie was an Asian man in his twenties with a dark complexion and short black hair that he wore plastered to his head in a style that was currently in fashion.

"What are you doing here?" Vennie asked with the uneasiness of the moment covering him like a bad suit of clothes.

"Me come to see you, been a long time nah. Don't you want to offer me a cup of tea or a drink, mon?"

"Sure, it's just that I wasn't expecting you. Yes, would you like a drink. I have beer here," Vennie said, reaching down to a fridge that sat beside his desk. He extracted a can of Foster's and placed it on the desk in front of The Burning Bush.

Bush nodded his gratitude and smiled.

"What brings you out here? A bit out of your way, innit?"

"Not really," Bush said, sipping from the can of beer. "I used to do a fair amount of business out here—remember when you worked for me?"

Vennie suddenly looked as nervous as a scalded cat. "Ye-Ye-Yeah, but that was a while ago, almost two years now," Vennie stammered nervously, avoiding direct eye contact.

Vennie sat down, thinking that it might help calm his nerves, which were jumping around inside his body like hot kernels of popping corn.

"How is Mr. Patel, I hear him all over now, expandin?"

" I suppose, I don't ever see him," Vennie said, shifting in his chair.

"Yeah, I want him to get a message from me."

"Yeah, well if I hear from him I'll relay it."

"Good." Bush finished drinking his beer, then stood up.

"You tell Mr. Patel I don't want him in my yard no more, yeah."

Vennie nodded dumbly. They both knew that Vennie was not about to deliver that kind of message to Patel. Bush looked Vennie straight in the eye as he pulled the long, heavy machete from the inside of his jacket.

Vennie's face contorted in instant fear as Bush raised the heavy knife above his head. Vennie almost managed to scream, but shock constricted his vocal chords, freezing the sound inside his throat. He tried to scramble away but he was trapped behind the desk.

"For fuck sake," Vennie barely managed, just as he raised his arm, hoping to deflect the blow. But it didn't do any good. The machete first struck him in the face. Then his neck, then his head, then again and again and again, until . . . The Burning Bush was burning hot as he chopped Vennie at least a hundred times or more. He chopped with exactly the kind of stroke he had learned and practiced as a kid in Trenchtown. It was the stroke used to break open coconuts. Vennie's green silk shirt was covered in blood, and his face resembled minced beef.

Bush put the machete back inside his jacket and left the room. As he descended the staircase, he glanced over toward the bar. The Australian bar man was busy. He spotted Marga stationed by the door.

Bush walked coolly down the stairs across to where Marga was sitting and nodded. Marga held open the door as Bush walked from the world of multicolored lights that illuminated Henry's back out into the dull, moonless night.

As Dennis drove the BMW back toward London, a thousand thoughts pushed their way into Bush's head.

His action had not been authorized by the Reverend. He would justify his actions by saying that he was eliminating the competition. The Reverend would understand that, surely.

Bush felt good. Somehow he felt more natural than he had an hour ago. More powerful. He had defended his territory. A natural instinct. The law of the jungle.

He lit a spliff, confident that Mr. Patel would get his message now.

CHAPTER 15

I slept four hours and woke up feeling like shit. My body clock was out of sync. It was still only 2:30 a.m. in New York, which meant that I had actually woken up before I'd gone to bed. It felt like I was living in the twilight zone.

I went back to bed and woke up again at 12:30 feeling a lot better. The phone was ringing. When I answered, Rhea's voice was at the other end.

"Hello Mr. Devil Barnett," she purred into the phone seductively.

"Hey, yourself," I said, happy to hear her voice.

"Are you busy tonight?"

"I wish I could answer that now, but I can't. I'm waiting on a few calls. Then I'll know more," I told her.

"Some things just don't change, do they?" she said sarcastically.

I remained silent. I figured what was the point. Why open up the door to another one of those 999 arguments?

"I'll have my mobile on all day and night, if you need to find out how things are coming, or I'll call you," I said, trying to soften the blow.

"I'll catch up with you," she said caustically, then hung up the phone.

"True, some things don't change, the same hotheaded woman," I mused to myself.

Munir picked me up around midnight and we headed for the all-night mini cab shop. Zubin was on the telephone when we walked in unannounced. As he looked up and saw us, an alarm bell went off inside his aging eyes. "Gentlemen," he said, forcing a smile.

"Sit down, Zubin, make yourself comfortable," Munir said.

"What brings you to see me again so soon?" Zubin inquired behind a shit-eating grin. He said something in Urdu, then hung up the phone.

"I want to do you a favor," Munir stated.

"Me?" Zubin said.

"I want you to make a link with Patel. Tell him I'm willing to eliminate his biggest competitor."

"How is that doing me a favor?"

"Listen, you are an old man. In a few years you will be past it. With just one deal of the kind I will offer Patel, you can make enough to retire. On the other hand, I can use someone else."

"No, I'll do it," Zubin said.

Munir had read him right. Zubin was so greedy that he would have rather chopped off his arm than let someone else get in on a deal and be left out in the cold.

"Just set a meeting for as soon as possible and let me take it from there, OK?" Munir instructed.

Zubin looked at Munir for a long while, then started to nod his bald head.

Diop Patel didn't look like I expected him to. He looked more like a cartoon character than a drug dealer. He was in his fifties, short, and thick, with long, thin spindly arms and legs, fat in the middle, with a perfectly round head that was attached to a neck that seemed too short for his body. Two bloodshot eyes popped out from behind thick glasses. His English was flawless, and he spoke with an upper-class British accent.

"You come highly recommended by Zubin," he said, smiling catlike.

"We think we might be able to help you. To put it simply we can make it very easy to move your product into the country. Risk-free in diplomatic pouches," Munir said. "We have a good contact at an embassy."

The funny-looking Asian man was quiet for what seemed like a long time.

"The question I have is what would you need to make you comfortable if we were to enter into a working relationship?" Patel said.

"We want our own territory."

"Your own territory," Patel said, raising his eyebrows.

"The territory I'm talking about is Hackney."

Patel said nothing, he just looked at each of us, then he began slowly. "That territory is already under control by my competition."

"Yes, we know, and that's a problem we are willing to take care of," I added.

A sly smile crept over Patel's nut brown features.

Back in my room, I ate and started to think about our plan. So far, it was working. The mobile phone rang, and Rhea's voice was on the other end.

"Hello, Mr. Devil Barnett," she said sexily.

"Hello, yourself. I'm sorry about last night," I said.

"No worries. What you up to tonight?" she asked.

"So far, not much. Just thinking about having a quiet night in," I answered.

"Feel like company?" she asked.

"Sounds good to me," I shot back immediately.

"Why don't you come over here, say around 9:00 p.m. I'll cook us dinner and we can watch a video."

"Not one of those videos from your sexy video collection," I teased.

"Maybe." She laughed coyly.

"Sounds good," I said.

"See you around 9:00 p.m.," she said.

Rhea lived in Ladbroke Grove, a trendy part of London,similar in spirit to Greenwich Village, only smaller. As I approached her house the steady drizzle that had been coming down escalated into a downpour.

Maybe it was was the sudden change in the weather and the wind violently blowing in my face that made it happen, I'm not sure. All I know was that my sixth sense kicked in, and not a moment too soon.

If the man had been more fit, I would have most likely been six feet in the grave by now, but his blubber conspired against him. It was the heavy breathing that made me turn to see the big man running toward me swinging something at my head. My reaction came so naturally, I didn't even have to think. It all came back, all the years, all the training, all of the assignments, all the dead men.

Instinct took over. I dropped to the ground and jackknifed 180 degrees and used my legs to clip his legs from under him. My attacker went down like a big bag of shit. His face hit the pavement with a bang, and the lead pipe he had planned to use as a weapon skidded across the asphalt. I could see that he was a white man.

He was big and powerfully built, but he was slow. Immediately he tried to regain his footing, but I was faster. By the time he had positioned his hands to draw himself up to his knees, I had placed my knee at the back of his elbow and grabbed his wrist. Then, with all my strength, I pulled back.

The snap of the big man's bone sounded like a dull firecracker.

He tried to cry out, but the pain caught in his throat and he only gurgled in agony. I stiffened my index and middle finger, held them together, and poked them directly into his right eye like a spear. Then, with a downward karate motion, the heel of my hand smashed against the bridge of his nose. More bones cracked. He grabbed his face and moaned "Ohhhhh," with his eyes rolling up into his skull.

As I moved my face closer to his, I dug into my jacket pocket until I felt my door key.

I took it out and placed the point of it into his left eye and pressed until he started to turn a shade of purple. "I'm going to ask you one time, just once," I said, keeping my voice cool as the rain beat us both in the face. "Who was it that sent you?"

The man tried to say something as his face contorted with pain. His lips pursed, and a gurgling sound emerged.

"The vicar, Jennings," he managed to say finally.

I pressed the key into his eyeball. "Oh God," the tough guy moaned.

"Go on," I said, pressing the key harder into his eye.

My instinct to kill him and leave him lying in the rain was

almost overpowering. He was helpless. I could have easily snapped the life out of him with just one blow to the windpipe. But I didn't. Something made me stop.

I grabbed his other arm and expertly broke it in two places. "Next time I see you, you're a dead man," I said quietly. Then I banged his head on the pavement and knocked him out.

I walked down the street past Rhea's house, ducked under a storefront awning, and waited at the end of the road. I thought about Christine's words again. That tickle I had been feeling had just turned into an itch, an itch that I knew I had to scratch.

I used my mobile phone to call Rhea to say the train had been delayed and that I was on my way. She said that the fish would be nice and hot whenever I arrived. I laughed at the double entendre and hung up. I went into a pub at the end of the road, straightened my clothes in the bathroom mirror, ordered a glass of orange juice, waited five minutes, then walked down to Rhea's address and rang the bell. The man I had left in the street was no longer there.

Rhea answered the door wearing a cool blue silk pantsuit with a see-through top. I stepped in out of the rain and she kissed me.

"Get out of those wet clothes. We don't want you to catch your death now do we, Mr. Devil Barnett," she purred, and winked.

I stripped down to my birthday suit.

Rhea took all my clothes and threw them into the washing machine.

"By the time we've finished watching the video, you'll be a brand-new man, Mr. Devil Barnett," she said.

She brought out a pair of men's extra-large sweatpants and a sweatshirt to match.

I looked at her with a raised eyebrow.

"I do have three brothers and a father, you know," she cautioned.

"I didn't say a mumbling word, I'm just grateful to be out of those wet clothes," I said, and laughed.

"I just bet you are Mr. Devil Barnett."

The dinner was delicious. Rhea was one of those women who had learned to cook in her early teens and grew up cooking for her brothers and father when her mother, who was a nurse, had to work shifts. She was able to do all of the West Indian dishes like ackee and saltfish, bread pudding, callaloo and rice and peas excellently; as well as others, including my favorite macaroni and cheese and corn bread dressing down-home Georgia style.

We ate and talked.

"I cooked corn bread dressing on December 13th," she said nonchalantly.

I looked up surprised.

"Why do you look so surprised? It's your favorite."

"I know, but why on that day?"

"Because it's your birthday, and I know that's what you would have asked me to cook if you'd been here. Strange, huh?" She smiled.

I didn't know quite what to say.

She ate in silence awhile before she spoke again.

"Problem is that I fancy you something awful, always have since I first laid eyes on you. But over the years I have had to learn to accept you for who you are. Believe it or not, I have come to terms with that."

I didn't respond. Not verbally, anyway.

"Don't worry, I won't pour beer on your head tonight— besides, I was drunk that night," she said, laughing.

I looked at her, trying to keep a straight face. We both tried but couldn't. We burst out laughing at the same time. Ten minutes later we sat down on the sofa and begin to watch a video— *Crimson Tide*, with Gene Hackman and Denzel Washington, one of my favorites. Twenty minutes into it we were both as naked as jaybirds and in each other's arms again.

Her smooth, slender fingers played against my body like she was Vanessa Mae and I was a rare Stradivarius, and I was working her body like I was Little Milton in a small, funky room on the Chitlin' Circuit:

> *If I don't love you baby, then grits ain't grocery, eggs*
> *ain't poultry and Mona Lisa was a man—Yeah,*
> *Yeah, Yeah.*

"Ooooh," she moaned, deep and throaty as we connected somewhere in a place that seemed beyond this earthly realm.

Rhea's natural body scent meshed with her perfume, giving me an erotic rush as I pushed deeper inside her. As I got a rhythm going, another blues song began playing inside my head. My body was grooving to the steady, syncopated motion of the bass and the beat of the drum simultaneously:

Rock me pretty baby, Rock me all night long,
Rock me pretty baby like my back ain't got no bone.

Passion exploded and lit up the room. Then we lay motionless in each other's arms, panting and spent. We kissed gently and continued to cuddle.

"You know what, Mr. Devil Barnett," she said.

"No."

"It's time like these that make me understand why I've always wanted you in my life permanently."

"Really," was all I could think of to say.

As much as I enjoyed her company, the emotions that I had for her were mixed. My head was speaking one language, and my heart another. As we caressed and cuddled each other, I could feel myself beginning to drift. I was drifting off into the land of ZZZs, a land filled with the flowers of peace. Flowers that emanated the fragrance of innocence.

When Munir called, it was in the afternoon, around 12:30 p.m.

"When do we move?" I asked.

"Nine o'clock tonight."

"It's all set, then," I said.

"All set," he confirmed.

"You talk to Dave and Ronnie?"

"Yes, they'll meet us, they're all set as well," Munir said.

"Excellent," I said.

The place Munir had decided on was a private club called The Gatsby, owned by a friend of his. The place was set up perfectly for what we were going to do.

The decor was old-time classic London, with oak pillars and plush furnishings. There were a number of people having dinner. We found a table near the back of the room and waited for Patel. He showed up about ten minutes later, accompanied by two bodyguards who looked around and sniffed the air for trouble as they walked in. Patel was shown to our table while his two men took a table to themselves nearby.

"Glad you could come," Munir greeted him.

"Has our guest arrived yet?" Patel wanted to know.

"Yes, but because he is a public figure, he can't afford to be seen talking to you in public, if you get my meaning?" Munir stated.

Patel smiled a bit and nodded his understanding.

"We've arranged for a private meeting just between us in a private room in the back. We can order our dinner there."

"OK," Patel said.

Munir led the way. As Patel followed with his two bodyguards in tow, Munir turned to him.

"No offense, but our guest wouldn't appreciate your companions. To him, they are just two more people with access to information who could expose him. It was difficult enough talking him into meeting with you. If he sees those two, it could blow the whole deal. He's the nervous type. Just have them wait here—they'll be safe, don't worry," Munir told Patel confidently.

Patel looked as if he was thinking about it for a moment, then motioned with his head for his bodyguard to sit back down at the table.

Patel followed me and Munir into the back of the club, toward private dining rooms.

Once we were out of the sight of the bodyguards, I grabbed Patel from the back, choking off his wind, and clamped a handkerchief filled with chloroform up to his face. He was as limp as a wet dishrag within ten seconds.

We carried him between us out through the back door and dumped him into the backseat of the car, where Ronnie was sitting. Munir jumped inside with Patel as Dave pulled up in his car, and I jumped in. The two cars pulled out and headed toward a place where we would execute the second part of our plan.

Munir checked his watch. He had arranged for two plain-clothes cop friends from Scotland Yard to enter the place with the intent of questioning the two bodyguards and to warn them off the premises.

We drove for another thirty-five minutes, until we had reached a warehouse in Harrow. Dave got out and opened the door, then drove the car inside. Munir and Ronnie with Patel in the backseat followed. Once inside he carried Patel to the centre of a large concrete room, where there were three straight-backed chairs.

Two large electric lights beamed down from the high ceiling to light the large room.

I sat him in a chair, then filled a small bucket that was near a sink at the corner of the room with cold water. I then dashed the with water into Patel's face as he sputtered awake. He responded with two beady eyes that pinned me with hatred.

"Let me go, you fucking bastards," Patel cursed as he squirmed. The upper-class accent was gone. "If you've brought me here to kill me, you will not walk away free—my bodyguards saw you," he reminded us.

"Oh, you mean the two men who are already dead by now," Munir told him.

Patel tried to tough it out, but Munir's words took some of the starch out of his sail. It showed visibly in his nervous expression.

"And if we wanted to kill you, you would already be dead by now," I told him.

"You'd better let me go. I'm a powerful man. You don't want to make an enemy of me."

I interrupted him by slapping him in the mouth.

"We'll see about that," Munir put in.

"What we want you to do is make a phone call," I said.

"No," he said defiantly.

I moved my face closer to his and spoke almost in a whisper.

"Believe me mister, my asking you is a favou to you rather than to me. You see, I could always—"

Then suddenly, with the speed of a striking serpent, Patel spat full into my face. I calmly walked over to the sink and washed his spittle from my face with a handkerchief. Nobody made even a murmur. Only the sound of my footsteps walking disturbed the silence of the room. I walked back slowly toward Patel. Then I pushed him with such force that it sent him sprawling backward over one of the chairs onto the floor. I then stepped over to him and kicked him hard in the kidney. He doubled over in pain and started to groan.

He turned and looked up toward me as I was pulling the hunting knife from the sheath underneath my shirt.

His eyes became the size of saucers as I stuck the knife directly into his knee and twisted it with all my strength.

He screamed like a banshee and almost passed out. But I wouldn't let him. I doused him with water again. Then I sat him up in the chair.

"Oh, God. Oh, God," he kept saying as he quivered from the pain and the shock of my attack.

Just as he was catching his breath and settling down, I plunged my knife into his other knee.

"We can keep this up all night, Mr. Patel. I don't mind if you don't," I said softly.

"Would you care to make that phone call now?" Munir asked him.

"Yes, yes," Patel managed to say.

"OK, this is exactly what I want you to say."

As Munir was telling him what to do, I walked over to where Dave was standing.

"He don't look like such a tough man now, does he?" Dave said to me.

"They never do when you get up close," I replied.

CHAPTER 16

The Reverend almost shit himself when the phone rang. His nerves were jangled and teetering on the razor's edge. The sound of the telephone almost sent him running for cover. He had been all right until he'd found out that the man he had hired to kill Devil Barnett was almost killed himself. Two broken arms, the loss of an eye, and a fractured skull. He reached for the bottle of scotch and poured himself a triple shot.

He downed it without thinking and then poured another. The phone rang again. Shit. The Reverend tried to decide whether or not he should answer it.

Damn, fuck, shit . . . if only this nightmare would just go the hell away. Reluctantly he answered the phone. "Yeah, uh-huh," he said. "Who, when? Oh, my God."

Suddenly he was wet with perspiration. Sweat poured down the Reverend's forehead and stung his eyes.

The voice at the other end knew something was very wrong because it was a voice that had seen him through thick and thin. Through the countless scams that he had perpetuated. In fact, more often than not he had been a part of those scams.

"Pull yourself together, Trevor," Reverend Waldorf counseled sternly.

"But why in hell would he want me to call him?" Reverend Jennings said, slurring his speech.

"How the hell would I know? You're there, and I'm here. The man said he wants you to call him right now."

"But I don't even know the man—not in person. I've only heard of him," Reverend Jennings whined in protest.

"You sound like you've been drinking. Trevor, what the hell's going on over there?" the midget Reverend Waldorf demanded.

"I'm OK, James. Everything's OK. Believe me, just keep the home fires burning until I come back."

As soon as he had put the phone down, he reached for the bottle of scotch again. It was almost empty. He emptied it and dialed the London telephone number that Waldorf had given him. A man's voice answered. At least the man had an English accent. It made him relax a little.

"Reverend Jennings, this is Diop Patel. Getting to the point, we have mutual interests to protect," the other voice said.

"I don't quite understand," Jennings responded.

"We can't afford to play games, Mr. Jennings. Both of our businesses are going to be affected badly if we don't find a way to stop this war between my people and The Burning Bush. I suggest that since you and I are at the top of the food chain in this situation, we sit down as businessmen and work out an amiable solution to our problems. Hold on just a minute."

Then another voice came on the phone.

"Mr. Jennings, I'm a Detective Inspector with Scotland Yard. We know about your warehouse full of bootleg CDs in Milton Keynes, and we also know about your café in Hackney. I asked Mr. Patel to contact you in the interest of striking a deal that we all can live with—otherwise you will be out of business by the morning. In addition to that, you will be facing some very severe charges, so I suggest that you listen to what Mr. Patel has to say."

Patel's voice came back on the phone. "I need to meet you as soon as possible. Otherwise, by tomorrow it could be too late and we both will be out of business. Meet me three hours from now. I think it would be better if you came alone."

Patel then gave the Reverend from God's Holy Tabernacle an address in Harrow.

"OK," Reverend Jennings said, not because he wanted to but because he didn't know what else to say.

Thirty minutes later, Bush arrived at the Reverend's apartment. It was almost 11:45 p.m. but the man was still wearing sunglasses.

When Bush received the call, he knew it must have been an emergency by the tone in the man's voice. The man sounded shaken.

"So what do you think?" The Reverend asked The Burning Bush.

"I think you got to meet with him, yeah."

"Alone?"

"I didn't say that," Bush replied. Already his scheming mind was hatching a plan. "Yeah, I'll dead him up, no problem?"

The Reverend's mind almost exploded at the suggestion. Dead him up? Bush was talking about killing Patel.

"I would have my men ready outside the meeting place. As soon as Patel showed, we would cut him down yeah," Bush said, with enthusiasm building in his voice and anticipation growing in his eyes.

"That might be a good thing, and on the other hand, it may not be," said the Reverend as he watched Bush's face closely.

"How do you mean? Bush asked.

"Um, the way I figure it, what you say has possibilities. Yes, it could work for us, but at the same time it could work against us," the Reverend said, making sure to sound as cool as he could.

"What do you suggest, then?" Bush responded.

"Not sure yet," the Reverend said, looking at his expensive watch. "We've got almost an hour to come up with a solution."

Bush nodded, shifted his weight on the expensive sofa, and lit a spliff. When the Reverend went into the bathroom to take a quick shower and change his clothes, Bush made a phone call.

CHAPTER 17

"Think the geezer will come?" The walkie-talkie crackled with Ronnie's voice.

"Who knows," Dave responded.

Dave looked at me, then down at his wrist watch.

"What we got, thirty minutes more or less?" he said, turning in my direction.

"More or less," I confirmed flatly.

Patel sat in one of the chairs, bent over with his head in his hands and his bloody legs extended in front of him. Munir had been kind enough to rip open his trouser legs and stop the bleeding in his knees by holding a cold compress to them that he had made from a thick wad of McDonald's restaurant napkins that Ronnie had collected in the glove compartment of his car. Now the Asian drug dealer sat doubled over in pain, making little moaning sounds from time to time. Sitting here like this reminded me of so many days and nights in my past when I had been involved in operations for the Agency. Back in the days before I grew my new conscience. Back when I believed in what I did as much as I believed in life itself. Back then, the American government was the end all and be all for me. In many ways, I guess I was a zealot even though I never thought of myself as anything but patriotic. But that was then and this was now. Now I did whatever I did because I wanted to help people. Not because I felt it was my duty and that I should be grateful for being lucky enough to have been born in the greatest country on the face of the earth, ever in the history of mankind. No question, I had been brainwashed with a very strong patriotic detergent. But again, that was then and this was now. I didn't feel bitter, I just saw things differently. Now I realied that America had its problems like any other country, with racism running at the head of the pack. I guess it had just taken me a long time to wake up. Still, I was an American and that was that. I wasn't ashamed of it or proud of it.

It was just another fact, like the fact that birds fly and grass grows. What I had become proud of, however, was that I had found a different person inside of me from what I'd ever known existed. Someone who actually cared enough about other people to go out on a limb to help. Frankly, it had come as a surprise.

My telephone rang.

I answered and was surprised to hear Christine's voice.

"Listen, Shelby Green just called me and said that he needed to talk to you right away. He said it was urgent," she said.

"Give him my number and tell him to call," I told her.

"Everything OK?"

"Yeah, right as rain, why?" I said.

"You must be getting lonely for Sonia," she said, and laughed.

I felt a slight tinge of emotional guilt but managed a laugh, anyway.

"That poor woman is still calling every day. What do you want me to tell her?" Christine continued.

"Tell her I'll be back within the week."

"You the boss, boss." Christine laughed again, then hung up.

I had been successful in pushing Sonia out of my mind for the past few days, with all that had been going on—not to mention the presence of Rhea. But now she was back. I could almost smell her scent as I sat in the darkness and lookied out into the emptiness of the large warehouse. Warm thoughts of her provided a comfort zone away from the cold and dampness that I could feel right through my clothes down to my skin.

A few minutes later, my phone rang again.

"What the fuck you doing in England, Tuffy?" Shelby Green said.

"I got a line on somebody connected with the killing of those rappers and I followed it here. I'm pretty sure either he killed those rappers or paid someone else to do it."

"I don't know, but I just got a call from Al Mack about a half hour ago. He called to tell me to tell you that they just found another one."

"Another one," I echoed.

"Yep, dead as a muthafucking doorknob in a hotel room down in the Village. The one called Goldfinger. Just thought you needed to know."

"Fuck," was my automatic emotional reaction. Shelby's words had just seared my brain.

"When you coming back?" Shelby asked.

"Soon, thanks for calling," I said.

"See you soon," he said, and hung up.

What if I had the wrong man? What if I'd screwed it up altogether? Maybe in my quest to run down the Reverend I had overlooked something crucial. I looked at my watch again. Ten minutes to go. The rain had started to beat down harder. I could hear it hitting steadily against the windows of the building.

A few minutes later, Ronnie's voice came through the walkie-talkie: "A black cab just pulled into the estate."

"OK," Dave responded.

"It's bit hard to see what he looks like with the rain, but somebody just got out and they're looking around. Now they just walked into the light of the building next door. I can see now he's a black bloke," Ronnie said.

"Must be him," Dave remarked.

"He's headed this way," Ronnie's voice crackled again.

"See anyone else with him?" I asked Ronnie.

"No."

"OK, show him in, we're ready. Keep your eyes open—I doubt if he came alone. The second you think there might be someone else out there, let us know," I cautioned.

"OK, mate," Ronnie said.

Within ten seconds there was a sound at the door. I eased myself back into the shadows and waited.

I recognized the Reverend as he stepped across the threshold of the door.

"Please come in. I'm Detective Inspector Shah," Munir greeted him.

The Reverend spotted Patel sitting in a chair under the light. Patel looked up at the Reverend. His weak eyes were red and bulging, and his face was covered in sweat. The Asian drug dealer grimaced in agony.

"Just a minor accident," Munir said, and smiled. "Sit down, Reverend."

As I stepped from the shadows and he recognized me, the panic rose in Jennings's face like a kite caught in a high wind.

"Don't worry, Rev," I said, walking toward him slowly. "I didn't come here to kill you, even though I should have."

The Reverend's feet shuffled quickly against the concrete floor as he attempted to find his footing for a quick dash away from me. But before he could make a move, Munir had his hand firmly on his shoulder, pushing him down into a nearby chair.

I kept coming slowly across the room, moving in the Reverend's direction.

"I didn't do anything. I swear before the living God Jehovah," the Reverend pleaded.

As I looked down at him looking back at me, my natural impulse was to slap him in his lying mouth, but I didn't.

"I suggest that you cooperate with us as much as possible," Munir stated, looking over to the corner where Dave stood watching silently and still like a man-size stone statue waiting to be called to life with a magic word. "My friend wants to know about the dead men who were killed from your rap group in New York."

"Who killed them?" was all I said.

"I swear I don't know," the Reverend pleaded.

Suddenly my natural impulses gave way and I backhanded him in the mouth with a slap so hard, it sent him sprawling backward and onto the floor.

"I'm giving you one chance to tell me the truth, which is one more than you gave me," I said, pulling the knife from its sheath under my shirt once again, "then I'm going to make a gelding out of you."

"And if you don't believe he knows how to use that knife properly, just ask Mr. Patel here what happened to his knees," Munir stated.

The Reverend became spastic and began to shiver and shake

his head as if he had some chronic nervous disorder. Huge tears started to roll down his smooth brown face as he started to sob uncontrollably.

"I don't know, I swear, one night they were at my church talking about some new music deal we were trying to do and the next day they were dead, that's all I know . . .That's all I know . . . please."

I wasn't sure whether to believe him or not.

"What were you talking about?" I said, looking down on him as he squirmed on the cold concrete floor.

"Man O War had started a production company and he wanted to start producing records for other acts. Then there was this issue about giving Fuzzy Martin some records that he could sell that he wasn't getting a percentage on and . . . That's what we were talking about," Trevor Jennings managed.

I leaned close enough to be within easy striking distance.

"They were under contract to me, so I wanted to cut myself in on the new deal, that's all. It was me who made it all possible," he squealed.

"So then what?" I asked. My voice was as flat and dangerous as the knife I held in my hand.

"Man O War didn't like it, but . . . but it wasn't anything we fell out about. We just came to the arrangement that he could produce the other acts without any legal interference from me if I could get exclusive rights to something he and Shogun had pro- duced in secret over in a studio in New Jersey," the Reverend said.

"Did you talk about any cash changing hands as compensation for Fuzzy Martin?"

"No," he said, shaking his head. By this time, snot had mixed with the tears and was running down into his mouth as he slobbered and spoke. He wiped his mouth with his sleeve and continued.

"What about the new project?" I inquired.

"It was an underground rap thing."

"Why did you bootleg it, then?" I wanted to know.

"The Global Corporation takes over thirty percent from me

just on distribution. On a hot record like this, a few hundred thousand copies is over a million dollars out of my pocket into theirs," he explained.

"Did they know about your bootlegging—is that why you agreed to pay them the money?" I asked.

"What money? I never agreed to pay them anything. And they didn't know about the bootlegging. Just Max Hammill, J. T., and myself. Man O War thought I was going to put the deal through Global like I had their other product. I was hoping to sell a million or so behind Global's back in Europe and blame it on somebody at the mastering plant and then take the project to Global afterward. Everybody would have still made a ton of money."

"Who was it who agreed to pay Man O War twenty-five grand in cash and for what?"

"I don't know. I swear, I don't," the Reverend cried, with tears still streaming down his face. He held up his arm and pointed to his watch and then he tried to say something, but as he looked up at me standing over him with a hunting knife glinting in my hand, fear overpowered him and he broke down crying again.

The Reverend was a scared man, and believe me I had seen enough to know. He wasn't the kind of man who had enough steel in him to lie under threat of mutilation—most men weren't. His stock in trade was bullshit. But I hadn't given him any room to operate. My bet was that the good Reverend knew in his heart of hearts that if he didn't come clean, he'd go home carrying his balls in a sack.

The Burning Bush sat in the 4 X 4 Jeep and looked at his watch. The deadline had passed over three minutes ago. The agreed plan between himself and the man was that the Reverend would go inside and come back out within ten minutes to let him know that everything was OK. If that didn't happen, Bush was supposed to make an emergency call to the police station to say a policeman was being attacked. That way, the police sirens would warn off any danger to the Reverend, who would tell Patel that he had called the police and that if he didn't walk away healthy, then his people who were waiting outside would make sure Patel never left the warehouse alive. This had been the Reverend's plan. Mostly because the Reverend wanted to avoid bloodshed at all costs. He was scared to face the fire. To The Burning Bush, this was a huge flaw in the man's character. Bush thought it a shame that the Reverend had not, like himself, acquired a taste for violence or bloodshed. The Bush pitied that aspect of The Reverend's character in the same way that an able-bodied athletic person might pity a cripple whom he sees struggling to walk.

Bush looked at his watch for the second time in three seconds. He knew what he wanted to do. In fact, he knew the right thing to do, even though the man had talked down his original idea.

As the seconds ticked by, Bush became more impatient. He looked over at Marga, who sat next to him motionlessly looking into the night with the Uzi resting on his lap.

During the next five seconds, Bush felt like he had waited no less than a million millenniums. His body tingled with anticipation, and his mind ached for satisfaction. Satisfaction. The satisfaction of knowing that he was on top, finally, after all of the years of hustling. First, items stolen from parked cars, then, the cars themselves; then small quantities of ganja, then small quantities of pills, and finally the mother of them all: the fast-moving moneymaker cocaine. His hatred for being at the bottom and having had to struggle all those years passed through his body and almost made him shudder. The thought that his long, hard struggle might be sabotaged by Patel magnified his hatred even more. So much that it made his head throb. Just when he felt he would bust at the seams, his mouth moved. "Let's go," he said.

"Seen," Marga answered.

As the first sounds of gunfire pierced the air, I ducked. I knew the sound instinctively as that of an Uzi. It was a short burst. That was quickly followed by a resounding crash at the front door.

The force of the Jeep crashing through the front of the warehouse door broke the building wide open.

Then more gunfire. Two men emerged from the Jeep, and I saw that one held an Uzi, which he fired again. This time, toward the middle of the room, where Patel sat.

"Hit the lights," I yelled, grabbing the Reverend by his collar and scrambling for cover into the shadows.

Dave made a move toward the far wall, and the room went black.

There was another short burst from the Uzi, and a man's scream answered by the sound of three shots from what sounded like a Glock.

Then the sound of a moan and a man's weak voiceg asping words in the Urdu language. I recognized it as Patel's voice.

Then there was silence except for the pounding of the rain against the crashed car at the front door. I knew I could depend on Dave and Munir to stay silent against the unknown. I clamped my hand over the Reverend's mouth and pressed my knife into his throat. I whispered into his ear. "Are they your men?"

The Reverend nodded his head up and down affirmatively.

Suddenly, three soft sounds penetrated through the darkness, shots muffled by a silencer.

"Ohhhhhh," the sound came low and coarse. "Me shot, me shot. Ohhhhh." The voice had a Jamaican accent.

There was the sound of metal clattering to the cement floor and more moaning.

I smiled to myself, glad to know that Munir had come prepared with night vision.

"Marga, Marga . . ." another Jamaican accent called out.

I moved forward, staying low, pushing the Reverend in front of me as a human shield. I reached the moaning and found a tall black man on the floor writhing in pain. Shot twice in the chest.

Another shot rang out. It was from the Glock again.

I picked up the Uzi that the dying man had dropped and I held it to the Reverend's head. I replaced my knife in its sheath and listened for movement. The other gunman didn't know it yet, but I did. He was already a dead man. Two more muffled shots sounded.

"Aiyee," another Jamaican voice cried.

Another hit. Good old Munir.

* * *

The Burning Bush cringed and fell backward as the bullet entered his right thigh. His mind prayed for light in the darkness of the room. The only thing he could think of was getting out alive. The pain burned from his thigh all the way up into his brain. As he fought to keep a clear head, he listened for sounds. A fleeting thought passed through his burning brain that he should have brought more men. But woulda . . . coulda . . . shoulda . . . was as worthless as a wet dream. The past was the past. His mind groped ahead of him, reaching in the darkness . . . stretching to grasp the slightest glimmer of light. He heard movement over by where he had heard Marga moan. He smelled fear: his own. His confused mind darted around the room like a ricocheting bullet.

He was nearly there.

He reached where the Jeep had crashed through the door. There was another gun inside, on the seat. Like a wounded cat and with one great leap, Bush bounded forward into the front seat of the Jeep. As he tried to back the Jeep out of the warehouse, there was a sharp sound and a crack in the windscreen. His wrist erupted with pain and a splash of blood flew up into his face, partially obscuring his vision. His mind told him he was shot again, but his will to escape pushed him forward. He managed to start the vehicle. As he released the clutch, the Jeep lurched backward, away from the door. His wrist was dead and incapable of manipulating the turn of the wheel, and by the time he thought of switching hands . . .

It was too late. The vehicle lurched again and stalled. The rain poured through the shattered windscreen, blocking his vision. His good hand grabbed for the gun. As he fell out of the car, the sound of an Uzi went off behind him. He turned, pointed the gun, and shot once.

A voice cried out.

"Don't . . . Don't shoot, please. Bush . . ."

The voice belonged to the Reverend. He didn't heed the voice and he didn't hesitate. He just shot again and kept moving toward the darkness of the industrial estate, toward escape, toward freedom and life, but the pain in his thigh, brain, and wrist had all conspired against him and coalesced into a great fireball of agony.

He couldn't move fast enough.

Another barrage of shots rang out. Bush turned again and fired. One time. Blam! Bush turned and moved forward again, then turned and fired. Five more or was it four more times. Blam! Blam! Blam! Blam . . .

I was already past the doorway and moving forward, the Reverend in front of me. The heavy rain made it almost impossible to see. The Reverend was screaming as the man ahead was firing back toward the door. When the Reverend gasped then wheezed and slumped forward, I knew he had been killed.

I let him go and continued moving toward the man, with the Uzi in my hand poised for a clean shot.

As I aimed, I felt the pain. It seared my upper body between my shoulder and my chest. I responded with a blast of my own. The man ahead in the distance stumbled and fell forward.

Between the fourth and the fifth rounds, Bush's escape was interrupted by the sound of the Uzi firing again. He heard the blast and felt it a nanosecond later. It tore through his chest and into his heart. He fell to the ground and cringed with pain and anger. But both his pain and anger quickly subsided as the fire that had always been inside him extinguished itself and the flame that had come to be known as The Burning Bush simply flickered and died away into the nothingness of a cold, rainy, moonless night somewhere on a dismal industrial estate in London.

I stumbled back and fell against the Jeep, suddenly drained of all my strength. My mind raced backward, then forward, then backward again to the first blast of the Uzi. I had heard it when I was inside the warehouse and I thought about Ronnie.

My mind turned my head in panic. I looked through the pouring rain, but I couldn't see. I remembered the blast, but I couldn't see. I felt it. Something had happened but I couldn't see. My breath became short, as acid pain filled my veins where blood once flowed. I shuddered and felt a loss of consciousness closing in on me. I struggled but couldn't hold on. The darkness reached out and swallowed me whole, just like in the story my grandmother used to tell to me, about Jonah and the whale.

CHAPTER 18

I was walking though a big green valley full of multicolored orange, pink, brown, and silver animals. Not any kind that I was sure I had ever seen before. There were dogs that resembled giraffes, and cats that looked like kangaroos. I didn't feel afraid, just intrigued by it all. I was amazed as the animals went about their business, for people walked among them freely like it was a big safari park that they regularly went to for a Sunday picnic.

Suddenly I looked up and I was standing next to my grandmother. She reached down and took my hand. I was nine years old.

"What you want to eat, baby?" she asked.

"Pancakes," was my answer.

"For dinner?"

I nodded my head.

"Don't nod your head. Say 'yes' and 'no,' that's what the good Lord gave you a mouth for," she said, the way she had at least a thousand times before.

"You want syrup or honey—the honey is fresh."

"Honey."

"OK." Grandmother laughed.

The sound from her voice filled up the valley and even made the animals take notice.

Suddenly I was full from eating my pancakes. I could still taste the honey on my lips, and then we started walking again. The places we walked through were green, peaceful, and beautiful. My grandmother sang a hymn as we walked, and I hummed some jazz tune. I think it was Herbie Hancock's "Maiden Voyage." We kept walking until we had reached the edge of the world. How I know it was, I'm not sure, I just know it was. We stood there on the edge of a great cliff looking over the precipice into a world of multicolored lights beyond.

My grandmother was still holding my hand. She was dressed

in her Sunday churchgoing clothes. A yellow summertime dress, with a big green and yellow hat with flowers and a large brim that kept her face hidden from the sun.

"Jesus will be along soon enough," she said, looking out into what was a crimson sky filled with blue, red, green, purple, and yellow lights.

From somewhere in the distance, a baby laughed. Then, from somewhere else came the smell of popcorn. I had always loved the smell of fresh popcorn. I smiled up at Grandmother, and she smiled back.

"Don't you worry, you all right now, heaven is right over there," she said, pointing to the multicolored lights "And, Junior, here you are standing on the very edge."

"Hey babydoll," a man's heavy, warm voice came from behind us. My grandmother turned toward the voice, and the eyes lit up inside her smooth brown face like two glowing candles. The voice belonged to a man I had seen only in an old photograph that she'd kept in her bedroom. His name was Marcus, whom I was named after. I had never met him before but I knew who he was. He was my grandfather.

"I checked and everything is ready," he told her, smiling.

He then looked down at me and smiled.

I could feel the warmth from his spirit as it went through me and gave me a warm, glowing sensation. I realized that's what made grandmother smile, too. I somehow identified the feeling without really needing to give it a name. But I knew that it was the feeling of love. Not the kind of love that I had ever known before, but the kind of love that went beyond human understanding. The kind of love that I heard my grandmother speak about when she told me about how God so loved the world that he gave his only son.

I wondered if my grandmother was going to give me to someone. I sensed that she was, but I wasn't scared. With her, I knew I had no need to be. I didn't know how I knew, I just did.

"Your daddy told me you were going to be up here, so I had to see for myself," Grandfather Marcus said, laughing down at me.

He seemed as big as a giant. Then he bent down and hugged me. His face was as smooth as glass and his eyes were deep and mellow and he smelled like the forest, strong and beautiful.

"Think he ready, babydoll?" Grandfather winked at my grandmother.

"Just gotta wait and see," she told him, still smiling.

Then from somewhere there was the sound of big band music. I recognized the tune. It was Duke Ellington's "Satin Doll."

I started to move back and forth to the beat of the music, and then both grandfather and grandmother started to dance. Their bodies were older, but they were moving together like two young kids, the way they had when they had met back in the thirties in Harlem's Savoy ballroom.

The song finished, and they fell into each other's arms laughing.

"I didn't know you could dance like that," I said to my grandmother, amazed.

Grandmother just laughed and nodded her head.

My grandfather took my hand and stood on the other side of me. There I was, standing on the edge of heaven between two people who loved me, listening to Duke Ellington.

"Where's Momma and Daddy?" I asked.

They both looked at each other and smiled again.

"Don't worry, they're waiting for you, too. They're all at the party," Grandfather Marcus said, and smiled.

"Remember old Mr. Epps?" Grandmother said.

"The one who got wounded in the big war," I responded.

"Yes, well, he told me that you was always his favorite boy, every since you found him sick that morning in the park. You were only eight years old but you had sense enough to call 911. The ambulance came and saved his life, remember?" Grandmother reminded me.

"I remember." I nodded.

"He's been one of your angels all these years. Him and me both," Grandfather Marcus said, and then smiled in that special way that sent that love thing through me again.

"Is there going to be a party?" I asked.

Both Grandmother and Grandfather starting laughing like they shared something between them that I didn't know about.

"Sure, puddin', they give a party to everybody that gets to heaven, otherwise how you gonna remember all your old friends and meet your new ones," Grandfather Marcus informed me. "You like Duke Ellington, don't you?"

"Yeah," I said, nodding my head.

"Well he said he wanted to be here, too. He's the one playing the piano." Grandfather smiled.

"His wife helped me with the cooking," Grandmother told me.

Suddenly I could smell all of the food from the party. All of my favorite dishes were there. Fried corn and perch with hush puppies the way Grandmother made them, and chili with big red beans and lots of hamburger the way Momma made it, and I caught the scent of fresh buttermilk biscuits and gravy, the way Saddy always made it. I smelled everything.

"Don't be afraid, Puddin', you with us now," Grandfather said.

And I wasn't afraid, either.

I kept watching the lights from heaven as they grew closer and closer. Blue and green, red, purple, and yellow. As they came closer, I felt warm inside. It was like that love thing my grandfather did, with his smile was warming up the whole world. Then suddenly it was the dead of winter and I was stark naked, The cold of a thousand arctic nights shot through my body, and I opened my eyes. The first thing I remember seeing were the white lights mixed in with the garbled voices and snatches of conversation: "Blood . . . Doctor . . . Charts . . . Intensive Care . . . Insurance . . ." The words came and went like a million mad flying phantoms. They mixed in with the sickening smell of clinical antiseptic medicines until finally I realized I was lying in a hospital bed. From the way my body felt, I knew the answer: I had suffered a sickle-cell crisis.

For the next two days I slept a lot.

It was a narcotic-induced sleep caused by the dihydrocodeine pills they used to treat my disease. They offered me the dihydrocodeine pills, but I refused because I didn't want to walk out of the hospital as a junkie dependent on my daily fix of medication until I could detox.

On the third day, I started to feel constant pain and the weak, sickly feeling. I fought it the best I could until I had to take the pills. On the fourth day, I began to feel better.

I opened my eyes and saw Munir standing by the bed.

"Glad to see you're back with us. The doctors thought they were going to lose you for a while."

I sat up as he plumped the pillow behind my back. For the first time, I felt the pain in my chest. "How bad was I hit?" I asked.

"Not terribly bad, but they had to operate to get the bullet out. You'll live." He smiled.

Suddenly, the thought of life grabbed something inside me and twisted my emotions as I recalled the first barrage of gunfire I had heard while inside the warehouse with the Reverend.

"How is Ronnie . . .?"

As the smile on Munir's face faded, I knew the answer.

"They apparently got him before they crashed the door," Munir said. "He was cremated yesterday."

"You talk to Dave?" I asked.

"Yeah."

"How is he holding up?"

"You know Dave. He'll be up later to see you."

The news of Ronnie's death seemed to sap all my energy. I fell into a deep sleep and didn't wake again until late in the afternoon, when I looked up to see Dave standing in the doorway.

He smiled and walked over to the bed. We embraced warmly.

"Sorry about Ronnie," I said, tears welling up inside of me.

"It couldn't be helped," Dave said.

We both sat in silent mourning for a while staring blankly into space. "Ronnie was a big man, he knew the risks. We all did," Dave said, trying to soften the blow.

"I'm sorry," I said again, not knowing what else to say.

"Ronnie is gone, but you still got me," Dave said.

I looked up as the tears began to roll down my face.

CHAPTER 19

I had only been away for ten days, but it seemed like a month. Shelby picked me up from JFK.

I gave him a rundown of what had taken place in London.

"So you think that the Reverend was innocent—well, of the killings, anyway?" he asked.

"I don't know what to think. He might not have committed the murders himself, but I'd bet a dollar to a doughnut that something about those murders had to do with the Reverend. There was too much smoke for there not to be any fire," I explained.

"Then just keep doin' what you think is best. I got your back. And Livingston is still willing to back you financially if you want to continue," Shelby said.

"Want to continue?" I echoed his words.

"Yeah. Why, you want to drop it?" Shelby asked, quickly averting his eyes from the road to me on the passenger's side for a split second.

"Oh yeah, I'd like to drop it, but my problem is I don't know how to quit," I admitted.

It was 1:39 p.m. when Shelby dropped me off at the Be-Bop. Duke was in the middle of the lunchtime rush and Benny Sweet-meat was hustling behind the sandwich bar slapping ham on rye, pork on wheat, and roast beef on white. Cowboy and Gerald stood at the end of the bar watching TV while Po Boy and Goose sat on their usual seats sipping beers and talking about who knows what.

Everyone greeted me as I entered, then I went into my office. I put on a Charlie Mingus CD and started to look through some bills that Christine had stacked neatly on my desk.

After writing a few checks, I lay down on the couch. I could still feel the effects of the sickle-cell crisis and suddenly I was tired again. I dropped off to sleep and began to dream.

Malik appeared with a wheelbarrow from a long way off in a

field and beckoned to me. As I walked toward him I saw that the wheelbarrow was full of faces. Faces I recognized. Dead faces. I saw the faces of the two dead rappers, the dead Jamaican, Patel's face, Ronnie's face and the face of the Reverend. The faces were dead but alive at the same time. They didn't laugh or speak—they were just alive and looking around the field as if to see who else was missing.

"Body count for the cause," Malik said.

"But why so many, why so damn many?" I kept asking him.

"We're at war, brotha. There are always casualties in war. Body count for the cause," Malik said.

A feeling of sadness passed over me. "But why so many," I asked again and again.

"Body count for the cause . . . Body count for the cause," was all that Malik kept saying.

I suddenly woke to the sound of the telephone ringing.

"Hello," I answered groggily.

"Hey man, how are you?" The voice belonged to Al Mack.

"I'm good, just back from England," I said.

"England," he exclaimed. "What the hell you lose over there?" He laughed.

I wanted to say one of my best friends, but I didn't.

"Just doing some work on this case. The Reverend ran over there and I followed him," I said.

"What did you come up with? Al asked.

"A lot of dead bodies, including the Reverend's," I said.

"No shit? Al remarked.

"No shit," I answered.

"As soon as we got the report on the latest killing, I got in touch with Shelby." He got the news before the newspapers did," Mack informed me.

"Yeah, I know. Thanks. Let's get together later and I'll fill you in," I said.

"Bet," Mack said.

"Later," I said, and hung up, grateful that I still had Mack on this side of heaven as a friend.

I called Grooveline and Monica answered.

"Hello, stranger," she greeted me.

"How are things going, what's the latest on the group, have you heard anything," I said, getting right to the point.

"Oh, things are in a total fucking mess. Goldfinger got killed, and J. T. disappeared, you know?" Monica said.

"No, I've been out of town, but I heard about Goldfinger. I'm sorry. Anybody say where J. T. went to?" I asked.

"No, some rumors had him going to Miami, but nobody's seen or heard from him."

"Was any money missing?"

"Uh-uh, not a cent. Just disappeared. But guess what?"

"You tell me."

"Guess whose managing the group now, yours truly," she said flatly.

"You lie. I guess congratulations are in order," I said.

"Don't congratulate me yet. First, I got to stop people from getting killed," Monica said.

"You becoming manager, how did that happen?" I inquired.

"Max is hardly ever around anymore, so the group started getting stressed with J. T. disappearing and all the murders and anything. So Max called from somewhere two days ago and made me manager. He gave me a contract and everything. I'm just answering the phones now 'cause the receptionist is on her break."

"Good for you. Tell me, what are you doing to protect the group?" I said.

"I've already got security for everybody twenty-four/seven, 'cause you know I can't have no more of that shit. Don't worry, I'm on the J-O-B. If I need some advice, can I call you?" she asked.

"You know you can," I told her.

"Thanks," she responded.

"Tell me, can you arrange for me to talk to the guys? I'm still trying to run down who is behind these killings," I said.

"Yeah, but you'll have to question them in front of my security. Nobody, I mean nobody, gets to see them alone, not even somebody as cute as you," she said with a smile in her voice.

"OK, I'm with that," I said.

"They're shooting a music video in SoHo tonight and tomorrow, so I'll call my head of security and hook you up. His name is Robert Trenchmore. But you know you owe me big-time right?"

"I know," I said, and smiled.

"Just as long as you know," Monica said.

I smiled again as I took down the number she gave me.

Then there was a knock at the door.

"Come in."

Christine entered with a big smile. She hugged me tightly. "Man, I'm glad to see you back in one piece." She grinned.

Her appearance had changed. She had changed the style and cut of her hair, lost a little weight, and was wearing a slightly classier cut of clothes.

"Thanks."

"What's the matter?" she asked as I looked her over.

"I don't know what it is, but something's going on. You must have a new boyfriend or something," I said, smiling.

"Duke said the same thing. All y'all men think the same. How come it's got to be a man involved? How come I can't look good just for me?" she said belligerently.

"I didn't say you couldn't," I said.

"Well, it ain't no man involved behind my new image. It's a self-expression thing. It's a feel-good-about-me thing, know what I'm saying. I'm the manager here now, so I want to look good and feel good about me. You can understand that," Christine explained.

"I can dig it." I grinned happily.

"OK then yeah, welcome back, boss—and oh yeah, speaking of a feel-good thing, when Sonia calls today like she has been calling every day since you've been gone, do you want me to tell her you're back?" she wanted to know.

"Yeah—in fact I'll give her a call later today," I told her.

"OK, Mr. Cool Breeze," Christine said, laughing as she left.

I felt good that my decision to make her manager had paid off. The job had given her more confidence in herself, and she was doing an excellent job. Profits were up, and problems were down. Couldn't ask for better than that.

I worked in the bar until 4:00, when I met Al Mack.

"Hey, Baby Boy, you looking OK. Tell me, did they fill you full of fish and chips over there?" Mack joked.

"I got by. The food in England ain't exactly a tourist attraction, if you know what I mean," I told him.

He laughed and ordered a coffee. I joined him in a booth at the back and reviewed all of the facts of the entire case, including what had taken place in the UK. This was good for Mack as well for me because it helped me to crystallize my thinking process.

The part I didn't include, however, was my visit to meet Malik.

At 5:07, we left the Be-Bop and headed for SoHo.

The place we eventually ended up was on 2nd Avenue, though. From the outside, the place looked like a plain old ordinary apartment building. That's one of the amazing things about New York City. A million things are going on all the time in places that you would never suspect.

Robert Trenchmore met us at the entrance to the building and conducted a personal search of us both. He told Al Mack that he would need to relieve him of his service revolver while we conducted the interview. He wrote out a receipt for the weapon, and Mack complied.

The soundstage and set for the music video was on the third floor. It was a fantasy set comprised of two scenes. One was of heaven and the other was of hell. They were working on the hell part when we arrived.

Wicked and Rebel were dressed in red from head to toe. Red sneakers, red pants, and matching sweatshirts. And they were rapping and dancing around five young women who looked like they had just jumped off the cover of a glamor magazine. The women were dressed in red Danskins, and on their heads they wore fake ruby studded tiaras with horns sticking out. As they danced around the pair, the women swayed back and forth and poked at the rappers with long, red pitchforks that had been painted a bright metallic red.

There were two movie cameras, and what looked like a thousand lights along with twenty different people running here and there, doing this and that. The director was a big black man in his early thirties with the kind of huge, unruly Afro I hadn't seen since the early seventies. Everybody called him Jamie. And by the way the crew was acting toward him, I figured that he must have been famous, too.

Jamie moved around the set calmly with two assistants in tow who carried clipboards as he told various members of the crew to make adjustments to the scene.

We watched them do the same scene three times from different angles, then Jamie said, "Cut."

Then one of his clipboard assistants made an announcement to everyone that it was time to break for lunch.

"Lunch," I said, looking at my watch. It was 9:05 p.m.

"No wonder these show business people are so weird. They're on a different time schedule than everybody else," Mack said, and laughed.

Robert Trenchmore came up and arranged for us to see Wicked, Rebel, Waxie Maxie, and Filthy Rich, the four remaining members of the group in a room that people kept referring to as the green room even though the color of the room was painted a bright blue.

"Gold was kilt in his own apartment can you believe that shit," Rebel said, using his strongest hip-hop intonations with just the slightest twinge of his native London accent left.

"Nobody safe from the killer eh, they said they could protect us but nobody safe," Wicked chimed in.

"According to our investigation with the doorman, nobody visited him after he got in that night. Which only leads to one other conclusion. The killer was either already there waiting, or he made his way into the apartment without coming in through the front door," Al Mack said.

"Can you guys think of anything or anyone who might have wanted to hurt Goldfinger?" I asked.

Nobody knew anything.

"I found out that Man O War and Shogun had worked on an underground project that the Reverend Jennings was bootlegging. Do any of you know about that?" I asked.

"Bootleg, What bootleg? Naw War wouldn't do nuthin' like that. He was down with us all the way. Doing an underground thing would have been like dissin' us. Naw, cuz, you must have got that wrong," Rebel said.

I looked around the room. The expressions on the faces told me that the general opinion was in lockstep with Rebel's. Trying to convince them otherwise was going to be an uphill battle, so I decided to let the dead dog lie.

"They way I see it, Gold getting killed is J. T.'s fault. He was supposed to be looking after us when he disappeared," Waxie Maxie said.

"Disappeared. Like I said before, the man dead," Wicked put in.

"Dead, why do you say that?" Mack argued.

"Listen, the man here every day and night, then suddenly him not here no more. No one hear from him, no one seen him. Even his mother don't see him. She call us checking him. Man don't disappear like that for nothing unless him dead," Wicked said authoritatively.

"And Max, he ain't hardly ever around no more," Rebel inserted.

"Every time he said we are going to hook, something comes up. We making him all this paper and he still be dissin' us," Rebel said.

"Monica is better than both of them, if you ask me—at least she's sorting things out," Filthy Rich said.

"Word," Rebel confirmed.

My mobile phone rang.

"Yeah," I answered.

"It's me, Chandra."

"Oh yeah, Chandra, how are you?"

"I've been trying to get you but you haven't been answering.

What's up—you stopped paying your bill and they cut you off or what?" There was a smirk in her voice.

"No, I've been out of town," I remarked.

"Have you been working on my little problem?" Chandra wanted to know.

My mind reached out to remember what the hell she was talking about, but I couldn't. "Refresh my memory," I said.

"I knew you was just talking shit, I knew it," she said, her voice rising in pitch.

"What are you talking about, Chandra?" I said irritably.

"About my car—you was supposed to be checking and seeing if you could swing it so that I could get some money from Gun's death so I could buy the car he promised me," she complained.

"Oh, yeah. No, I didn't forget you, but if I remember, you was supposed to deliver on some other things, too. And from where I sit, you haven't come through."

"That's why I've been calling you, yo," Chandra said.

"So what you got?" I said.

"What I got, what you got?" she said.

"Come on, Chandra, I don't need this right now. I'm in the middle of something. If you got something, just tell me."

"You ain't going to try and dog me out, are you?"

"No, Chandra," I said.

"OK, I'm still trusting you, 'cause I don't really know you or nothing."

"I know, OK."

"OK, promise me you going to follow up and not forget about me," she insisted.

"I promise."

"OK," she said. "I found Peaches and she ain't who you think she is, either."

CHAPTER 20

Ten minutes later, Mack and I were headed back uptown toward Harlem. He dropped me off at the Be-Bop. He had to get home— it was almost 11:30 p.m. As I walked the block to the bar, I passed two cross-dressers having a conversation. They were definitely men, but both had tits, tight pants, and long wigs. On a dark night with a few drinks, they could have fooled some men for sure.

"Sorry, but I've got to love you and leave you, girlfriend, 'cause my sugar daddy's coming over at twelve. Talk to you tomorrow," said the taller one to the other as he/she broke off and began to walk in the opposite direction.

"Call me tomorrow, girl, OK?" the shorter one called, waving demurely as he/she swished on down the street.

There were only a few regulars drinking when I arrived. Christine was working the bar. I had a drink and was reading the paper when Chandra walked through the door with a woman I recognized. At first I was thrown because the two people walking in didn't fit together, but I recovered quickly as they sat down.

"Say hello to Peaches," Chandra said, smiling.

"Hi," I said, smiling at the woman I had only known as Thelma, the secretary at God's Holy Tabernacle.

"Hi yourself." Thelma smiled back.

"I didn't know they called you Peaches," I said to her.

"Peaches is like my street name. But I use Thelma when I'm working at the church. It sounds better."

"A drink?" I offered.

Chandra ordered a double Jack Daniel's, and Thelma had a whiskey sour on the rocks.

"So it was you and Chandra who were having a party with Shogun on the day that he died," I queried.

"Uh-huh," Thelma admitted, cautiously sipping her drink.

"Did you see or hear anything out of the ordinary that might have been a tip-off that something may have been wrong?" I asked.

"No, like Chandra said, we were just freaking off in the Jacuzzi and he got this phone call and got dressed and left," Thelma told me.

"Did you see a lot of him?" I asked.

Chandra rolled her eyes at Peaches.

"Well, I saw him, but I wasn't like his woman or nothin, we was just friends."

"On the day that you were last together, who arrived first?"

"I did," said Peaches, "at least I think I did."

"Yeah, you were there when I came by," Chandra said.

"What time was that?" I asked.

"I guess around lunchtime," Peaches told me.

"You took off work that day, then?"

"Yeah," said Thelma

I questioned them both as to what took place, what was said, and what wasn't said, but got no new information.

They both agreed on the same story, which means they had rehearsed. The only thing Peaches added was that before Chandra came, Shogun was on a long telephone conversation with the producer Bobby P. But she couldn't tell me what they had talked about other than to say it had to do with some music.

"So I came through, right? So you're going to hook me up, right?" Chandra said.

"Yeah, I'll talk to someone tomorrow," I promised.

When the pair left, it was almost 12:15 a.m.

I got a coffee, selected a Jonathan Butler tune on the jukebox, and sat down in one of the back booths alone. I wanted to just let the impressions of what I had just experienced with the two women wash over me.

As I played back our meeting in my mind, I remembered that when I'd asked if there had been anything that might have been a tip-off on the day Shogun died, Thelma had hesitated slightly. The hesitation wasn't even slight enough that most people would have noticed, but I did. My interrogation training and experience had taught me to read when people were lying. And Thelma was lying. But the reason behind the lie was the missing part.

As I continued to contemplate what Thelma was trying to hide and why, I suddenly I felt another presence and I glanced up to find myself looking at Sonia.

"So you're back from your big mystery adventure?" she said.

"Yeah."

"May I?" she asked, indicating if she could sit down.

"Sure," I said, sipping my coffee.

She looked at me without speaking for a long time. "I've been trying to call you," she said.

"I know, Christine told me," I said.

"I was worried."

"Thanks. Would you like something to drink?"

"No thanks."

She looked beautiful, maybe even more beautiful than I had remembered.

"I guess you think I'm a real pain in the ass," Sonia said.

"Sometimes yes, but usually not at all," I said, and smiled.

She smiled a little, too.

"I'm really sorry about the way I acted before you left. Is that why you never contacted me when you were away?" she asked.

"No, that's not really the only reason—well, actually that may be part of the reason but definitely not the whole reason. I didn't contact you primarily because I was so caught up in this case I was working on and . . ."

"And that was the primary reason?" Sonia said.

"Yeah."

"And the secondary reason?"

I remained silent.

"Another woman?" she asked.

I looked at her for a few moments without speaking, but my expression answered her question.

"Is that important? You ended the relationship, remember? I

didn't get a chance to have a say in it one way or another," I reminded her.

"I guess I deserved that," she conceded.

I sighed heavily, not knowing exactly what to say next. I wasn't feeling trapped or even uncomfortable, I was just laying my cards on the table.

"I'm very sorry for the way I acted. But I felt that you put your damn detective business ahead of me and it was making me jealous. I know it might sound silly, but that's the truth," Sonia said.

"I don't think it's silly. I can understand it. Listen, Sonia, everything I've ever told you I've meant. I said I cared for you enough to have a future with you and I meant it, but that didn't mean I was willing to change who I am in order to do that. Like I wouldn't expect you to change who you are to accommodate me. I don't think that would be fair," I explained.

"I'll tell you honestly. I really struggle with you taking all your time and even risking your safety for people you don't even know—People who don't even care about you—when you don't have to. Especially when you have someone like me who is willing to devote her life to you and provide a comfortable and safe home for you," she explained.

"I appreciate that, I really do, but why I have to do this goes much deeper than choosing between a safe life and a life free of any possible danger. For fifteen years of my life I gave my loyalty unquestioningly to a system that didn't give a fuck about me. They didn't appreciate the fact that every hour of every day, my life was in danger for them. And when the chips were down, they abandoned me—or worse still, conspired to sabotage me. That hurt me a lot. That and my father getting killed together made me decide to start rethinking my life and return to Harlem. Now, the things I do for people I do because I realize that without my involvement, certain things that need finding out wouldn't happen if I didn't get involved. And most importantly, the people that I help now, whether I know them or not, care. What I do makes a difference in their lives, and as a result it makes a difference in my life," I confessed.

"So what you do makes you feel needed?" she stated.

I let her words sink in deeply.

"Yeah, I guess you could say that. When all is said and done, I'm no different from anyone else. Everyone needs to be needed in some way, I guess," I admitted.

"What about me needing you? What about the girls—they need you in their lives. You make a huge difference in our lives, you know," she said.

"I appreciate that, and I enjoy that and I need that, too, but there's that other part of me that just needs what it needs. I can't explain it, but it just exists and I have to deal with it. I guess it's like an artist who has to paint every day whether or not he has enough to eat or pay the rent.

"It's such a part of who I am that I'm not sure I know how to give it up—or even if I could, I'm not sure that I would want to," I told her honestly.

She started to cry softly.

"What can I say except that I love you and I know it, and that I'm sorry for the way I acted. I know I have this jealously thing and it doesn't make any sense," Sonia remarked.

"That's OK, I understand. If I were in your shoes maybe I would act the same way. But try to think of it this way: You've got two beautiful children. God forbid if someone attacked them or hurt them in any way. But let's just say something like that happened and the suspect wasn't picked up immediately. Who could you turn to here in Harlem to find out the truth or get justice? You know yourself that the police will only respond if it's a white person or a big-shot involved. If you're an ordinary black or Latino person, you're dead in the water. You know that's true as well as I do.

"If something like that should ever happen to you or even to any one you know, then you can come to me," I told her.

"I'll see you later," she said, and stood up to leave.

I stood up to kiss her good-bye but before I could she turned with tears flowing down her pretty face and walked away.

I felt bad but I didn't know what else to do or say. I knew deep in my heart who I was. More importantly, the person I had become, no matter the price, was of my own choosing.

With Sonia's voice still ringing in my head, I started to help Christine with the cleanup detail. When I finished it was 2:00 a.m.

I drove home and crawled into bed. There was no more pain in my body, but there was pain nevertheless.

The picture that I still had in my mind of Sonia walking away with tears in her eyes held me tightly and created a stinging agony in the deepest part of me.

I changed the dressing on my shoulder, which had started to heal nicely, then I made myself a sandwich from a piece of ham I brought home from the bar.

I ate and sat in the dark and listened to the sounds of the night, which included a cat in heat screaming below my window, a street-sweeping machine on the prowl, a garbage truck making a commercial pickup, and a Delfonics tune floating through the atmosphere from somewhere in the distance.

As I soaked in the nocturnal essence, my thoughts ping-ponged from London to Peaches, to Sonia to Ronnie, to the Dance-hall Dogz, to Max Hammill to Bobby P to God's Holy Tabernacle.

Nothing had materialized that wasn't there before. No new clues, no new information—yet there was a difference. As if something was on the verge of happening. It was an old feeling. A feeling that I knew inside out. A feeling that had never let me down before. The same feeling that had kept me alive during all my years as an agent. A sixth sense, maybe. A guardian angel, perhaps. I knew that the answer was out there, and I knew that I would eventually find it. Where I once faced a brick wall, I now faced the same wall with one less brick. I was getting there, wherever there was. I could feel it. Closer and closer, step by step, inch by inch.

CHAPTER 21

It was just after 2:30 p.m. and the lunchtime crowd at the Be-Bop Tavern was just thinning out.

Po Boy and Goose were at their normal places, drinking as they normally did.

"Well can you or can't you?" Sheila wanted to know. She was getting hotter and hotter under the collar minute by minute.

"Baby, just relax, these things take time," Po Boy placated.

"My sister's birthday is next week and we're ready to go. You said you was gonna get us Benny Sweetmeat for our party. And I ain't hardly going to pay no five hundred dollars for nobody else, either," she said with steam almost coming from her ears.

"I'll handle it, don't worry, he just out of practice, you know he need to get his confidence back. You know how these artists is." Po Boy grinned and winked his good eye at the attractive woman some fifteen years his junior.

I was washing glasses and pretended I was minding my own business, but I wasn't. I was listening to every syllable.

"Well, either you let me know by tonight or I'm going to get someone else," Sheila told him.

"Don't worry, baby, I'm on the case," Po Boy assured her.

"You said you was working on it and I believed you," Sheila pouted with a tinge of flirtatiousness in her voice.

Po Boy, who was an old hand at picking up on such gestures, rose to the bait like a hungry catfish grabbing a fat grub worm.

"Don't you worry, I'm working on it. And I'll get him, too," Po Boy stated confidently as she turned and walked out.

Po Boy strained his neck back toward the kitchen, where Benny Sweetmeat had gone about five minutes before, carrying a big load of pans.

"Look like that five hundred dollars is gone," Goose stated matter-of-factly.

Po Boy looked at his friend of over forty years with dismay. "What you mean gone." Po Boy grimaced.

"Just what I said, gone. And if I'm lyin', I'm flyin'," Goose reiterated, and drank another sip of his beer. "You heard her. If you can't get Benny, then she ain't interested, and you got 'bout much chance of getting him as you do getting the president of the United States. Fact is, the president might be easier," he said, laughing at his own joke.

"Man, you ain't got no faith, that's your problem." Po Boy scowled toward his old friend.

"I don't have to have no faith 'cause I know Benny Sweetmeat," Goose reminded him.

Just at that moment, Benny came through the doorway. "Who calling my name?" He smiled at his two old friends.

"Benny, we was just talking about faith," Po Boy told him.

"Faith?" Benny's face screwed itself into a question mark.

"Yeah, faith. I was just telling Goose that if a man have faith, he can do just about anything," Po Boy remarked.

"You ain't going to get me to argue there. I've seen that myself," Benny said as he continued his cleanup.

Goose just sipped his beer and watched to see how Po Boy was going to work his way around to where he was headed.

"Let's say a man was once a legend and he lost faith in himself, so he thought he couldn't live up to the legend no more. My question is, how do you get that man to get his faith back?" Po Boy queried.

"That's a tough one, Po. I guess it all depends on the person. Different people take different things to get them going," Benny advised.

"Yeah," Po Boy said.

From the corner of my eye I could see him watching Benny for a reaction like a hunting dog watching for the slightest rustle of a bird in the bush.

"Well, let's say, uh . . . let's just say that there was this fellow who was the best at something and his friends still knew he could do it but he had lost faith in hisself, well for one reason or another. And let's say this fellow had the opportunity to become great again but he didn't know quite how to get his greatness back. My question to you is, what would you suggest his friends do to help him out?" Po Boy asked, pinning Benny Sweetmeat with his good eye.

Benny didn't even look up from his cleaning when he spoke. "I know what you working up to Po, and it ain't gon' work," Benny said flatly.

"Them days is gone forever. Besides' what would I look like trying to tell my little granddaughter to keep her dresstail down if she was to hear that her own granddaddy was helping hisself to three or four womens at one time."

"Told yuh," Goose quipped' a big grin breaking out on his face.

Po Boy didn't respond immediately. He just screwed up his face like someone had slipped him a nasty dose of castor oil.

Goose looked at his friend and broke out laughing. He laughed so hard that it caused him to start coughing.

Benny Sweetmeat just looked at Po Boy and shook his head as if to say poor misguided old fool.

"I told you that five hundred dollars is gone," Goose guffawed. "Gone like a turkey running through the corn." Then he started to laugh again.

After Goose had finished laughing, Benny turned to Po Boy and stopped working for a moment.

"You know your problem, Po, you don't understand nothing about principles."

"Principles, what that got to do with anything. I was just trying to help you out, man. Trying to help a friend get back into his stride, and what do I get, a kick in the teeth," Po Boy said irritably.

"I know you doing what you think is right, but you got to look at it like this: Them good times that we had back thirty years ago, them days gone forever. And you can't go back to relive the past. That's all," Benny explained. "The principles I live by now don't allow me to do that kind of thing no more. That's all," Benny explained.

Po Boy was quiet as he soaked up Benny's words.

He motioned for two more beers, and I served him without comment.

When Benny Sweetmeat took another stack of dishes back into the kitchen, Bertha Darby—one of the senior citizen regulars—walked over to where Po Boy and Goose were sitting. "You dirty old men should be ashamed of yourselves, talking under women's clothes," she said, directing her comment at Po Boy.

"What you talking about, woman?" Po Boy scowled at her grimy appearance.

"I heard it all. I been sitting right over there, and I heard it all. You trying to get next to that nice woman with your dirty scheming. You two old men should be ashamed. Who you think would want y'all, anyway. Don't nobody want no old man. Like Moms Mabley said, "ain't nothin' an old man can do for a woman except to show her the way to a young man." Bertha laughed raucously.

"Woman you done lost it. Just cause there's snow on the roof don't mean there ain't no fire in the stove," Po Boy said defending the sexuality virility of the over-seventy set.

"Hah, whatever little fire you might have had going at one time done gone out a long, long time ago, hah. Give me another Bud, honey," she said, and laughed in my direction.

"And you just remember one thing: A woman can look up longer than a man can look down," Bertha added.

"Amen to that," Duke said, and grinned.

Bertha took her drink from me and, with a smile on her weather-worn face, returned to her regular corner table and dug back into a pile of reading material.

Cowboy stood at the end of the bar having a drink and going through his pockets over and over again.

"What you lose, Cowboy?" Duke asked him.

"I don't know but I know I had it this morning but I ain't got it no more," was all he said in a strained voice as he continued to search his many pockets. He had pockets in his poncho, his army fatigue jacket, and his army pants. He didn't say a word to anybody, he just continued to go through pocket by pocket meticulously.

Duke shrugged at me and I shrugged back. We knew enough not to bother Cowboy when he was in one of these moods. The other customers knew it, too. Nobody wanted Cowboy up in their face screaming obscenities with spit flying everywhere like he was prone to do when he got upset. Today he was obviously agitated about something.

"What a woman got between her legs done caused more trouble in this world than the atom bomb." The comment came out of the blue and it came from Goose Jones.

Goose Jones!

Even Po Boy, who was still sulking and looking out into space over his aborted business opportunity, had to look over at his old friend with astonishment. Cowboy even stopped searching his pockets for a moment and gave Goose a strange gaze. Benny, who was by this time having a cup of coffee and a sandwich, looked up and stopped chewing.

"What was that, Goose?" Po Boy said, looking abruptly at his friend, not understanding why Goose needed to announce his comment to the entire room.

Goose was usually the side man of the duo who only commented on conversations initiated either by Po Boy or other people. As far as anybody knew, this grand declaration was a first.

"Sex," Goose stated unequivocally. "I been thinking, look at all the trouble in the world back through time and even now. Almost every murder or theft got something or other to do with sex. Think about it. If a man kills another man or steals from another man, it's either about a woman or money, and if it's for money, ninety-nine times out of a hundred that man is going to use that money so he can go and buy hisself a nice house and a fancy car so it will attract sex to him like bees to honey," Goose announced.

Po Boy wasn't sure how to respond. In fact, nobody did. Not

even Bertha Darby, who was looking at Goose Jones from her corner table as if he had just landed in a spaceship.

"Give him a drink, a double of Old Crow," Po Boy said.

Goose took the drink and downed it in one gulp without comment. The whiskey seemed to do the trick because Goose went quietly back to reading the sport pages without another word about the deeper ramifications of sex as it contributed to the general mayhem in society.

The phone rang.

"Be-Bop Tavern," Duke answered.

"Yeah, just a minute," Duke said, looking at me and passing me the receiver.

"Is this Mr. Barnett?" the voice on the other end said in a distinct English accent.

"Yes."

"This is Neville," the English accent said. "Neville Turner." Remember me, Trevor Jennings's cousin. I've got something you might be interested in."

"Go on."

"The solicitor contacted us . . . I mean contacted Aunty Stella after Trevor's death and told us that there was a will that left most of what Trevor had to a daughter in New York. The only trouble was, nobody knew of a daughter. To be honest, I think it's a dodgy will," Neville said.

"Why should you give a shit who gets his money?" I responded.

"Well, you see, most of that should have come to us, I mean his family here in the UK. He was an only child and there is only his mother left, you see."

"So you think that if you can prove the will is a fake, then you can claim the money for his mother as the next of kin, then can use the money to make the old lady comfortable for the rest of her life?" I said.

"Yeah, exactly," Neville said.

"Tell me, Neville, how much was in Trevor's estate?"

"The solicitor said a half million pounds. If you come up with something, I'll make sure you get a nice fee out of it, don't worry mate," Neville told me.

I really didn't give a shit about helping Neville get his hands on the dead Reverend's money, but I figured maybe I could find something else about the murders of the rappers by approaching this thing from a different angle. I really had nothing to lose. "What's the name of the daughter as mentioned in the will?"I asked.

"Thelma Rodgers."

"Thelma Rodgers?" I echoed.

"Yeah, but I've never heard of her before now, is what I'm saying," Neville said.

"Yeah, I'll check it out and get back to you," I told him.

"Thanks, mate," Neville said.

"By the way, how did you get my number here?"

"I rang Trevor's church, and his assistant, a bloke named Wendell, gave it to me.

"Like I said, I'll check it out and get back to you."

I hung up the phone and started to think.

So what else was new.

Thelma probably was the dead Reverend's daughter, but so what. Preachers have always had a history of having children out of wedlock.

I suddenly remembered Chandra's car and I put in a call to Oliver Reems. "Hi Oliver, Devil Barnett."

"Hello, how are you? Believe it not I just put you on my list to call," he said.

"Why is that?" I inquired.

"I was going to call you to thank you for a new client you brought to me."

"Me?"

"Yeah, Doug Anderson is a friend of yours, right?" Reems inquired.

"Oh yeah, Doug, I gave him your number."

"And he became my client. He's a very knowledgeable guy.

He's already taught me a few things," Reems acknowledged.

"He knows the music business inside out," I confirmed.

"Did you find anything out about the deaths?" Reems asked me.

"No not yet, but . . . I called you to find out if there is any way I could get a few thousand dollars from Shogun's estate to give a girlfriend of his who he promised to buy a car for before he died. She's been helping me pull together some information and I told her I'd look into it," I said.

"Mmmm, I might be able to do something. Let me call you back in a few days. I'm working on something, and if it works out, I'll give you the money myself."

"You'll give me the money?" I was stunned with curiosity.

"Yeah, I'm working on a very big deal that could easily make it worth my while," Reems said.

"I guess you know what you're doing," I said, and left it at that.

"Don't nobody do nothin' for him but me," Cowboy said, fixing a miniature coat and hat on the raggedy teddy bear in the baby carriage known to the world as his son Gerald.

Cowboy looked around the bar anxiously, then walked over to the window and looked out.

Both Duke and I noticed that he was acting stranger than usual, but we thought better of mentioning it.

Our agreed policy with him was that as long as Cowboy didn't upset the other customers, we would leave him alone. But with psychos, it's always hard to judge. Generally, Cowboy wasn't usually dangerous, but there was always that outside chance that his mind would snap, sending him all the way straight to Berserksville.

"His mammy don't care nothin' about him, all he got is me and the damn hospital telling me he got to have insurance if he get sick. But they don't want to help me get it. Damn people make me sick. But we gonna make it, ain't we boy, me and you. We gonna make it," Cowboy muttered to his motionless son.

Cowboy unbuckled the strap on the baby carriage and took Gerald out. He sat on one of the barstools and placed the teddy bear in his lap. He took off the miniature coat and hat, then took a small brush from his pocket and gently brushed the soiled fur of the bear.

When he had finished grooming his son, Cowboy replaced the teddy bear's coat and hat and sat Gerald back inside the baby carriage. He then finished his drink and walked out into the street.

"And I remember when he used to walk around in Harlem with a pocket of full money. Damn shame, ain't it, used to be a top man with figures, now he's walking around here nutsy as a betsy bug 'cause a piece of snatch drove him crazy. You know what happened, don't you? Po Boy said in Duke's direction.

"I heard," Duke said.

"I knew the girl. Pretty girl from Louisiana, long pretty hair, skin like butter, she was near 'bout twenty-two or twenty-three. He met her when he was in the army, stationed down there. He married her and brought her back up here. She got her head turned while he was out making a living.

"She used to hang out in the bar of the old Satin Hotel. Some young slick dude turned her head, and Cowboy heard about it. He went and found her one day in one of them rooms with some young dude. She was selling pussy out of both panty legs. Cowboy caught hold of the dude and cut him so bad, he almost died. Messed him up for life, damn near cut his manhood off. You know Big Quinn. Naw, you probably don't remember him. He dead now, but he used to be the bouncer at the Satin.

"Only thing saved Cowboy from a murder charge was Big Quinn knocking him over the head with a two-by-four.

"That's musta what knocked his brains loose," Goose observed seriously.

"Like I said befo', that thing between a woman's legs done done more damage to the world than the atom bomb," Goose said.

I was behind the bar, checking the stock for the evening shift, when a man with skin as black as I had ever seen walked in.

He walked over to Duke, who was wiping down the bar and emptying ashtrays. "You Mr. Barnett?" the man asked Duke.

"No, that's him there," Duke said nodding in my direction.

The man's face looked familiar, but I couldn't immediately place it.

"Mr. Barnett, Mr. Devil Barnett? the man said. He was in his early to mid thirties, and his face bore a childlike expression. His light brown eyes sparkled as he showed off a row of perfectly even white teeth. "Irma told me to come find you," he said.

"Irma?"

"Irma Madison, my wife," he said, nodding his head.

OK, I knew immediately who I was talking to now. It was Irma Madison's husband, Stokley, the one she couldn't help referring to as a damn fool. She told me to bring this to you," he said with the distinct twang of a Southern accent as he passed me a cream-colored business-size envelope with embossed gold lettering in the corner that read GOD'S HOLY TABERNACLE.

"S-S- She told me to wait till you read it and come back with an answer," Stokley stuttered.

I opened the enveloped. The letter was neatly typed.

Dear Mr. Barnett,

You told me to contact you if I came up with something else.
I am writing you cause I been trying to telephone you but you ain't been at work.

I found out something I am sure you want to see right away.
This something I got is hotter than July.
Bring money.

Irma

"OK, tell her I can meet later tonight."

"Ah, s-s-s-she can't, not t-t-tonight," Stokley said.

"She said right away," I said.

"That maybe, but she just can't, not t-t-onight," Stokley stuttered, then smiled sheepishly.

"Did she tell you to say she couldn't meet tonight?" I asked him as if he were a child bearing a note from his mother.

"No, but I just know sh-she c-can't. She can tomorrow, but not t-tonight, please," Stokley said.

"When, then?"

"Tomorrow anytime, night is better, but not t-tonight," he repeated.

"OK, tell her tomorrow night then," I said.

"What time?"

"Eight."

"OK, eight?" he said. "Thanks, Mr. Barnett, I 'preciate it." He smiled, then winked at me.

"Want a drink, Stokley?" I asked.

His sparkling eyes swept the bar, then he looked back at me like a kid in a candy store. "On the house, you mean?" he asked.

"Yeah."

"OK, I'll have a-a g-g-gin and t-t-t-onic, thanks very m-much." He smiled and licked his lips.

I watched him as he stood at the bar sipping his drink and smiling and winking and blinking idiotically at every pretty woman who walked into the bar.

"Man, if I saw these many fine womens all the time, I d-d-d-don't believe I would have t-t-time to s-s-s-sleep," he said, and grinned.

He eventually finished his drink and left. It was hard not to like Stokley. He had a certain simple, childlike, endearing quality about him. But then again, so do a lot of murderers.

CHAPTER 22

Roachie looked down at his hands wrapped around the woman's throat. He had great faith in these hands because he knew exactly what they were capable of. As the dedicated servants of the cause, each time he had called on these hands to kill, they had answered their master without question. They had never failed him. Now, all he had to do was squeeze and his problems would be over. At least he could sleep at night. At least maybe the torture and the pain of love would dissolve and his heart and soul could rest in peace. The words from a song that his mother used to play on their old, beat-up record player." "LOVE LOVE LOVE CAN MAKE YOU DO FOOLISH THINGS," ran through his mind.

His killing hands gently caressed the soft brown neck of the woman and slid downward over her smooth, warm shoulders onto her small but well-formed breasts.

"I'm expecting somebody," she said.

"I don't give a damn. I'm here now. Who is it, another one of them goddamn rappers?" Roachie spat angrily.

"No, it's business," she said, defensively.

"Why don't you treat me like you do them—just 'cause they're famous, you treat them with respect and you dis me," Roachie said, fully conscious of his hands and their schizophrenic personality.

"That ain't true."

"They keep you high—that's why you hang out with them, ain't it," he insisted.

"No," she said.

"You lyin."

"No, they're my friends."

"Only friend a crackhead got is the pipe." As soon as the words were out of his mouth, he wished that he could take them back.

"Don't call me no crackhead," Thelma spat.

"I didn't call you no crackhead," Roachie backpedaled." "I just said—"

"You did, that's fucked up. You know I'm clean. I stopped that shit," Thelma said with hurt in her voice.

"I'm sorry," Roachie said.

"Get up off me, that was fucked up," Thelma said as the tears began to stream down her face.

"I'm sorry I told you," Roachie said. "You know I love you. I'm sorry."

"That was a fucked-up thing to say," she repeated.

"I wasn't talking about you."

"You just jealous of them, that's all," Thelma said.

"They can see you whenever they want. I can't, so that's how I feel. Yeah, I'm jealous, so what," Roachie conceded.

"So stop talking about me being a crackhead. You think I wanted to be strung out. There's a lot of shit that happened you don't understand," Thelma flared.

"Well, tell me and then I'll understand."

"It ain't that easy. If I told you you, would really think I was fucked up."

"Listen Thelma, I love you. And I always will. Can't nothin' you do or say change that," he assured her.

"Listen, I ain't ready yet. When I am we'll sit down and talk about it, OK? There's a lot of shit you don't even know about me. Shit, some of it I'm ashamed of telling anybody, even you, and you're the closest one to me," she said.

Suddenly there was a sound of something outside the door. Instinctively Roachie jumped up from the bed where he was lying buck naked and grabbed his pistol.

"It's those fuckin' rappers, ain't it. That's who you expecting?" Roachie whispered with murder in his voice.

"No, put that gun down, please." She sounded scared.

Stepping cautiously, Roachie approached the sound. As he threw open the door, he heard a door slam. Following the sound, he ran to the exit door and looked down the stairs but was too late. Whoever had been listening at Thelma's door had disappeared.

"Who the hell was that, then?" Roachie said to Thelma, who was by this time sitting up naked on the bed.

"How the hell would I know? My appointment is business. The doorman would have called up," she said defensively.

"You would think that in a nice apartment building like this, they would have better fucking security," he said.

Thelma stood up and walked across the room. She was still naked. Roachie was standing by the door. Her slender dancer's body caught the dull glow of moonlight that pierced the window of the high-rise apartment. To Roachie, Thelma Rodgers was the most beautiful thing God had ever made. And in his heart and mind he believed that she had been especially made just for him. When she hugged him, he remembered all of the tender times that they had shared before Max Hammill and J. T. Brown had strung her out on crack. He would never forgive them for that. How could he, for all of the hurt and pain it had brought into both their lives. He felt better knowing that he would soon settle that score completely. J. T. Brown was already dead and buried in a grave deep in the woods of Connecticut. His ever faithful killing hands had seen to that. He would never string anyone out again.

But Max Hammill was still alive.

One down and one to go.

"What would you say if I told you that I was coming into some money?" Thelma asked.

"Money, what kind of money?" Roachie looked puzzled.

Enough money that would let you set up your own business and move away from Harlem," she said.

"Where the hell you going to get that kind of money from?"

"The church."

"The church? What the hell would the church be doing giving away that kind of money. Oh, you mean one of those church programs?"

"In a way, yeah. What would you do if it happened?" she asked.

"You mean if I was offered would I take it and move away?"

"Yeah."

"Only if you would go with me," he said. "I still want to marry you, you know that. We could put the past behind us," he said, pulling her close to him.

"I've told you before, Roachie, what we had is in the past. I still love you, but I ain't no good for you. I ain't no good for nobody, not even myself. Besides, I'm a whore. Who likes being with a whore? I don't know why I even do it, maybe 'cause I'm good at it," she said, pushing him away.

"Naw naw, baby, don't say that, you ain't no whore," Roachie said, shaking his head.

"It's true, men like what I give them, I don't know why, but they do. I'm fucked up and I know it. And you a good man and you deserve something much better than me. I really love you, Roachie, that's why I'm saying this. Maybe one day I'll change, I don't know, but now I'm just the way I am. Besides I still like to get high," Thelma admitted.

"Baby, you just need some help, that's all. We can go to a psychiatrist together. I love you that much," Roachie pleaded, with tears welling up in his eyes.

Thelma turned toward the window and looked out into the moonlit night.

Roachie hugged her tightly and let himself feel their special kind of love.

Mixed in with the beauty of the moment was an anger that started to rise inside him. He had killed J. T. as much for her and him as he had for the cause and he knew that without hesitation he would kill for her again and again. Anything to keep her safe.

The sprint down the two flights of stairs from the ninth floor to the seventh and down the hall into the laundry room and then through the back corridor of the building down through the basement and out of the back entrance had Reverend Waldorf out of breath when he reached the street. He had narrowly escaped being caught listening at the door of Thelma's apartment by her ex-boyfriend, a big, muscular man with a bad temper. He was upset not only by the fact that Roachie was in the apartment making love to Thelma but by what he heard her saying while she was doing it. She kept saying that she loved him. And what's worse, she sounded as if she really meant it.

Even though the midget was more than twice her age, in his heart, Reverend Waldorf wanted Thelma's love to be reserved only for him. When the midget had first started sleeping with Thelma, he knew that she had only consented to his wishes in return for the drugs he gave her. But that was more than two years ago, when she was really hooked *on crack. In the time between then and now, things had changed and the relationship had grown into something else. For him anyway.*

She was clean now, but she still liked to get high from alcohol and weed, which is why he carried a bottle of Dom Pérignon and two big Jamaican style spliffs in the deep pocket of his thick winter coat.

The bitter cold of the winter night wind bit through his clothes and into his skin. How he wished that he could go inside of the building, where Thelma's warm, open arms and legs would be waiting for him.

But that was an impossibility. He didn't dare go back to her apartment while her ex-boyfriend was still there. Roachie had a reputation all over Harlem as a mean bastard who carried a gun, and everyone who knew him knew that he was crazy about Thelma.

That's why he had stood at the door and listened. His thick ring of keys slipping from his pocket to the floor had caused the noise that had sent him running through the building in fear for his life. Now all he could do was wait in the bus shelter and keep an eye on the apartment building entrance until he saw Roachie leave. In the meantime, he was freezing his balls off.

My instincts told me two things, number one, that Irma was a long, long way from being stupid. She may have been a lot of things, but stupid wasn't one of them. And number two, after meeting Stokley, she was probably right: Stokley was a damned fool. That's why I chose to ignore Stokley's request and go straight over to Irma's house. Whatever she wanted to tell me was important enough for her to send Stokley to find me.

Irma was cooking when I arrived.

"Where's Stokley?" she asked as I entered her kitchen.

"I don't know," I said, and shrugged my shoulders.

"Damn fool," she mumbled.

"So what have you got?"

"You bring the money?"

I reached down in my pocket and showed her a hundred-dollar bill.

"Is that all?"

"I haven't seen what you have for me yet."

"We have to go over to the church," Irma informed me.

"The church?"

"Uh-huh, that's where it's at," she said.

Five minutes later we were headed toward God's Holy Tabernacle.

"This is gonna blow your mind," she said with a twinkle in her eye.

We reached the church, and Irma used her keys to open the door to the back entrance.

"It's all right, the regular janitor had to go away for a few days and Stokley's supposed to be filling in for this week." We climbed two flights of stairs and walked down a corridor until we came to a door with a nameplate that read REV. JAMES WALDORF. Irma opened the door and showed me a flashlight, which she removed from her purse.

"We had better use this just in case someone is snooping around outside—I wouldn't want them to see no light in here," Irma explained.

She shone the beam of the flashlight toward a small desk in the corner of the room.

"He so little he can't even use a regular desk like real folks," Irma said, chuckling.

From the elaborate set of locks and the high quality wood carvings around the top edges, the desk obviously had been especially made for the midget Reverend. Irma removed a set of two keys from a small brown envelope and opened one of the desk drawers. Inside the drawer was a small red strongbox secured with a padlock.

She unlocked the box and removed a small green cloth bag. "Here it is," she said, her eyes gleaming with anticipation like an alley cat in heat.

I took a package from inside the bag and opened it slowly.

Inside the package were seven photographs. Three of the photographs were of Thelma naked and performing oral sex on Shogun, another two were of her having sex with both Goldfinger and Man O War together, and and the other two were of Thelma and Chandra performing the sixty-nine on each other.

"Tolja he was a nasty little somethin', didn't I," Irma pointed out.

I put the photographs inside my pocket and started to replace the strongbox back into the drawer of the desk.

"You ain't going to take them?" Irma blurted, almost panic stricken.

"Why not?"

"'Cause he'll know "

"So what, he won't know who took them," I defended.

"But he knows Stokley's got the keys, and sooner or later somebody will put two and two together. I can't take that chance, I could lose my job. That is, unless you got something else lined up for me that's better?" I could hear the hope in her voice.

"I'll leave them," I said, replacing photos.

"Tell me something, how did you find out about these photographs in the first place and how did you get the key to the Reverend's drawer?" I asked, shining the flashlight in her face.

"Let's get out of here first," she said.

She relocked the Reverend's drawer, and we went back out the way that we had come in.

"Where we headed?" I asked when we got back into the car.

"Home, I want to go home. That must be worth at least three hundred, ain't it?" she asked, looking at me with anticipation.

"We'll see," was all I said.

My mind was racing. The implications of something ugly had emerged. Why were naked pictures of the Reverend Jennings's secret daughter in the private possession of the midget assistant Reverend's desk?

When we got back to Irma's house, she fixed me a cup of coffee and sat down across the table from me.

"Now tell me what I asked before," I said.

"Before? Oh, you mean how did I find out about the pictures?"

"Yeah."

"Somebody left a letter and two keys."

"A letter and and keys?"

"Yeah, with instructions."

"Where is the letter now?"

Without another word she got up and left the room. Within three seconds she had returned with an envelope in her hand. The letter was typed on plain white paper. It read:

Irma,

Take these keys and look in the office and the strongbox in Rev. Waldorf's desk. Left hand side, middle drawer.

Then show this note to Mr. Barnett at Be-Bop Tavern. Show him what you've found. Keep your mouth shut and you will get paid. Rodger Lenard Rice 77 65 6.

Where were you when you got this letter?" I asked.

I was here at home," Irma said.

"You mean somebody brought it?"

"Must have, I went to get the mail in the morning like I usually do and there was this envelope with two keys and this letter. I just did what it told me to do."

"When did it come?"

"Today is, let's see, must have been Wednesday."

"Did Stokley see the letter?" I asked.

"Yeah. He was here when I opened it."

"Did you tell anyone else about the letter?"

"No, the letter said to keep my mouth shut, didn't it? I want to get paid, so I didn't tell nobody else. I wish I didn't have to tell Stokley but he was here when I opened it," she reiterated.

"Did he see the photographs?"

"Weak as Stokley is for stray womens, Lord no, I wasn't 'bout to show that damn fool no naked pictures of Thelma. I went to look in the drawer when Stokley was working down in the boiler room. It ain't good to let everybody know everything, not even your husband," she said.

"Can you think of anyone who might have sent this?"

"As God is in heaven, I can't Mr. Barnett. At first, to tell you the truth, I was scared to death when I saw those pictures 'cause I recognized the pictures of those two rappers right away—I mean, who wouldn't, they was famous. But then I remember our meeting and you seemed like a man who would take care of business—you know, nice but not the type to be nobody's fool—so I figured I had better do exactly what the letter said to do, cause whoever sent it must have known I could get up to Waldorf's office on the Q.T., know what I'm saying," Irma explained.

"I know what you're saying," I agreed.

"How much is that worth—got to be worth at least three don't you think?"

"OK, you got it. I'll get it to you tomorrow, stop by the bar, I'll have it for you in an envelope."

"Thank you. I knew you were all right, Mr. Barnett." She smiled, pushing her torpedo breasts flirtatiously in my direction.

"Tell me, what do you know about Thelma? I asked.

"Thelma . . . child, Thelma ain't nothing but a mess," she said and laughed.

"She 'bout as hot as a two-dollar pistol. Anything wearing pants with something hanging between their legs got a chance with Thelma. Before she come to the church, I heard she was a crackhead out on the street selling it," Irma said.

"When did she come into the church?"

"Maybe a year ago. She used to drive Reverend Jennings crazy messing around with lots of different men. But he never did nothing but just holler at her and she would holler back, then everything would cool down and a few weeks later she was right back at it again." Irma chortled.

"What do you think those photographs were doing in Reverend Waldorf's drawer?"

"You know, I've been trying to figure that one out, but I can't. Knowing that nasty little devil, it wouldn't surprise me if he ain't dipped his little wick in Thelma's honey pot. But why he had the pictures, I can't say. I thought maybe he was trying to blackmail Thelma, but that don't make sense 'cause Thelma don't give a damn who knows what she is. In fact, she proud of it," Irma said, chuckling.

"Did you know she was also known as Peaches?"

"Oh yeah, sometimes men used to call the church looking for Peaches until Reverend Jennings's put a stop to it."

"Have you heard any rumors around as to who her parents were?"

"Rumours? I've heard two or three stories. Some said she was the child of Reverend Jennings best friend, and another said she was his niece, but those in the know, know the deal, if you know what I'm saying," Irma informed me, winking her eye.

"I'm not sure, but I can guess."

"It ain't hard to figure out. Thelma is Reverend Jennings's daughter sure as I'm standing here—that's why he put up with so much stuff from her. He couldn't very well turn his own daughter out into the street now, could he?"

"Did Reverend Waldorf know it?" I asked.

"Of course, he did. Him and Reverend Jennings been friends since before Thelma was born, didn't you know that?"

"No, I didn't," I admitted.

"It's a shame about the Reverend, ain't it. Got shot over there in England trying to stop some Jamaicans from selling drugs in the church," she said.

"That's what you heard?"

"Yeah. Mother Hinton said so—she's gone to England to bury him, didn't you know?"

"No, I didn't."

"I don't know what the church is gonna do for a Reverend now, I'll tell you, the Reverend's shoes is going to be hard to fill," Irma mused.

I thanked Irma and went back to the bar. I looked at the number on the letter: 77656. It wasn't a telephone number. I called information, but nobody had a Rodger Lenard Rice listed. I called a Rodger L. Rice only to find out his middle name was Lindsey. And I called two numbers for R. L. Rice and another for R. Len Rice, but without any luck.

I helped Christine close up and went home to bed.

I couldn't go to sleep, though, because there were too many unanswered questions floating around the room just out of reach.

I finally got up from my bed and made a phone call.

"Stokley, I don't even want to hear it, you better get your butt home right this minute," Irma answered the phone with fire in her voice.

"This is Devil Barnett," I said calmly.

"Oh, I thought you was that damned fool husband of mine. Three in the morning and he still ain't home. He must think I'm a damned fool," Irma complained.

"Do you have Reverend Waldorf's Social Security number at home?" I asked.

There was silence for a few seconds. "As a matter of fact, I do," she said.

She gave it to me and I immediately called Onion, who I knew could hack his way into any computer file that had ever been designed.

The Reverend Waldorf was damned near frozen stiff by the time he saw Roachie leave the building where Thelma lived.

He started across the street in a stomping run, which was meant to warm his body and rejuvenate his circulation. He reached Thelma's floor and used his key to enter.

She was wearing only a T-shirt.

"I had to wait out there for over an hour," Waldorf complained, shivering.

"Don't you start with me, James, I ain't in the mood. I told you I was busy tonight and you made the decision that you had to come by, not me," Thelma said curtly.

"Well, don't get mad," Waldorf said. "I just had to see you."

"That was your call, not mine, what did you bring?" she said coldly.

"These." Waldorf beamed, holding out the two spliffs and the champagne as if they were offerings to a goddess.

"All right." Thelma's dull expression lit up slightly as she reached for the joints.

He flicked the lighter for her, and the fire flared in front of her face illuminating fine brown features. She leaned forward, ignited the marijuana and inhaled the weed deeply into her lungs. "Nice," she said after she had exhaled.

Waldorf grinned back happily.

Just then, the buzzer rang.

"Who the hell is that?" Waldorf asked. "It ain't Roachie, is it?"

His mind was fogged by fear. It grabbed his brain and extended downward to his feet.

"Maybe he left something," Waldorf said, his nervous voice raising an octave as Thelma pressed the talk-back buzzer.

"Who is it?" she said.

"It's me, Stoke," the voice seemed to say, but it was hard to tell.

"OK. Come on," Thelma said, brightening.

"Who?" Waldorf said.

"Just a friend of mine. Go into the bedroom and wait," she commanded.

"The bedroom?" Waldorf scowled.

"Yeah, we got some business to take care of. Just go inside and wait. I won't be but a little while."

Waldorf looked hesitant and started to complain.

"Do what I say or get the fuck out," Thelma said. To Waldorf, her features had turned into a death mask.

"OK, OK, just don't be too long, OK?"

She didn't answer him. She just sucked her teeth and watched as he did as he was told.

A few minutes later, there was a knock at the door.

Thelma opened the door, and a man's face lit up as he stepped across the threshold.

Stokley looked first at Thelma wearing only the T-shirt, then around the room and begin smiling as if he were a kid in a candy shop.

"Listen, I ain't got but a little while. I got some other business I'm doing tonight OK," Thelma said.

"OK," Stokley said as he pulled out three ten-dollar bills from his pocket and handed them over to her. She took the money and put it into a brown and blue ceramic jar on the wooden cocktail table and motioned with her head for him to get undressed.

Within three seconds Stokley was out of his clothes and standing buck naked.

He had always had an eye for Thelma, as he had for most women, but him and Thelma had a different kind of thing going on.

It had started when she was still on the street, before she got herself straightened out and started working at the church. They met one night when Stokley was cruising for crack whores. Imagine his surprise when he saw her all cleaned up and working for the church. He was nice about it, he never tried to embarrass her for the life she used to lead, and they kept in touch and became friends, well sort of . . . Every now and then he would show up with a few joints or a bottle of champagne. She liked champagne. In return, she left things open so that he could get his ashes hauled every now and then. Of course that was on the condition he provided her with a little loan, which he never expected to get back at the time of the hauling. He rationalized it by saying that if he took a regular woman out on a date, he would end up paying thirty or forty dollars, anyway, and there still wasn't no guarantee. At least with Thelma he knew where he stood. Plus, she made him laugh and feel good about things. Stokley knew he was a long way from being the smartest man around. Being raised on a farm in Alabama with almost no education, he never had much of a chance for advancement. In fact, he knew he wasn't smart at all, but in Thelma's company he didn't feel inadequate. In fact, in her company he felt real halfway smart, even. At least he didn't feel like a damned fool like when was with his wife. Sometimes after him and Thelma had gotten high and had sex, he felt as handsome and cool as one of those guys on a billboard advertisement, dressed in a tuxedo, driving a sports car, and drinking top-shelf scotch.

Thelma had a certain quality with men that only a few women shared, in his experience. She knew how to make a man feel special even when he was digging in his pocket. Once she even explained to him in detail why a woman shouldn't give away the most valuable thing she owned.

She said it would be the same as him going to work five days a week and giving the sweat off his brow and not expecting to get a paycheck on Friday. To him, it made perfect sense.

He just loved the way Thelma laid her loving on him.

As he lay against her on the carpet and started to kiss her slender, brown body, Stokley was completely unaware of the midget standing in the door watching them. Though the little man's complexion was a deep brown, his face had grown almost beet red from rage. Without warning, he toddled over to where Stokley was making love and crashed the bottle of Dom Perignon down on top of Stokley's head. The bottle broke, sending Stokley into unconsciousness and glass all over the floor.

"What the fuck, you crazy?" Thelma screamed, jumping up and looking at the little Reverend as if he had lost his mind.

"That muthafucker doing that to you, I won't have it, I won't," Waldorf screamed, hopping nervously around the room as if a colony of angry termites were lodged in his anus.

"You ain't got no fucking right to tell me what to do. Get out," Thelma said.

"I won't have it, I won't. This one and that one, like stray cats in heat they roam in and out of your life, but no goddamn more, no more, I'm sick and tired of it," he told her, tears streaming down his face.

"Just get the fuck out," she repeated.

He looked at her and made a threatening step in her direction, but she halted him with the sternest of looks. Thelma was a she-devil lion tamer, and Waldorf was the wild, roaring lion. Then, suddenly, like a cowered animal he sighed and all of the fight was gone. With one crack of the whip he was tame again.

"Please don't make me go," Waldorf said, and started to whimper like a baby.

Thelma looked at him pitifully.

"Please," the Reverend cried, and fell to his knees looking up at her like she was the holy Madonna. "I didn't mean it, I didn't."

"You pathetic. Go on, get in the goddamn room," she commanded disgustedly as she might have to a dog who had just shit in the middle of the floor.

Obediently and without another word, Reverend Waldorf walked into the bedroom.

Thelma looked at Stokley naked spread-eagle on the floor and checked *to see if he was still breathing. He was. Then she turned her attention to the bedroom.*

The Reverend Waldorf was sitting on the king-size bed with his legs crossed and crying his eyes out.

Thelma went over and started to hug him tenderly. He wept openly and unashamedly like a child as she kissed his tears away.

The more she comforted him, the harder he cried. He lost himself inside her arms. To James Gregory Waldorf, Thelma was everything good on this earth. Her tender acceptance of him had erased forty-nine years of ridicule he had experienced on this earth for being born a midget.

He had often wondered why God had played such a mean joke on him? Making him half a man with full-man-size instincts.

Only Thelma had ever been able to make him feel like a whole man. Only she had been able to erase the hurt of those years as a teenager when he had made his living in a traveling circus running around and acting like an idiot for crowds of people who saw him as nothing more than a freak of nature. Through her. he had gained humanity. Salvation. even. He was writing a poem for her that he planned to give her on her birthday. It said, "I can almost feel the magic of the first time that we kissed. I remember all the . . ." He hadn't finished it yet, though. In Thelma's arms, he had found peace. He even knew exactly what she was but he didn't care, because that's just the way love is.

"You can't go around conkin' people over the head with bottles, James, you know better than that," Thelma scolded.

"I know, but I was jealous. I'm sorry, but I love you so much," Waldorf managed to say through his tears.

"Damn, you'll have the police up here after you if you ain't careful. You could have killed him if he didn't have such a hard head," Thelma reminded him.

"I know, I'm sorry. I was jealous, plus I'm so lonely, I miss Trevor," the midget said, and started to cry again.

Thelma undressed the midget and maneuvered him under the sheets. She slipped her T-shirt off and rubbed her smooth brown frame against his misshapen, miniature body. Reverend Waldorf grabbed up at her firm breasts with child-size hands. He sucked her breasts gently until she felt a warm, tingling sexual sensation. This was the third time she had made love today, but it still felt good. Thelma expertly maneuvered Reverend Waldorf's little-boy-size penis into her and with a few pumps from her thighs he came quickly and was completely drained of energy. His eyes rolled back into his head, and he dropped off to sleep.

When she thought about Stokley lying in the middle of the floor, Thelma quickly slipped on her T-shirt and went out into the living room, but to her surprise he was gone.

When I got to the bar around 9:30 the next morning, the r egular customers were already present for their morning oiling.

At 10:17 a.m., I received a five-page fax from Onion.

One of the pages was a copy of a birth certificate on a James Gregory Waldorf Garrett born in Kingston, Jamaica. In addition there was the birth and death certificates of a Margaret Louise Garrett, who was also born in Kingston, Jamaica. I felt better knowing that at least I had gotten part of it right.

I continued helping Duke at the bar during the morning. Someone ordered a J.D. and Coke and someone else ordered an E&J straight up, water on the side. As I was pouring someone out a double of C.C. and coke. I was thinking that nobody asked for the proper name of the brands anymore, everything was initials. Then it suddenly hit me who Rodgers Leonard Rice was.

I dialed a number that I had remembered by heart.

"Can you get into Waldorf's office now?" I asked into the phone.

"Now?" Irma responded.

"Yeah."

"Everyone's getting ready for the memorial service, there won't be many people around but . . ."

"All I need is about ten minutes, it's important," I told her.

"I can get you in, but once you're in you're on your own," Irma warned.

"Just get me in and I'll deal with it from there. By the way, do you know if Waldorf has a safe in his office?" I stated.

"I don't know, he may have one, but the only place I know

about for sure is in Reverend Jennings's office, why?"

"What time would be best to come around?" I asked.

"I would think around noon, 'cause I heard Waldorf say he has a pastor's luncheon somewhere else. Hey, how much do I get for this, this is high-risk stuff you asking," Irma said.

"Another hundred," I answered.

"That's in addition to the two I already got coming, OK," she added.

"OK, I'll see you in thirty minutes," I said, and hung up the telephone.

At 11:58, Irma met me at the back door of the church. She had been right, almost no one was around. I didn't even see the ever-present, sloe-eyed, effeminate-looking Wendell, who was usually Johnny on the spot whenever I arrived.

I used the key Irma handed me to let myself into Waldorf's office, but I couldn't find what I was looking for. So I quickly climbed the stairs to where the Reverend Jennings's office was located. The door was unlocked and there was no one around. It only took me a second to locate what I needed.

I used the information in the letter to open a wall safe that was hidden behind a mirror: 77 Right, 6 Left, 56 Right. I had figured out that the name Roger Leonard Rice was simply a code for Right, Left, Right. People asking for initials of drinks rather than the whole names had triggered something and made me think of LRL, which when put with the numbers made perfect sense.

Inside the safe I found a letter that told me all that I needed to know. I dropped it into my pocket and called Al Mack. "Can you meet me as soon as possible?"

"Make it an hour," Mack said.

I walked out of the God's Holy Tabernacle more satisfied than I had felt in weeks."

I met Al at the Be-Bop Tavern and filled him in on what I had discovered, then handed over the letter from the safe along with the fax I had received from Onion.

He read the letter. "You just never can tell about people, can you?" he said.

"No, you can't," I agreed.

AT 3:25 p.m. we were sitting in the office of the Reverend Waldorf along with Thelma, waiting for him to appear. He had called earlier to say he was expected back at the church at around 3:30 p.m.

"So what's all this drama about?" Thelma complained. "I got to get back to work. People are calling every minute about the memorial service."

Neither of us spoke. We just sat and waited.

Reverend Waldorf walked in at 3:47 p.m.

A look of mild surprise spread across his face as he saw Al Mack and me.

"I believe you have the advantage on me," the midget said in his most distinguished tone.

"My name is Barnett. We met in passing once before," I said.

"I'm Detective Al Mack, from the Harlem precinct," Mack informed him.

Waldorf's eyes rested on Thelma. He sighed and shook his head slightly. "Gentlemen, if there has been any little problem, believe me we will do our best to make the situation right. We know our Thelma here has difficulties from time to time, but we understand her and we will do our best to make sure whatever she's done doesn't happen again," he said with a disapproving look in Thelma's direction.

"Thelma is not what brings us here," I said.

Waldorf looked puzzled. "What, then?" he inquired .

"Murder," Mack said.

"Murder." The little man's brow furrowed in confusion.

"Uh-huh," Mack said.

Before he could say another word, Mack produced the letter that I had taken from the safe and passed it to the Reverend.

At the sight of the letter, the little preacher visibly weakened and seemed to lose his ability to stand up. He sat down at his desk as tears began to fill his eyes.

"What's wrong, James?" Thelma asked with genuine concern.

"I did it all for you," Waldorf said pitifully, looking up at Thelma.

"Did what?" she asked.

"I couldn't let them keep fucking with you. They would have messed up everything. They knew too much, don't you see?" Waldorf stated.

"What's he talking about?" Thelma asked, turning to Mack.

"What he's talking about is the three rappers he killed to protect you."

"Me, killed . . ." A look of horror spread over Thelma's face and she seemed to lose her capacity for speech. Her mouth gaped open like a fish out of water sucking air, but the words didn't come.

"Why?" Mack asked.

"'Cause they knew. That fucking Man O War and Shogun, they knew," Waldorf said.

"Knew what, James?" Thelma inquired.

"Tell her," Mack said, looking sternly."

The midget was dumbstruck, for a minute, anyway.

"When you got involved with those English rapping fuckers, I told you they weren't any good. You were having orgies with them," Waldorf said, bursting into tears.

"So fuckin' what, I do what I want to do, I'm grown," Thelma said defiantly.

"Well, you must have told them about us and . . . Man O War must have mentioned it to his mother in Jamaica, who knew about . . ."

His voice trailed off.

"About what?" Thelma said.

The Reverend stopped talking, and I took up where he left off.

"About your father, Reverend Jennings, who got your mother Margaret pregnant when he was a preacher back in England. Apparently your mother came to America with your father and gave birth you. But she got sick, so your father put you under the care of his friend's family and sent your mother back to Jamaica, where she died. Back in Jamaica, your mother had a friend named Sarah Mainwaring, who knew your mother's brother, who had also emigrated from Jamaica to America. Sarah Mainwaring was Man O War's mother."

"I knew Jennings was my real father, so what?" Thelma said.

Waldorf looked up sadly with a pleading expression on his face.

"Your mother's brother was a long-time friend of your father, the late Reverend Jennings, wasn't he?" I said to Thelma.

Waldorf was quiet for a long time, then spoke in a weak voice barely above a whisper.

"Yes, Trevor and I became friends from the time we attended seminary together one summer in England," Waldorf whined painfully, placing his hands against the sides of his head.

"When did you leave Jamaica for America?" I asked.

"I came here two years before my sister Margaret did," James Gregory Waldorf Garret admitted.

"You, my uncle . . . You mean you, my own blood and you been fucking me? Oh shit, that's fucked up," Thelma exploded. "Oh, shit," she wailed, then broke down crying.

"I'm sorry, Thelma, I'm so sorry," Waldorf cried. "But I had to kill those dirty rappers, that Man O War, him and Shogun came to me and Man O War told me that his mother knew who I was and he showed me a letter from her saying that I was Thelma's uncle. Then they showed me the photographs they had taken.

"Then Man O War and Shogun started laughing at me and they threatened to tell the whole congregation on me and show the photographs around if I didn't give them money. Don't you understand," Waldorf pleaded. "I had to, don't you see. I had to because I don't know who else they had told about us. I knew that she had been messing around with the whole group, so I figured the only way would be to kill them all. I had to cut the link, don't you understand. It was either that or lose the only woman I ever loved and who had ever loved me," Waldorf said.

"Did the Reverend Jennings know about the murders?" Mack asked.

"No, but that was the other reason I had to do it. If Trevor had found out, he never would have trusted me again. Don't you see, I had to do it for the good of everyone. Trevor trusted me, everybody did," the midget Reverend reported.

"Why did you put the letter in the safe?" Mack asked.

"After Trevor died, I figured it was the safest place. No one else had the combination, or at least I didn't think they did."

"You dirty little freak," Thelma said as she crossed the room. As quick as a flash she hauled off and slapped the midget across the face, knocking him off the chair.

I grabbed Thelma as the midget sat on the floor looking lost.

"We'll get the rest of the story down at the station," Mack said as he stood up and took out his cuffs.

Then, without warning, like a bullet shot from a gun, the little Reverend jumped up and made a mad dash past Mack toward the door. I grabbed at him but, he was too quick.

He went out of the door and down the corridor, moving from side to side on short legs that seemed to churn faster than a speeding locomotive.

By the time Mack had drawn his gun, the dwarf was out of the door and moving down the street. Both Mack and I gave chase, but he had gotten a good head start. Both of us ran at full speed, but Waldorf was still opening the gap between us as we neared the corner of 137th.

"Police, move out," Mack shouted as he ran with his pistol in hand. He narrowly missed running over an old lady who was carrying two large shopping bags. The midget Reverend was ducking and dodging as he ran, making himself a difficult target to hit.

I gave it all I had and managed to get within about two yards of the little man. He looked back and darted quickly toward the subway entrance, but just as he changed direction he ran smack into a baby carriage. The man pushing the carriage was dressed in a large cowboy hat, a filthy green poncho, and brown army fatigues.

Seeing that the baby carriage contained only a dirty teddy

bear, the little Reverend grabbed the carriage with both hands and flung the baby carriage behind him in hopes that I would stumble over it. The carriage sailed through the air and bumped into a lightpost, jarring the teddy bear loose from its secure place in the carriage. Gerald the mangy teddy bear was thrown out into the street into traffic, where a car ran across its face.

"Noooooooooo." The sound of the man screaming was enough to make the Reverend look up for a moment. But that moment was more than enough time to seal his doom. Cowboy leaped into the air as if his legs were made of springs and reached out to grab the little Reverend's neck just as the midget was about to descend the staircase down into the subway.

One look in the leaping man's face confirmed to the midget Reverend that he was stark-raving mad.

Cowboy lifted the Reverend high above his head and flung him down the subway stairs like a rubber ball.

Cowboy followed him down with another great leap and grabbed him by the collar with one hand while expertly flicking out his pocketknife with the other.

Mack was right behind me as we both headed toward the bottom of the stairs.

"Cowboy," I shouted. "Don't kill him, please don't."

Cowboy looked up and stared into the barrel of the service revolver than Mack had trained on his head.

"Don't kill him," I repeated.

"Let him go," I heard Mack's voice behind me.

"Cowboy, let him go," I repeated.

Cowboy paused, saw it was me. He looked as confused as ever. His expression contained surprise and outrage mixed in with the craziness and hurt of a thousand lifetimes.

"He ain't worth it," I said. "Don't kill him, Cowboy, don't."

I couldn't seem to find other words.

"He hurt my boy, he deserve to die," Cowboy said.

"I know he does, but don't kill him. This is the police I have here with me. Let them handle it."

Reverend Waldorf was only half conscious from the fall, but he looked up toward the sound of the voices weak and trembling.

People coming up from the train steps scattered in all directions when they saw Mack with his gun trained on Cowboy.

A uniformed cop ran up with his revolver drawn.

I spotted him first and yelled out, "Police! Police! We're the police Don't shoot, just be cool."

Mack saw the uniform and echoed my warning. "I'm a Police officer, I got it. Back off."

Cowboy looked down into the face of the midget Reverend, who was wet from sweating.

"Let him go and everything's gonna be all right, Cowboy," I said as I moved closer down the stairs toward him.

"But this muthafucker deserve to die," Cowboy insisted, still holding the knife over the midget's head.

I stopped talking and looked Cowboy straight in the eye. It took a few seconds before we connected, but we did.

I reached out slowly towards, him and Cowboy eventually placed the pocketknife into my open hand.

Al Mack walked down and cuffed the Reverend while Cowboy picked up Gerald from the street and hugged him close to his chest in a deep demonstration of fatherly love.

"We taking both of them in?" the uniformed cop asked Mack.

"No, the other one was just assisting the arrest," Mack said.

"OK, cool," the cop said, and replaced his service revolver.

"Call for a pickup," Mack said to the uniformed cop as he tightened the cuffs on Waldorf.

"You got it," the cop said, and walked off.

"You did good today. You stopped two men from being killed," Mack said.

"Yeah, I guess some days are better than others," I responded.

CHAPTER 23

After I had accompanied Mack back to the station and signed a citizen's report that I witnessed the confession, I was tired. It was only 6:30 p.m. when I finished, but I felt like I had just worked a double shift on the world's hardest job. But at the same time I felt relieved, like the pressure had been lifted. I called Livingston Holmes and Shelby Green and gave them the news, then picked up some Chinese food from the corner joint and headed home. I got in, took a quick shower, and put on a CD by Gilberto Gill and let his smooth Brazilian rhythms soothe and move me as far away as possible from the images of death that I had carried in my head all during the time I had worked on this case.

I was sick to death of death. I turned off the ringer on the phone and dropped off into a deep sleep.

When I woke up, the clock next to my bed read 7:30 a.m.

I was starving. Just as I was turning the phone back on, it rang.

It was Sonia on the other end. "You still talking to me?" she asked.

"Yeah, why shouldn't I be?"

"Because of the way I acted the other day," she said.

"Yeah, I guess we were both pretty uptight," I remarked.

"I'd like to apologize," she said softly.

"No need, you were just feeling what you were feeling," I consoled her.

"I still love you and want you, you know? You don't have to say anything back. I just wanted you to know," she told me.

"Thank you." I was happy to hear the words.

"About those tickets to the Bahamas. What if I were to pay for them—would you still go with me?"

"You don't have to do that, and we can still go. I think the trip can do us both good."

"Do you mean it?" she asked.

"Yeah, I do."

"I'll call the travel agency and then call you back after lunch," Sonia said.

"Cool," I said, and hung up.

I got myself ready for work and left the house. I was in my car when my phone rang again.

"'Morning to you, sir. This is Oliver Reems," the voice on the other end chimed.

"Good morning," I answered.

"I called to say the deal I had been working on went through yesterday and I can give you five thousand to help that young lady buy that car you said she wants. Is that OK?"

My ears perked up. "The deal must have been very sweet if you're taking five grand out of your own pocket."

"Sweeter than you can believe. Doug was able to track down Max Hammill, the owner of record for the Dancehall Dogz, and got Max to sell his management and ownership contract to him for almost nothing.

"In addition, Doug had me contact the parents of Man O War and Shogun and we were able to make a deal with them to allow the release of the CD that Man O War and Shogun had produced with Bobby P."

"Doug, then, he took the deal to Global Distributors and picked up a half million for giving them the right to distribute worldwide. As the lawyer for Doug, I picked up two hundred thousand. Your part of this is fifty thousand for introducing us."

"Fifty grand." I almost bit my tongue.

"Ten percent as a agent's fee. Doug and myself won't have it any other way," Reems said.

"Doug, that sly old fox, had dealt Max a nice one. That's fantastic. Congratulations," I said, and laughed.

I admired the way Doug had made his moves.

"By the way, I saw the morning papers. So Waldorf actually confessed to holding a gun to Lee's head while making him drink the whiskey laced with barbiturates and then chopping off the other one's head with an ax, gruesome," Reems said.

"Yeah, that's what he confessed to," I confirmed.

When I parked, it was 8:36 a.m. My body and mind needed a big breakfast, so I walked around the corner to a joint called the Harlem Diner and Grill, where they serve soul food from 6:00 in the morning until 4:00 the following morning.

I was a regular customer there.

Marty, the daytime short order cook, was busy behind the grill flipping pancakes and filling large orders piled high with bacon, sausages, and biscuits. The smell of the place made my mouth water. There were ten small tables in the room, and the restaurant was about half full.

I took a table by the window as the waitress named Laney came over. "Would you like to start with coffee, Mr. Barnett?" Laney asked.

"Yes, thanks."

"Back in a minute," she said, and smiled.

Laney handed me a menu and left the *Daily News* on the table and walked away. I opened the newspaper to find an article about the capture of Waldorf, along with his photograph and details of his confession.

I looked out at the Harlem morning. People were busy moving along the street on their way to work, school, and various other places.

"Dream-chasing time" is what my dad used to call rush hour in Harlem. I smiled at the thought of him standing behind the sandwich bar of the Be-Bop Tavern filling orders and serving drinks day in and day out.

"Mind if I join you?" A voice reached out to disturb my reminisces. I looked up and was surprised to see Malik standing by the table. He sat down as Laney returned with the coffee.

She poured us both a cup. "Have you gentlemen decided yet?" Laney asked.

"Not quite—give me just a few more minutes," I said.

"Just a few more minutes, please," Malik also said.

"OK," she said, walking away with the coffeepot in hand.

"You've been busy, I hear," Malik said as we sipped the hot coffee.

"News travels fast. This is Harlem, you know how it is," I said.

We continued sipping our coffee for a while in silence.

"I got a lot of help from somebody who led me to certain incriminating documents. I figured that somebody was you," I said frankly.

"If we can help, we're glad to oblige. Like I told you before, we're all in this thing together, like it or not," Malik said.

"The way I figure it, your person was inside the church. Maybe the Reverend's assistant Wendell, Mother Hinton, the former janitor Wallace Budrow, or possibly even Irma playing a clever double role."

"I won't say yes to who it was, but I will say yes to the fact that we did provide the letter that Irma gave to you. But on the other hand, you helped us out a lot, too."

"How was that?" I asked.

"We had our suspicions about the Reverend Jennings but your investigation forced him out into the open so we could see where the connections were."

"You mean Max Hammill and J. T. Brown?"

"Exactly."

"I hear J. T. has disappeared. Am I correct in thinking that's probably on a permanent basis?"

"We warned him twice and twice he ignored us. In addition, he was looking for someone to put a hit out on you," Malik confirmed.

"I heard," I said, looking up at him and nodding appreciatively. "What about Max Hammill?"

"He's leaving the country for good this afternoon: 6:10 flight from JFK," Malik said.

"I see, and the beat goes on . . .," I muttered.

"And the beat goes on," Malik echoed.

"What put you onto Waldorf as the killer?" I asked Malik point blank.

"We didn't know he was the killer. We only suspected him of dealing drugs. But what made us look at him in the first place was you," he said.

"Me," I spouted, surprised.

"When you put the pressure on Max Hammill and made Jennings run to England, we started looking more closely at Waldorf because we figured if Hammill was telling the truth about Jennings, then it would stand to reason that Waldorf would continue operating in Jennings's place as a behind-the-scenes drug man. But we were wrong. Instead, we found out that Waldorf had been doing a lot of strange things. One, he took a large amount of money from the church funds and put it back without explanation—fifty thousand, to be exact. And two, our people overheard him on the phone talking to Goldfinger. Apparently Goldfinger also knew about the deal that Man O War and Shogun were making with Waldorf involving the photographs, the money, and the letter," Malik explained.

"Your people inside did a damn good job," I commented.

"All for the cause," Malik said. "But you had suspicions of your own about Waldorf, I'm sure."

"Yeah, things started getting clearer after Goldfinger got killed while I was in England."

"That meant that killer had to still be in New York," Malik said.

"Not only that, but Waldorf had been in the back of my mind ever since a little girl who lived in Maxie Waxie's apartment said she saw a 'big big teddy bear man' climbing up the building outside her window. Also, I remembered seeing Waldorf chase down a naked man outside the church with murder in his eyes. But the main thing that really kept nagging at me was that Irma said Waldorf had known Jennings since before Thelma was born, which led me to believe there was a long and checkered past that he shared with Jennings. You know the saying 'birds of a feather flock together'."

"The newspapers says he did it all for love," Malik said sarcastically, grimacing.

"That's what the man said," I confirmed.

"Like my father used to say 'where love goes, disaster often follows,'" Malik mused philosophically.

"A lot of truth to that one," I said, thinking about Sonia and me.

The waitress returned. "Ready yet?"

Then suddenly I thought about Ronnie. "Yes tell me ,do you have any beans?" I inquired.

"Beans?" Laney echoed quizzically.

"Yeah, like pork and beans."

"I'm sure we do."

"Then give me four pieces of toast with some beans on top," I said.

Laney's face went into an amused grimace. "Is that all?"

"That's all, beans on toast," I clarified.

"OK." She smiled weirdly and walked over and spoke to the cook, who looked out from behind the grill.

"Devil Barnett, man, what you ordering? Beans on toast. Where you get that one from," Marty inquired with puzzlement on his fat face.

"Beans on toast, that's the kind of thing you eat at the end of the month when you run out of food Dev, not something you order in a restaurant." Henry, the owner, laughed from behind the cash register.

"Make that two orders," Malik said loud enough for Marty to hear.

"Did you hear that, Henry? I can't believe what I'm hearing. Another man done got his tastebuds all mixed up, too. This thing might become an epidemic," Marty cackled.

"We must never forget that the world is a strange and mysterious place," Malik said.

"You can say that again," I mused to myself as I thought about my friend Ronnie, whose glowing smile could light up a whole damn room.